ERICK S. GRAY

GUN

BLACK ODYSSEY MEDIA

WWW.BLACKODYSSEY.NET

Published by
BLACK ODYSSEY MEDIA

www.blackodyssey.net
Email: info@blackodyssey.net

Library of Congress Control Number: 2023900479
First Trade Paperback Printing: November 2023
ISBN: 978-1-957950-01-3
ISBN: 978-1-957950-02-0 (e-book)
Cover Design by Navi' Robins

10 9 8 7 6 5 4 3 2 1

Manufactured in the United States of America

Distributed by Kensington Publishing Corp.

Dear Reader,

I want to thank you immensely for supporting Black Odyssey Media authors, and our ongoing efforts to spotlight more minority storytellers. The scariest and most challenging task for many writers is getting the story, or characters, out of our heads and onto the page. Having admitted that, with every manuscript that Kreceda and I acquire, we believe that it took talent, discipline, and remarkable courage to construct that story, flesh out those characters, and prepare it for the world. Debut or seasoned, our authors are the real heroes and heroines in *OUR* story. And for them, we are eternally grateful.

Whether you are new to Erick S. Gray or Black Odyssey Media, we hope that you are here to stay. We also welcome your feedback and kindly ask that you leave a review. For upcoming releases, announcements, submission guidelines, etc., please be sure to visit our website at www.blackodyssey.net or scan the QR code below. We can also be found on social media using @iamblackodyssey. Until next time, take care and enjoy the journey!

Joyfully,

Shawanda Williams

Shawanda "N'Tyse" Williams
Founder/Publisher

Gun, it means power and destruction. Gun, it means murder and death. Gun, it can equal wealth and prosperity. Gun, it can mean life-changing. Gun, it means protection from danger. Gun! It's our constitutional right to own one, the Second Amendment— "being necessary to the security of a free State, the right of the people to keep and bear Arms, shall not be infringed."

PROLOGUE

IT LOOKED LIKE rain in Brooklyn as dark clouds hovered over the entire city like an invading alien spacecraft, ready to release hell upon the people below. Staring into the sky, the community witnessed black clouds sprawling across the sky, billowing in from the west. The sky just about looked ominous as the clouds' brassy glare drained the color from buildings and trees, leaving neighborhoods tinted bronze in faltering light. The air started to grow heavy in the community as the humidity pressed down . . . suffocating. The scent of not just rain but trouble became dark and heady. A flickering flash lit up the sky. Then the earth-shattering sound of thunder boomed above, like a cannon going off in the war.

Sean Black seethed by the bedroom window as he gripped a revolver in his hand. They were coming for him. They were coming to take everything he owned and valued—they were coming for his soul. He wasn't going to allow it. He was king of the neighborhood—a violent drug lord that came to rise by sheer bloodshed, violence, intimidation, and implementing fear. He had power, he felt immortal, and he felt nothing could stop him—especially the DEA.

"*Kill 'em all!*" a voice boomed to him.

"I will. I promise. I will, for our bond will never divide," Sean Black replied hotly.

His thirst for implementing bloodshed became ravenous, and the expression on his face became demonic. It was as if hell were written across his face. Those closest to him believed he had gone crazy a long time ago. He would talk to himself—talk to the revolver as if it were an intimate companion—an advisor to him.

The flesh of his fingers tightly wrapped around the handle of the .357 he clutched. The revolver was a chromed Colt Python .357 Magnum with a six-inch barrel, the Rolls-Royce of revolvers. Its markings were distinctive: a black handle. A demonic eye was inside a fiery pyramid (a triangle) on both sides, as seen on the back of a dollar bill—The Eye of Providence. The Eye of Providence is supposed to represent the eye of God watching over humanity, mankind. But this demonic eye was watching over something else. It was something sinister and unbecoming, and it was corrupting of man.

The .357 was impressive and custom-made; it was appealing and undoubtedly hypnotic in someone's hands. Rumors of the gun say that it was perfectly handcrafted by the devil himself, forged in hellfire, and made from the bones of damned souls. It was believed that the devil himself traveled from hell to earth into humanity's realm to deliver his gift personally. He placed the hellish tool into men's hands and watched them become kings and rulers with extreme wealth. In return, he would devour their souls, strengthening his demonic hold on civilization. And it was said that if one stared long enough at the hellish tool, they could see their soul becoming contorted and consumed by looming demons. Their forthcoming future is engulfed in brimstone and hellfire. But men didn't care because they all craved power and wealth—and there was a certain hunger that they needed to subsist. So, for lengthy possession of the .357 came perpetual unrest, a ravenous thirst for violence . . . and a one-way ticket to absolute damnation.

"*Kill 'em all!*" the voice continued. "*Bring them to me.*"

Sean Black pressed his top and bottom teeth together and gritted his teeth in silent fury. He continued to seethe. He started to strip away his clothing, becoming butt-naked inside the room. A burning sensation and a threatening intensity became overwhelming, like the room was on fire.

"Let 'em come! Let 'em fuckin' come! I'm ready for them! I am. I'm ready to kill 'em all!" he ranted and shouted.

All but one of his men had abandoned the place. C.C. stood poised by the front door, gripping an AK-47, ready for action. He was prepared to cut down cops, agents, and Marshalls; it didn't matter. Under Sean Black's influence, he was ready to slaughter for his boss.

DEA agents and local cops came up the stairs like a swarm of bees ready to attack. Sean Black was dangerous. He was a notorious and cold-blooded killer. He had a large body count, and Brooklyn and the city feared him tremendously. It was almost as if he were addicted to killing. In the past three years, Sean Black controlled Brooklyn, and he seemed untouchable. Whenever the government or prosecutors tried to indict him, witnesses would disappear or end up dead. Some were utterly charred and unrecognizable, and evidence would turn up missing, their stories would change, etc. Cops started to believe that Sean Black was the luckiest sonofabitch around. Maybe he was too smart to get caught. And they steadily grew frustrated with his reign of crime and violent pedigree. But his luck ran out. The grand jury issued an indictment, and an arrest warrant was implemented for his immediate arrest. A witness was ready to testify against Sean Black. The witness was prepared to turn state evidence against the violent crime syndicate.

Every cop in town felt it was time to take this maniac off the streets—dead or alive. Cops in the city were ready to take him down fast and hard. And that included a heavily armed task force. The DEA task force stood poised outside the black steel door with their insignia pompously boasted across their uniforms. And on the other side of that door, they swore the devil himself awaited them.

Their radios crackled inside the silent hallway.

"Team One in position," someone announced into the radio.

It was a tense situation with their automatic weapons ready to kill if necessary and combat boots ready to storm aggressively into the apartment.

"Take that sonofabitch down," a voice crackled through the radio.

They had their orders. They charged for the door with their commands and assertiveness, ready to take it off the hinges with a battering ram. But to their shock, the steel door wildly swung open, and C.C. started to open fire with the AK-47 on the looming agents.

"Fuck you bitches! Fuck you bitches!" he heatedly shouted. "Y'all want some of this?! Huh? Come get some!"

The AK-47 cut loose in his hands like he was in a Rambo movie.

Brata-tat-tat-tat-tat-tat-tat-tat.

Two agents were immediately hit before the gunfire was returned. A brief shootout ensued, and a barrage of gunfire hastily took down C.C. His body lay sprawled in the doorway, contorted by a gruesome death. Chaos followed. Several task force agents hurried into the apartment. They immediately swarmed every area of the three-bedroom residence as their radios continued to crackle—*men down—men down*. Their adrenaline amplified, and their final destination . . . the main bedroom where Sean Black had barricaded himself inside. He stood naked and had become disoriented and enraged. He trembled almost sickly and had become frantic. He scowled as he gripped the .357 Magnum tighter in his hand. He could feel its power coursing through his veins. He felt supernatural, and he wasn't going down without a fight.

Sean Black seethed. He heard his enemies looming closer. He could almost hear their raging heartbeats and their cavernous growling. They were coming for him. It felt like the gates of hell had opened wide, and demons were spilling out into his area, yearning to gnaw at his bones and flesh. They were coming to take away his power—his precious. They were coming to snatch away his soul. He heard them outside the door—the demonic souls, the damned gathering and plotting to devour him, ready to destroy him, prepared to drag him to hell. Sean Black could hear their giant claws scratching and scraping at the bedroom door. He could smell death. His eyes danced wildly around his head with insanity and paranoia. He stood poised by the door, waving the demonic tool wildly, screaming out gibberish but what appeared to be another language—a foreign language—the devil's tongue.

"أنا لعنة لك. أنا لعنة لك," he screamed, saying in Arabic, "*I curse you. I curse you!*"

The bedroom door rapidly crashed open, and agents urgently spilled into the room with their weapons drawn. Two were instantly met with a gruesome fate as Sean Black aimed and shot them point-blank in the head at a frightening speed with the .357. A naked Sean Black howled at them as he continued his fierce attack, and utter pandemonium followed. Sean continued to open fire at the threat coming for him, and the agents let loose a barrage of bullets that tore into his naked frame like it was paper-thin. Surprisingly, he didn't go down. He continued to seethe and bled heavily. Then he charged at them with such a ferocious and demonic ability that everyone was astonished.

"What the fuck!" one man shouted.

The .357 went off in Sean's hand, killing another man. Then he suicidally leaped at law enforcement like a lion onto its prey. Before one man could react, Sean Black's jaw was in his throat, and he madly sank his teeth into the man's neck and violently tore away a chunk of his flesh. Blood spewed from the man's neck uncontrollably as his fellow agents violently wrestled Sean Black away from him. He continued to scream and taunt them in a different language . . . الجحيم يدعو الجحيم يدعو

"Hell is calling! Aaaaaaaahh!"

He acted possessed, and it seemed like there was no stopping him. Shot to shit, Sean Black was still on his feet and ready to kill 'em all. He pivoted with the gun still in his hand and was prepared to shoot again. This time, over a dozen DEA agents let loose on Sean Black with a volley of gunfire that could have taken down a small building. Each bullet cut through him like a shard of glass. Finally, the gunfire forced him through the window. He spilled out onto the fire escape with the .357 released from his grip. It dropped three stories below into a mound of rubbish. Sean Black shrieked, the gun gone from his reach, his possession. He had built an empire with it, but at what price? It contorted his reality. It warped his soul, and now the devil was coming to collect what was owed to him.

He was dying. His breathing had become sparse, and his heartbeat was fluttering and fading. The demons he fought were now upon him, towering over his bullet-riddled frame, snarling at him and ready to shred him to pieces, Sean Black believed. He could feel his flesh on fire, burning profoundly. He could feel the demons begin to gnaw at his bones and flesh—tearing and ripping into his carcass with pleasurable desire. He screamed in agony.

"You hear that?" one agent asked out of the blue.

They did. Each man standing over Sean Black's body heard the terrifying screams. They stood there on the fire escape in utter bewilderment. They gazed at the body, but how was it possible that they could still hear his screams? He was dead. It was unnatural. What they heard was the echo of Sean Black's perpetual torture and suffering. It gave each man a deep chill. It was unlike anything they had witnessed before.

In the rubble below, the gun had sunk into obscurity in the narrow alley. It cloaked into a shadow of darkness while a dozen agents searched painstakingly for the weapon. They knew it had fallen into the trash somewhere, but where was it? The .357 Magnum had killed several of their fellow officers, and now it was nowhere to be found. Impossible. Since the shooting, the agents had eyes on the entire area, and no one came or went. They went through every alley area and came up empty—nothing!

"How the fuck does a gun like that just up and disappear?" a superior asked his subordinates. "And you sure no one else was around?"

"I'm sure, sir. We had eyes on the entire area, securing the vicinity. There's no way."

"And there are no sewage drains or cracks anywhere it could have fallen into?"

"No. We checked."

It left them scratching their heads, baffled. What weren't they seeing?

The .357 was only a heartbeat away from its previous owner. It wasn't meant to be bagged and tagged into evidence. Instead, it was meant to become forged into someone's hands and create power and destruction. It was meant to be owned by a human soul and for that soul to be transformed so the devil could collect his next dying soul.

PART ONE

No man chooses evil because it is evil; he only mistakes it for happiness, the good he seeks.

CHAPTER ONE

THE CHURCH ON the corner of Livonia Avenue and Watkins Street was lively and vibrant, with singing, clapping, praising, and dancing inside the pews. The choir standing on the small platform behind the pastor joyfully bellowed out, "*This little light of mine*," and the small congregation clapped their hands together in joy and sang along with the choir.

"*This little light of mine, I'm gonna let it shine. This little light of mine, I'm gonna let it shine. Jesus is the light; I'm gonna let Him shine; Jesus is the light; I'm gonna let Him shine. Let Him shine, let Him shine, let Him shine, let Him shine*," the people sang.

The Tabernacle Church was situated on the urban Brooklyn block and across the street from the towering projects in Brownsville, Brooklyn. Under the train trestle was a praiseful escape for its members from the violence and drugs that plagued the rough and venomous neighborhood. And though its members were few, they were faithful, loyal, and generous in offering and tithes. And they also implemented many outreach programs to help their troubled community, including feeding the homeless and mentoring at-risk teenagers. Pastor Richard Morgan was their guide. He was a stout, short, and breathless man, and he was also an energetic man with a magnetic personality. He constantly had his members believing that they could walk on water and change anything for the greater good with just God and faith.

"Amen! Amen! Amen! Hallelujah!" Pastor Morgan shouted ecstatically. "Listening to this choir makes you lift your feet and jump for joy. Don't they? Give them a hand. We might be few, but God almighty, we are powerful. We are influential! We are God's children, and we are His voice and angels. We won't quit on them because God will never quit on us!"

"Yes! Amen! Hallelujah!" a woman shouted blissfully. She agreed wholeheartedly with the pastor's words, repeatedly clapping her hands, smiling, and praiseful. "God will never quit on us!"

"Repeat it, Sister Richards," Pastor Morgan hollered as he pointed her way.

"God will never quit on us," repeated the woman.

"Yes! Yes! And that's why I'm so grateful, so happy, and energetic because our God almighty will never quit on us. Just give Him a chance, and you'll see . . . You'll see what He's about and what He's capable of . . . God is love, God is guidance, and God is powerful and forgiving!"

"Yes! Hallelujah!" Ms. Richards praised.

She was a thin, brown-skinned lady, a lovely-looking woman in her early forties with slight Cherokee Indian features. Her grandmother was a full-blooded Menominee. Her hair was long, soft, black, and styled into a ponytail. Her full name was Anika Richards, and standing next to her, equally clapping his hands and giving praise, was Omar—her son, her only child.

"Amen!" Omar uttered. "Amen!"

Ms. Richards smiled at her son. She was his pride and joy.

Omar was a thin man. He had a thin face and short, nappy hair, and he stood five foot ten but carried an honest look and personality. He was twenty years old but remained a mama's boy. His life was simple: home, church, and working at the local grocery store to help his mother pay the bills. They were behind on everything from the rent to the light bill. Their struggles and debt were massive, but Ms. Richards believed everything always happened for a reason. She felt their efforts in the projects and life only brought them closer to God and closer to each other.

She was a devoted Christian, had been so for many years, and she made sure that Omar was a man of God too. She didn't have much to give, but she gave faithfully to the church via offerings, tithes, and her time volunteering every week. She always told Omar, "I know we don't have much, but remember. There is always someone out there with less than us . . . who is more unfortunate than us. So we need to be grateful for what we have. It is God's plan and His will."

However, they were poor—nickel-and-dime needy and on the verge of eviction. Omar wondered how anyone could have it worse than them. They had nothing. Some nights, they would struggle to put food on the table. But his mama continued to instill in him to have blind faith and courage.

After the benediction, Ms. Richards and Omar went to have a few words with the pastor. She looked at the man like he was the Messiah himself.

"Wonderful service, Pastor Morgan. Beautiful words," she praised him.

"Thank you, Sister Richards. Seeing you and your son here every Sunday is always a pleasure. God is good, isn't He?"

"Yes, He is," she agreed.

"And, Omar, how have you been?"

"I'm doing fine, Pastor," Omar answered nonchalantly.

"And the job at the grocery store, how is that coming along?"

"It's coming along okay."

"Good to hear. Whatever helps, right? God has blessed you with employment to help your mother, and I know it isn't much.

But still, with faith and patience, better things will come," the pastor proclaimed wholeheartedly.

Omar wanted to believe that.

"And, Sister Richards, I hope to add a few of your famous sweet potato pies at our bake sale next week to help raise money for a new roof."

"Of course. I'll have at least five pies baked and ready," replied Ms. Richards.

The pastor smiled. "Such a blessing. We probably could afford a whole new church with your baking and cooking alone."

She laughed.

"Pastor Morgan, I need a word with you about next week," one of the female members uttered, interrupting his moment with the Richards.

"Yes. Yes. Of course," he said. Then he turned to Ms. Richards and her son. He said, "I need to handle some immediate business; God's work is twenty-four-seven and unconditional."

"Yes, I understand."

"But contact me sometime during the week, and we'll talk. Y'all get home safe," he said.

"We will, Pastor. Thank you," she replied.

Ms. Richards and her son left the church. She had a pleased smile on her face as they stepped foot into the outside world again—Brownsville, Brooklyn. The number 3 train roared above on the elevated railway. The two-way traffic on Livonia was constant on a Sunday afternoon. Residents were out and about that sunny day. Across the street, the drug dealers and drug users were already out and about at the Tilden Housing Projects where they resided. The dealers were addicted to the money, and the users were addicted to the drugs.

Brownsville was dominated by public housing developments of various types, mainly in a small area bounded by Powell Street and Rockaway, Livonia, and Sutter avenues, composed of multiple inward-facing developments located on six superblocks. Thus, the urban community included the most densely concentrated public housing area in the United States. And the Tilden Houses, which was the Richards' residence, had eight sixteen-story buildings.

Brownsville, many times, had the dubious distinction of being the murder capital of New York City. And the social problems associated with poverty, from crime to drug addiction, plagued the area for decades. It still had a severe problem with crack and heroin, and violent crimes and gang-related gun violence seemed to rise. Vacant storefronts and empty lots were standard in the community. And some of the playgrounds were poorly maintained, with broken lights, dilapidated structures, and unlocked gates. For many residents, their community felt like Baghdad—the terrorists were the gangs and drug lords—even the police and their community had been held hostage for years. Things were so dangerous in the community that a UPS driver who had been robbed at gunpoint needed an armed security guard to accompany him on numerous occasions. And along with poverty and violence, the neighborhood suffered from significant health disparities compared to the rest of the city.

As Omar walked with his mother to their building, she suddenly went into a violent cough. She had to grab the railing nearby to avoid falling over, becoming hunched over, and trying to seize her next breath.

"Ma, are you okay?" Omar asked worriedly.

Finally catching her breath, she stared at her son and replied, "Yes . . . I'm fine. There's nothing to worry about, Omar."

He knew she wasn't okay. She was sick. But she didn't want to admit how poor her health was. It was the third time that day that she went into a violent cough, couldn't breathe, and became weak at the knees.

"Maybe we need to go to the clinic again to have you looked at," he suggested.

"No. There's no need for that. It's Sunday anyway; they aren't open." She took another breath and continued, "And besides, I want to get home and cook you a nice meal. I'm not trying to spend this glorious afternoon in some emergency room."

Omar sighed. His mother was pigheaded.

They continued their walk back to the apartment. Omar eyed several young men playing dice in the rundown park in the near distance. They were in a semicircle, gambling, cursing, and drinking. One particular thug that Omar saw was named Brice. He wasn't fond of Brice. He hated the man—although God said they should love their enemies. As stated in Matthew 5:43, "*But I say to you, Love your enemies and pray for those who persecute you, so that you may be sons of your Father who is in heaven.*"

However, Brice was a menacing bully that terrorized the housing area and the community with violence and intimidation. And for some reason, Brice didn't like Omar. He was set on making Omar's life absolutely miserable via physical violence or heatedly mocking him while they were in each other's presence.

Omar felt that he had stared in that direction too long. Still, before he could turn away, Brice was looking his way, and a smirk formed on the bully's face seeing Omar walking home with his mother. He continued to gamble, though.

"I know you're hungry, Omar," said Ms. Richards, entering their poorly furnished apartment.

"What you gonna cook?" he asked. His stomach was growling. They had been in church all morning until early afternoon, and neither one had any breakfast.

She walked into the kitchen and opened the fridge, peeking inside. There wasn't much inside but snippets of stuff. But she was a whiz at making something from nothing.

"Omar, I'm gonna need you to go down to the store and pick me up some butter, cheese, and milk," she said.

"Okay. What you plan on making, Ma?"

She smiled his way. "You'll see."

It was all he needed to hear. His mother was a good cook. And though they were poor, she could produce magic in the kitchen on a shoestring budget when it came to feeding her son.

"Let me change clothes first," he said.

He went into his bedroom to snatch off his tie, his only tie for church, and his good dress shirt. Like the entire apartment, his bedroom was furnished on a meager budget. He didn't have a bed frame, only a single mattress on the floor placed against the wall, and no drapery curtains hung at the window, only shabby blinds. There were no pictures or posters on the walls. The sun had been pouring down and percolating through the window, and the small room was as hot as an oven. The only cooling the place had was an open window. The only other furniture decorating the bedroom was a wobbly straight-backed chair next to a folding table used for an impromptu desk.

Omar tossed his tie onto the mattress and stripped away his fine dress shirt, replacing it with an unpretentious T-shirt. Along with a pair of denim jeans and his off-brand sneakers, he was the personification of a poor kid clad in Salvation Army and hand-me-downs. He had no flash or style, not even a pierced ear and an earring. Having any jewelry or nice things was far-fetched to his reality. They lived off government assistance, welfare, food stamps, and Medicaid.

"I'll be right back, Ma," he said.

He stepped into the narrow hallway covered in graffiti and heard rap music blaring from a neighboring apartment. Dink and his friends were always in the living room with alcohol and weed-fused arguments over NBA 2K. Omar could smell the purple haze they smoked leaching from the apartment into the hallway. He grimaced at the smell of it. The whiff was strong, catching a slight contact from it. He didn't smoke weed. He never understood what the pleasure was from it.

"Hey, big head," he heard her say.

Omar turned around to see Kizzie coming out of her apartment, smiling his way. She lived next door to him with her grandmother and was the one person he considered a friend. Kizzie's smile was bright, like the morning sun illuminating the world. She was a petite and cute girl with thin glasses and long, thick black hair that most ladies would kill to have. She rarely did anything but style it into a simple ponytail or keep it bushy. She was a simple girl that the world would laugh with her when she laughed.

"Hey," Omar smiled. "I didn't see you in church today."

"Finals are tomorrow. I've been studying all morning for them," she replied. "But anyway, what kind of church hat did Ms. Brown wear today?"

"If I had a camera, I would have taken a picture of it. Her hat was purple, big, and had its own orbit," he joked.

Kizzie laughed. "Ms. Brown loves her some extravagant church hats."

"She does. And Pastor Morgan preached a good service today."

"About what . . .?"

"About faith and guidance and never giving up," Omar replied.

"You going to the store for your moms?" she asked.

"Yeah, she's making something special for dinner today. You wanna come by later?"

"I'll try. I have three finals to take tomorrow morning. College is rough."

"At least you're in school, trying to do something with your life. It feels like I'm gonna be poor and stay stuck here in this neighborhood all my life," Omar said reflectively.

"Hey, what was that about faith, guidance, and never giving up you said the pastor preached about this morning? Don't let your faith falter. Your time will come, Omar. You're smart, caring, and you're my best friend."

He smiled again. "You always know what to say to me, Kizzie."

"That's what friends are for. Oh, can you bring me back a pack of chewing gum? For some reason, it helps me study."

"Chewing gum?" he replied with some slight bafflement.

"Hey, I'm weird like that, Omar. You know," she chuckled.

She handed him two dollars, spun around, and dashed back into her apartment. Then Omar entered the stairwell and descended the concrete steps. Unfortunately, he had to pass someone's fresh urine and empty beer bottles. It was the reality of the ghetto—people's nastiness.

Outside, the sun felt brighter and hotter. A heat wave had dominated the city for the past several days. And it felt like it wasn't cooling off anytime soon. The blazing sun was giving the city of New York a personal bear hug, and it was hanging on tight. Those unfortunate to tolerate the heat without any air condition loitered on the front concrete steps of their buildings dressed loosely in sundresses, T-shirts, shorts, and flip-flops and repeatedly fanned themselves to keep cool as sweat dripped from every pore of their body. Successions of fire hydrants were opened up. The kids and adults took advantage of the gushing water pouring out onto the city street. People did whatever they could to keep themselves cool.

Omar cut through the small, broken glass-covered playground located in the courtyard. He watched as a woman lazily swaggered across the same playground toward a group of men loitering on a bench nearby. She was clad in dirty black shorts, a spaghetti-strapped blouse, and house shoes. Her hair was matted and uncombed, her lips were dry and chapped, and her eyes were sunken deeply into her head. It was no mistake that she was a crackhead searching for her next high. Omar shot her a brief look and minded his business. It was the cost of living in the projects.

He moved with a mission, wanting to hurry to the corner bodega and back. His stomach growled. He was eager to enjoy his mother's cooking. They didn't have much, but his mother always made sure that they had enough. Being poor, Ms. Richards learned how to become creative in the kitchen, and the outcome was masterpieces that seemed impossible to make with the little she had to work with.

"You should write a cookbook," Omar always told his mother.

She would chuckle at the idea and reply with, "Boy, don't anybody wanna know about any recipes coming from the ghetto."

She always shrugged off the idea.

The local bodega on the busy street was the neighborhood landmark. It always had a cash flow of local customers. It was also part of the neighborhood hangout spot.

Fernando had been the owner of the bodega for years. Everyone in the area knew him, and he knew everyone, including Omar. Nice and sweet boy, Fernando always spoke about Omar. Besides Kizzie, Fernando was the second friend in Omar's life. The two had an affinity for Japanese anime—their favorites being *Dragon Ball Z, One-Punch Man, Ghost in the Shell, Naruto Shippuden*, and *Eureka Seven*.

"Have you seen the new episodes of *Dragon Ball* yet?" Fernando asked Omar as he placed the items for purchase on the counter.

"No. Not yet."

"You're missing out. Unfortunately, Goku goes down, and Frieza and Android 17 face off against Jiren. It's an epic battle," said Fernando.

"Wow! I need to see it."

"Yes, my friend. See it soon so we can talk about it," Fernando replied.

The items came to $6.29. Omar stared at the five-dollar bill in his hand; he was short. Fernando smiled. "It's okay; give me the five and pay me the rest when you can."

"You sure, Fernando?" he asked, skeptical.

"You're a friend, and we look out for each other. Besides, your mother makes the best pies in the neighborhood. And when she makes another sweet potato pie, bring me a few slices, okay? Call it even."

Omar smiled. "I definitely will do that."

Omar exited the bodega with the things he needed and wanted to hurry back home. His mother was waiting, and he was starving. But that trip back home wasn't going to be quick. But the moment he exited the bodega, he heard Brice say, "Look at that bitch-ass faggot here! What you got for a nigga?"

Omar stood face-to-face with his worst nightmare.

Brice.

CHAPTER TWO

"I DON'T WANT ANY trouble, Brice. I need to get home," Omar said timidly.

"Nigga, you dissin' me, muthafucka!" Brice exclaimed. "Home is mo' important than me, nigga?"

"No, my mother's cooking, and she needs these items."

"Items . . .?" Brice quickly snatched the plastic bag from Omar's hand and looked inside. "What, milk, butter, cheese . . . What the fuck is this? What ya moms tryin' to cook up? Shit!"

"No . . .no, um . . ." Omar stammered.

"Yeah, I saw you n' ya moms earlier. Bitch is fine fo' her age n' shit. She fuckin'? Nah, it doesn't look like she fuckin'. She could be, though. Tell ya moms if she wants some good dick, then I'll come through, spread them legs, n' stretch my big dick out n' dat aged pussy. Shit, I might fuck da bitch so good dat she might make me ya new stepdaddy." He laughed. "How 'bout that, nigga? Me becomin' ya stepdaddy, n' I start beatin' you like you my stepchild."

Omar remained quiet. He didn't like the vulgar comments about his mother, but he felt helpless. He was outnumbered, and Brice was a muscled thug that got off from bullying everyone and fighting. He stood at six-one and was black as a chalkboard. He was also swathed with tattoos and some battle scars, sported a bald head, and had a face like the back of a tack with two eyes.

"What, faggot? You ain't got shit to say, huh? I just said I wanna fuck da shit outta ya moms, maybe shoot my thick cum down her throat after she finishes suckin' my big, black dick, n' you ain't got shit to say 'bout that, muthafucka? You that pussy, nigga?"

Omar frowned slightly.

Brice continued with, "Yeah, you that pussy, nigga . . . so pussy, lookin' at you got my dick hard."

His gang laughed.

"Look, I don't want any trouble," Omar timidly repeated.

"What . . .? You don't want any trouble. Nigga, fuck ya trouble," Brice shouted. Then he signaled to one of his goons and uttered, "Yo, Tip, snatch dat nigga up fo' me n' let's do this shit."

Tip aggressively grabbed Omar into a treacherous choke hold. He dragged him off the busy street and into a back alleyway where they could continue to bully and torment Omar without anyone seeing them. Omar struggled, but it was futile. Tip was a brute with powerful arms, and if he wanted to, he could break Omar's neck with one slight jolt. The choke hold Omar was in started to restrict his breathing. He tussled with his aggressor, but Tip refused to let up as Omar gasped and became teary-eyed.

"You like that feeling, faggot? Huh, pussy . . . You like that shit, don't you?" Brice taunted.

Tip squeezed harder. Omar felt like he was about to pass out. He begged with his eyes to be released as Tip seemed to enjoy the torture he bestowed on his victim. Brice gave his goon the signal, and right away, Tip released his compelling grip from around Omar's neck. Omar dropped to his knees, huffing and puffing, soothing his neck. He was relieved, but it was only the beginning of the storm.

"My nigga could break ya neck right now n' not bat an eye," said Brice.

Omar's eyes were glued to the ground. He was afraid to look up—to lock eyes with his bully. He didn't want to fight. He wanted to go home.

"You know what, Omar? I'll make you a deal. You let me fuck ya moms once or twice, n' I'll leave you alone for a month. How that shit sounds, huh? You like dat deal?"

Omar remained silent.

Brice was a pervert too. It was known in the neighborhood that his appetite for sex and other sexual vices was outlandish—young or old, he didn't care. It was rumored that he was into young boys too. Growing up, he spent a lot of time in boys' homes and reform schools and was turned out by the older boys when he was an adolescent.

"How 'bout this, since ya moms ain't suckin' dick right now, you suck dick, nigga? Yeah, you do. You a faggot, right?"

"I just wanna go home, Brice, please," Omar begged.

"Home? Muthafucka, you owe me sumthin'," said Brice.

"Owe you what . . .?"

"You walkin' these streets, in this neighborhood, breathin' n' shit. Shit ain't free, nigga. Taxes, muthafucka!"

Omar didn't see it coming. A rapid punch from Brice to his face blindsided him and landed him on his side. His jaw felt like it was on fire.

Brice ominously crouched down near Omar.

"I don't like you, nigga. I never did," Brice expressed. "You just look so fuckin' stupid n' pathetic, nigga. You know what, faggot? . . . Just to prove you a faggot, suck my dick, nigga."

He stood up, unzipped his pants, and pulled it out. It was flaccid and lengthy, and the look on Brice's face told Omar that he was serious.

"No," uttered Omar, his only defiance. "I'm not doing that."

"What, faggot?" Brice shot back, grimacing at what Omar said to him. "You not doin' what . . .?"

He stood there with his dick out, and his crew stood there like it was natural for them to witness Brice force himself on other men—young for the most part—and coerce them into giving him sexual pleasure. What Brice said goes, and no one questioned his sexuality or called him a faggot. He was a ruthless thug that didn't give a fuck—a shot caller.

Omar was terrified. But he was determined not to relinquish to such debauchery. There was no way he would give his bully any oral pleasure.

"You not gonna suck my dick, nigga?" Brice exclaimed.

"I can't do that," Omar cried, his eyes tearing up.

Brice punched him in the face again. It was so hard that Omar felt dizzy and faint and spewed blood from his mouth. Then Brice slapped him in the face twice. He was determined to humiliate and embarrass Omar.

"How 'bout this, faggot? You don't suck it now, you ain't gonna walk again," Brice threatened him.

He stepped closer to Omar with his dick in his hand and was ready to force it down Omar's throat. But then a loud whistle sounded. It came from one of their lookouts at the end of the alleyway, indicating trouble was looming—most likely the police—beat cops, they assumed.

It was time to go. But before his departure, Brice had one more act of cruelty to implement on Omar. He reached into the plastic bag and removed the half gallon of milk purchased for his mother to cook with. He undid the top and menacingly poured it all over Omar, completely wasting it—every drop. And then, to add insult to injury, Brice took aim with his dick in hand and started to piss all over Omar, spewing out his golden stream and dousing him with urine from head to toe. Alerted, Brice zipped it back into his pants and smirked at Omar. And everyone laughed at the cruel act.

"To be continued, faggot-ass nigga, fo' real," Brice warned him.

He pivoted and walked away, leaving Omar on his knees, drenched in milk and piss. The only thing Omar could do was linger there until they were completely gone. And he cried. He had never felt so humiliated in his life. He reeked of piss, but to know that he almost had a dick shoved into his mouth was horrifying. He wasn't gay but felt like a punk—and violated. He was growing tired of being bullied and perpetually helpless against Brice and his gang.

Finally, he picked himself up but was ashamed to go home. It was a long walk to the apartment, but he had no choice. The summer heat wave made him reek boisterously, as every step he took felt agonizing. So many eyes on him were critical and judgmental. He thought that they all were laughing at him, mocking him. He felt like a loser and a victim.

Walking into the apartment, the moment his mother set eyes on her son, she was taken aback. He looked a hot mess, reeking of foulness. Omar looked at her and immediately broke down in tears and hurt. He trembled still from the humiliation he'd suffered. Ms. Richards didn't hesitate to rush her son's way to console him. There weren't any questions about who did this to him or why. She was familiar with the bullies in their neighborhood and that her son had become a prime target for most of them. She helped him remove every bit of soiled clothing and told him to shower. But not before he cried like a baby in her arms and asked, "Why do they keep messing with me, Mama? What did I do to them? Huh? Why?"

Like always, she spewed out a Bible verse to him, proclaiming, "Recompense to no man even for evil. Provide things honest in the sight of all men." And "But I say unto you, Love your enemies, bless them that curse you, do good to them that hate you, and pray for them which despitefully use you, and persecute you."

Omar didn't want to love his enemies at the moment. What he went through was still stuck in his head like superglue. And how can anyone love a menace like Brice? He felt the man was evil, a demon in human skin.

"I want to move," Omar told Kizzie.

He lingered by his bedroom window and gazed at the activity in the courtyard below, observing dealers' transactions with drug users in public. The playground was so littered with trash and dilapidation that it was unsafe for any child to play on. The ghetto felt like hell for Omar. It was hell for him.

"Move? Move to where?" she asked him.

"Anywhere. I would rather be anywhere than here. I hate it here, Kizzie, I do."

She sighed. "Brice is just a lost soul, Omar. Forgive him."

"He's a psychopath," Omar returned.

"Still, the Bible says we need to forgive our enemies. 'For if you forgive others when they sin against you, your heavenly Father will also forgive you. But if you do not forgive others their sins, our Father will not forgive your sins,'" she proclaimed.

"Forgive," he uttered with distaste. "How can you forgive a demon like him? You know what he almost made me do . . .?"

The thought of it brought tears to Omar's eyes. If they hadn't been interrupted by approaching beat cops, there was no doubt in Omar's mind that Brice would have made him do the unthinkable. It was the first time Brice ever committed such perversions against him. Usually, the physical abuse, the mocking, the stealing from him, the beatings, and so on, but it was a disgrace to coerce another man into giving him oral pleasures. He didn't mention it to Kizzie or his mother; he felt embarrassed to bring it up. So, he kept that incident to himself, yearning to lock it away somewhere subterranean and never think about it again. But it was nearly impossible as it was haunting him every day.

Kizzie stared at him empathetically and asked, "What else did he do to you, Omar? What happened?"

Omar shied away from the question and uttered, "Nothing!"

"Something is bothering you."

"Look, I don't wanna talk about it, okay?" he spat.

"Okay. Fine."

Omar continued his profound gaze out his bedroom window. He fixed his eyes on a young female addict disappearing with a dealer behind the city dumpster. They wanted some privacy where she would trade sex for drugs. He watched her drop to her knees to undo his jeans, and she was ready to give him a blow job. Omar turned away from witnessing the sexual act from afar and closed his eyes.

"You sure you're okay, Omar?"

He heaved a heavy sigh and responded with, "Yeah. I'm okay."

Kizzie moved closer to him to give comfort from one friend to another. She was ready to soothe whatever uneasiness he was going through. She sat on his bed near him, her eyes fixed on him, prepared to be an ear to him. She was ready to listen—to talk.

"Omar, I'm your friend, and I'm always gonna be here for you if you need anything . . . even if it is to talk. You're a good man with a good soul, and I want you to know that. And this storm is only temporary. You know God doesn't give us more than we can handle, right?"

He sighed after hearing it. Then, he sarcastically replied, "Well, apparently, God must think I'm some kind of badass then . . . because I've been handling shit since I was born, and it doesn't seem to be getting any better."

"You just need to have faith and patience," she said.

"I wish God would just make Brice go away."

"Things will only happen in His time," she said.

Omar wanted to reply, well, I wish He would hurry up, but he shut his mouth. Kizzie regularly carried an optimistic attitude despite everything she'd been through. She had seen her fair share of pain and misery since she was young. Her mother was a heroin addict, and when Kizzie was four years old, her mother tried to sell her to a local pervert for five hundred dollars. Her grandmother intervened and nearly beat the pervert to death. When she was eight, her mother was supposedly clean and had a new man in her life. Kizzie felt like things were finally looking up for the family. Unfortunately, the boyfriend tried to molest and fondle Kizzie. When she was twelve, her father was brutally murdered. At fourteen, her mother was raped and murdered. When she was sixteen, she was in a terrible car accident and couldn't walk for months. She had physical therapy that her grandmother could barely pay for. When she was eighteen, she was diagnosed with Lupus. It's a deadly disease affecting one's immune system that attacks your own tissues and organs. And yet, having been through all that, Kizzie kept her faith and kept going. She remained optimistic and vibrant.

Omar knew Kizzie had a right to be angry, depressed, pessimistic, and glum, but she wasn't. Instead, she believed God was her healer and would deliver her from anything.

"How do you do it, Kizzie?" he asked. "After everything you've been through, how do you keep going?"

"I just pray a lot, Omar. All I can do is pray and have faith. I know things will work out for me. I'm still here, right?" She smiled.

He smiled. "Yeah. I'm glad you are. What would I do without you?"

"Probably something stupid," she joked.

He laughed. The two had an extraordinary bond that no one understood or could break. Their friendship was as solid as the walls of Ft. Knox.

Kizzie continued to make Omar laugh, and she helped take his mind off his trouble—for the moment.

"You know best friends are like walls," Kizzie started.

"Say what?" Omar replied with a raised eyebrow—baffled by her comment.

"Sometimes you lean on them, and sometimes it's good just knowing they're there," she continued.

Cute. He smiled.

"Best friend," he said.

"Best friends forever . . . Pinky swear," she said.

"Pinky swear."

The two wrapped their pinkies around each other joyfully, laughing and smiling.

CHAPTER THREE

THE MESS ON aisle three was extensive. Someone had accidentally dropped a 1.5 gallon of liquid detergent on the floor, and it was a mess, spilling everywhere. Omar was assigned the task of cleaning it up. He sighed at the spectacle. But it was one of his jobs at the supermarket, cleaning. His duties included guiding customers to items they needed, replenishing the grocery shelves, assisting with checkout, helping customers load their groceries into their vehicles, and cleaning the store. It was mundane work, but he needed the money. In addition, he needed to help pay the bills. His mother worked two jobs; her first was a cashier at the Family Dollar near their home. Her second job was being a waitress during the graveyard shift at a diner, where she had to take two buses and walk two blocks. With three incomes coming into their home, it still wasn't enough, as their debt continued to pile up, and it seemed like they were late every month with their rent.

After cleaning up the mess on aisle three, Omar's shift was almost over. It had been a long day. Work felt uncomfortable for him. He assumed his coworkers and the shoppers were mocking him behind his back. It felt like they knew what had happened to him the other day with Brice. He thought the word was out that Brice almost made him perform oral sex. He knew it was blasphemy and went against everything he stood for. Nevertheless, the immoral act was eating away at him. Omar wanted to snatch off the green smock he wore and hurry home.

He didn't want to become paranoid, but he was becoming paranoid.

"You did a good job today, Omar. You can leave early," said his supervisor.

"Thanks," Omar replied.

"Are you still looking to do overtime tomorrow?"

"Of course. I need the money," said Omar.

"Well, I'm gonna need you to stay and help close up. And this Saturday, the truck will arrive early; I'm gonna also need you to help unload everything."

Omar smiled. "You can count on me, Mr. Palmer."

He removed his smock and rushed to clock out. It was early evening in the summer. The heat wave was still gripping the city. The streets of Brownsville were hot from the scorching sun and a drug war that was escalating because of the death of Sean Black.

Omar grabbed his book bag and changed his shoes. He clocked out and left the neighborhood supermarket in a hurry. As he went home, the Brooklyn streets were bustling with folks and activity. As he crossed Rockaway Avenue, several police cars flew by him in haste, with their overhead police sirens blaring, indicating something terrible had happened. Omar kept his eyes on the screaming cop cars until they turned the corner two blocks down. The summer heat brought out craziness and violence.

It didn't take him long to find out where the cops were headed and what had happened. Nearby where he lived, two men lay dead in the front seat of a dark green BMW, their bodies riddled with bullets and contorted in death, with their blood, brains, and flesh grotesquely splashed everywhere. They had been hit with semiautomatic rifles that left a mess. Cops were ubiquitous, and a crowd had gathered around the crime scene.

The dead men were part of a drug crew and an escalating drug war. Since Sean Black's demise, two confrontations started to surface in the neighborhood. One, Sean Black's crew was in a civil war for supremacy over the organization. The latter, a rival gang, had moved in, seeing opportunity and growth with the drug kingpin dead.

Omar awkwardly walked by the crime scene and saw the bodies sprawled out in the car. He had seen death before, and it always made him uncomfortable. *Why kill each other?* he thought. Brownsville was plagued with death and violence, and he was tired of it.

The only thing he wanted to do was go home, eat something, and relax. His bedroom was an escape from it all—the chaos happening in the community. It was the one place where he felt truly safe. There, he could watch his anime on his old DVD player, something he had saved up for, and fantasize about a world far from his own.

"Ma, I'm home," Omar announced when he crossed the threshold into the apartment. There was no response. "Ma, you home?"

He moved through the living room and into the kitchen, where he gasped abruptly and became shocked. His mother was sprawled out across the kitchen floor facedown, a broken plate and spilled food spewed everywhere. She had collapsed.

"Ma!" Omar cried out, immediately rushing to her aid.

He dropped to his knees and cradled his mother into his arms. Tears started to well in his eyes as he flew into an absolute panic.

"Ma, wake up! Wake up!" he shouted. "C'mon, wake up. Please!"

She was unresponsive. Omar hurried out of the apartment and frantically banged on Kizzie's door in a full-blown panic. It opened with Kizzie seeing a hysterical Omar. His eyes were drenched with tears, and his face was soaked with fear.

"Omar, what's happening? What's wrong?" she asked promptly.

"It's my mother. She passed out. Call 911," he cried out.

"Ohmygod!" she uttered and instantly sprang into action. Unfortunately, the Richards didn't have a phone in their apartment, so Kizzie hurried and grabbed her cordless phone, raced out of her apartment, and dashed into Omar's. She speedily dialed 911 while doing so and was on the phone with the 911 dispatcher.

"Ma'am, is she still breathing?" the dispatcher asked.

"I don't know!" Kizzie exclaimed.

"If she's not, then I'm gonna need you to perform CPR. I can coach you through it," said the dispatcher.

"Please, help her!" Omar shouted.

"The paramedics and police are on their way. But I need for you to check for a pulse."

Kizzie was doing everything in her power to save her neighbor's life. She was scared. Omar was powerless and continued to panic. He paced around the area, crying and praying to God to save his mother's life. Kizzie checked for a pulse, and startlingly, she was still breathing.

"She's breathing," Kizzie animatedly told the dispatcher.

"That's good. Help is on the way."

Kizzie and Omar sat in the waiting area of Brookdale Hospital. Their nerves were on high. Kizzie held Omar's hands inside hers as the two sat closely together and kept Ms. Richards in their prayers. They were silent. She was his comfort—his support when it felt like the walls were collapsing on Omar—what could go wrong was going wrong. They both were worried, but it was Kizzie who remained composed. The two felt alone and deserted, even with the waiting area bustling with people. Omar's mother had been rushed into the emergency room over an hour ago, and there still hadn't been any word from any person about her condition.

"She's gonna be fine, Omar," Kizzie finally spoke.

"I hope so. I don't know what I'm gonna do without her, Kizzie," Omar replied despondently. "Where are these doctors? They need to tell us something."

"God's got this. He's in control. He's gonna pull your mother through," she assured him.

He didn't respond to her statement. Instead, he was a nervous wreck and couldn't think straight. He wanted to charge into the back room to see about his mother's condition, maybe become aggressive toward the staff, and demand answers. It was a rare time when he showed assertiveness. But Kizzie kept him seated, somewhat calm, and in prayer.

"I know you got this, God. I know you do," said Kizzie.

Finally, after waiting an hour, a doctor emerged from the double doors separating them from the emergency room and came their way, his eyes blank. Omar and Kizzie didn't take their eyes off him. He was a Caucasian, tall, clad in blue scrubs with a stethoscope around his neck, with blue eyes with dark, cropped hair. His attention was on the two young adults. Omar stood, and Kizzie followed. Before he could stop in their presence, Omar immediately asked him with apprehension, "How is she?"

A brief silence followed by the grim news. "Your mother suffered from a hemorrhagic stroke," said the doctor.

Omar never heard of the condition.

"She had a stroke?" he uttered incredulously and in a distressing tone. "But is she okay?"

"Unfortunately, she's in a medically induced coma. Blood flow to a certain area of the brain had been cut off . . . meaning her brain cells were deprived of oxygen and began to die. We're doing our best for her, but it's bleak," the doctor proclaimed.

The news was upsetting.

"Can we go see her?" Kizzie asked.

The doctor nodded.

Seeing his mother in such a grim condition made Omar shed more tears. It was a hurtful sight. His mother had a stroke, and her chances of survival weren't good. About ten to fifteen percent of people who suffer from such a stroke die before they reach the hospital, and forty percent die within the first week. It was known that fifty percent die within the first six months.

Omar sat next to his mother and took her hand into his. He squeezed it gently, wishing she would squeeze his hand back. But there was no reaction. His mother looked like a vegetable lying on the hospital gurney, and Kizzie stood over them, sad also. She placed her hand on Omar's shoulder, closed her eyes, and prayed for her neighbor's condition. Troubled, Omar sat there, staring at his mother.

"Please don't leave me," he said quietly to her.

And he continued to pray with Kizzie.

CHAPTER FOUR

IT WAS DAY three of Ms. Richards being in a vegetative state. She would lie there, having not gained any awareness. But she always had company. Omar visited his mother at the hospital every day, talking to her, praying for her, and trying to have faith that she would recover. The medical staff checked her vitals regularly. However, Omar had another problem. They didn't have any medical insurance. So, every day his mother spent at the hospital being treated was becoming costly. The extra price tag was thrusting him into more debt. His supervisor understood his situation, but no money came in. Omar didn't work. It was a step closer to him and his mother becoming homeless. But his priority was his mother's health.

It was the umpteenth day of what seemed to be an endless heat wave. Brownsville was teeming with positive and negative activity from block to block. The sun felt like it was in a conspiracy against the city. The streets and sidewalks felt like someone could fry an egg on them and could cause a third-degree burn if skin touched any part of the asphalt. It was so hot that the mayor could cry out a state of emergency.

Omar exited the elevated train station onto Rockaway Avenue with a heavy heart. He hated to leave his mother at the hospital but visiting hours had ended. Back in the concrete jungle of Brownsville, he hurried across the busy avenue and made his way home. But unbeknownst to him, it wouldn't be a simple walk home. His mind was elsewhere as he walked the urban blocks and became distracted by stress and worries. He moved mindlessly, unaware of his surroundings and not knowing he was being followed. It was a mistake he would come to regret.

Brice and his crew tailed Omar since he descended from the train station. Brice was craving to catch Omar alone and continue or finish what they'd started a week ago. They subtly shadowed Omar into the towering projects. They planned on attacking him once he was in the lobby of his building. There, they planned on dragging him into the stairwell and fucking him up. Brice wanted to take his time punishing and torturing Omar. He figured they wouldn't be interrupted in the project stairwell. There, they all could take their time fuckin' up the nigga, and Brice was ready to take things further. Something about Omar made Brice want to humiliate him, not just with a swift beating, either.

Oddly, he wanted to come in that fool's mouth.

Omar was attacked as soon as he swung open the weathered doors to his building and stepped into the lobby. Several thugs swarmed Omar like flies to shit. He was overwhelmed with punches and aggressively forced into the stairwell as Brice had planned.

"Yeah, muthafucka!" Brice shouted. "To be continued right now, nigga."

He was queerly excited.

Omar became wide-eyed with panic. Five of them were there; he was outnumbered, outmuscled, and no match for any of them. Brice had a sinister look on his face that uncovered his perversions and iniquity. He was eager to beat, torture, and do unnatural things to Omar.

"I told you, nigga, we gon' catch up again. N' this time, ain't no interruptions, muthafucka. We got *all* evening," said Brice with a cocksure smile.

They held Omar down submissively.

"Let me go!" Omar shouted, trying to wrestle himself free.

Tip kicked him in the ribs twice, and it was a crippling hit that shot severe pain through Omar's body and made it feel like something had broken inside of him. He cringed from the pain and wailed.

"I'm 'bout to make you my fuckin' bitch right now, nigga," said Brice in an ominous tone.

"Brice, please, don't do this to me!" Omar begged.

"What, nigga . . . Don't do what?" Brice continued to taunt him as he started to unzip his pants. "I'm gonna make you suck my dick until you spit out cum."

It was a nightmare coming true for Omar. How could Brice's crew allow such a thing to happen? Omar wanted to know. It was baffling. It was homosexual; it was gay, which was utterly frowned upon in the hood, especially in the Ville. Yet, they were about to force Omar to suck dick and maybe rape him in the stairwell.

"No! Let me go!" Omar screamed. "I can't do that. No!"

"Nigga, like you got a choice," replied Brice, who gripped his lengthy erection and was ready to implement the bestial act. "And if you bite me, nigga, I swear to God I'm gon' knock out ya teeth and fuck you up real bad."

His goons laughed. It was going to be a captivating thing to see. Omar deduced that they were all gay—in the closet, and that's why they didn't have a problem with what was about to happen.

"My mother's in the hospital!" Omar exclaimed.

"Yeah, I heard 'bout dat bitch. Guess what? When I'm done wit' you, how 'bout I pay that bitch a visit n' fuck that bitch in the ass?" he laughed. "Yeah, that probably will bring the bitch back to life. Fuck her good too. She needs that dick."

The insult made Omar fume. *How dare he disrespect my mother like that*, he thought. She meant everything to him. She was his world, and Brice insulted her like she wasn't shit—like she was shit at the bottom of his shoe. He mocked her condition, and something suddenly came over him. Seething from the rudeness Brice implemented, somehow, Omar could jerk his way free. With Brice towering over him with his manhood exposed, Omar clenched his fingers into a tight fist and swung away with all his might. He aimed directly at the genitals and punched Brice in his balls so hard that the man was suddenly overcome with pain. Brice folded over and dropped to his knees, wailing like a child. Omar then sprang to his feet and ran. He bolted up the stairwell onto the second floor and fled down the hallway. Brice's goons gave chase, and so did Brice himself when he finally recovered from the pain.

"We gonna fuck you up, muthafucka!" Brice heatedly screamed.

Omar ran to the second stairwell at the other end of the hallway and descended the iron stairs so fast that he nearly tripped and fell. But he caught his footing and ran as fast as possible, knowing his life depended on it. Brice and his goons were right behind him. If caught, they might kill him.

Omar hurried out into the public from the building, and he scampered and zigzagged through the courtyard and playground. It was a wild chase, and he dared not to look back. His heart pounded against his chest, and his legs and arms moved feverishly. He moved so fast that it felt like he was running on air. He daringly dashed across the busy avenue into heavy traffic, nearly getting hit by a moving car. Car horns blew Omar's way, and drivers cursed at him while his foes were still in heated pursuit. Omar scurried and crisscrossed through the urban landscape and spun into a narrow alley. He soon found the turn was a mistake. It led him to a dead end, and he tripped over something, stumbled, and hit the ground hard on his side.

Brice and his crew caught up to him in a hurry. It had been a long and winded chase, but now, they had Omar right where they wanted him, cornered like a trapped stag. They were flustered with rage. They were ready to beat him to death and do ungodly things to him. Omar was on the ground on his side, helpless. It was palpable to him that hell was about to rain down on him like in Revelation, and there was no way he would survive it. The way Brice glared at him, it was murderous.

"You punch me 'n my dick, nigga! I swear to God I'm 'bout kill ya ass right now," he growled through his clenched teeth.

Omar cowered near the small pile of trash and rubble stacked against a brick wall. He outstretched his arm against the ground for some reason . . . and his hand came across something strange—something hard—something metal. His fingers wrapped around the handle of a pistol—a .357 Magnum that lay obscured beneath the rubbish. Brice ominously charged his way with the intent to tear him apart with absolute rage. His crew was ready to do the same. Omar sprang from the ground with the gun in his hand and aimed at a stampeding Brice and the others. The weapon was unexpected, and Brice was caught off guard. He was in awe of the weapon in Omar's hand.

"Don't come any closer!" Omar warned them, waving the gun around wildly.

Brice scowled at Omar and snarled, "What da fuck you gon' do wit' that shit, bitch? You ain't got da fuckin' balls to shoot me!"

It was a daring statement from Brice.

"I swear, Brice, I'll shoot you right now," Omar cried.

His heart was racing, and his palms became clammy. It was the first time he ever held a weapon in his hands. He was still shaken, jumpy, and breathing heavily.

Stepping angrily closer to Omar, Brice exclaimed, "You know what I'ma do to you, faggot? I'm gon' snatch dat fuckin' gun away from you n' fuck you wit' it. How 'bout *that*, muthafucka?"

"I'm warning you, Brice!" Omar shouted.

Brice was ready to challenge him, call out his bluff.

Omar kept his arm outstretched with the revolver at the end of it. He had enough! He felt this sudden rage prevail over him. It was a feeling he had never felt before. He abruptly felt absolute power consuming him. The .357 became squeezed tighter in his grip, and he seethed. He was ready to react and pull the trigger, fearing what they wanted to do to him and being afraid to walk in his neighborhood. He finally had the advantage, going from prey to predator. His lucid thinking encouraged him to kill Brice immediately, and it would all disappear. A voice in his mind said, "*Go ahead and kill him. Kill him!*"

It was a daunting thought for Omar, taking someone's life. The sudden voice inside his head was mesmerizing and manipulating. It empowered him with hatred and rage to execute revenge.

"You will no longer feel weak."

Every wrong they had done to him all started to amplify with the gun clutched in his hand. Omar looked fiercely at Brice and his cronies and wanted that power never to feel weak or vulnerable again.

"Kill them!"

Brice continued to believe that Omar was bluffing. Finally, he had enough of the idle threat—the pussy with the gun in his hand. He took a few steps closer to Omar and wanted to snatch away the gun and fuck him up with it. But Omar cocked back the hammer to the .357 like he knew what he was doing. The fierce look in his eyes finally registered to Brice that he had had enough. A scared dog backed into a corner will suddenly become a vicious threat.

Brice halted his action.

Omar had no more words to eject; the rising intensity in his eyes showed the actual threat. The way he suddenly held the gun in his grasp, unexpectedly looking undaunted by Brice and his crew and having the hammer to the gun cocked back and ready to fire. *Where did this sudden cockiness come from?* they all thought.

"A'ight, nigga, you got this one," Brice finally relented. "But I'ma see you around, pussy. You wanna pull out guns on niggas? I got you, pussy." He chuckled bizarrely.

Brice coolly backed away from Omar. He didn't have a choice. The barrel was aimed directly at his head, and a bullet coming from that size of a barrel would make a mess of him at close range. His cronies followed his submission, retreating from the alley. Brice angrily kept his eyes on Omar, and Omar did the same. Finally, Omar lowered the gun and sighed with relief when they were gone. The weapon had saved his life, and he was grateful. He stood there and gazed at it for a while. It was an intriguing gun. The markings on its sides were creative and spellbinding. The weapon felt rhythmic in his hand—almost singing or cooing to him. Briefly, he thought about tossing the gun back into the rubbish, but he didn't. The allure was there. Omar felt he needed the weapon. So he tucked it into his waistband, concealing it, and cautiously returned home.

Once there, he removed the gun from his waistband and sat at the foot of his bed. His eyes remained fixed on the weapon.

"You are a beautiful piece of work," he announced out loud, becoming intrigued. "Wow."

That night, he placed the gun underneath his pillow and slept with it close to him. He would wake up tomorrow, and it would feel like a brand-new day to him—a day of Genesis—his rebirth.

CHAPTER FIVE

THE SKY WAS black with tranquility fastened to the poetry of stars. It was a warm, black night that hugged you no matter what, with an alluring full moon above. The heat wave that had gripped the city the past several days had subsided some, giving the town a slightly needed break from the oppressive humidity. Every inch of the city was buzzing with summer activities. The summer night became abuzz with what made the city and Brooklyn the concrete jungle. It was a beautiful night to enjoy, but it wasn't picturesque for everyone.

Omar stood on the gravel rooftop of his building and aimlessly gazed out at the sprawling scenery. This urban concrete jungle constantly rumbled with crime, poverty, grief, and heartache. Brooklyn was illuminated for the sky to see. But there was gaping darkness inside Omar—darkness gripped him like death. He stood aloof. He was grieving heavily, becoming filled with anguish. His eyes were saturated with tears. It felt like his world had ended, his life spent. The tears continued to pour out. His mother had died today—early in the afternoon, finally succumbing to her stroke.

"I'm sorry," uttered the doctor despondently to Omar. "We did everything we could do for her."

The news had hit Omar heavily, like a speeding 18-wheeler on the highway. He became a mess. He felt splattered everywhere with profound grief, misery, heartache, and sorrow. First, he hunched over and wailed so loudly that it sounded like a screaming banshee. Then suddenly, his legs became weak, soft, and wobbly like Jell-O, and he fell to his knees, overcome with grief. *No. She can't be dead*, he believed.

"Mama!" he cried out. "Mama! Mama!"

Kizzie rushed to console him. She too was grieving, Ms. Richards was like a mother to her, but she needed to be there for Omar. She crouched with him and wrapped her arms around him like a blanket. It was hard to believe that she was gone. Her tears poured out too.

"It's going to be okay, Omar," she said.

"She's gone, Kizzie. My mama's gone," he cried out.

"It's going to be okay. God has His reasons. He does."

"No. It's not gonna be okay, Kizzie. She's gone! She's gone! Oh God," he belted out.

His tears continued to fall, creating a small puddle near him. The thought of never seeing his mother again was crushing. It was unimaginable.

"I need to see her," he said.

Omar walked into the hospital room and fixed his eyes on his mother's still body on the bed. It was like she was resting, being in peace. But she would never open her eyes again. He would never hear her voice, feel her hug, enjoy her laugh, or receive her words of comfort again. He was alone now. It was a daunting feeling. It was a feeling that gripped him and made him shudder like it was a cold winter night.

He neared her body, took her motionless hand into his, leaned forward with copious tears in his eyes, and gently kissed her forever.

"I love you, Mama, and . . . and I'm gonna miss you so much," he wholeheartedly proclaimed.

Just seeing her still and lifeless was tearing him apart. Kizzie stood by his side, and she took his hand into hers. She was teary-eyed too, her eyes on Ms. Richards and her heart in sizeable sorrow. She sighed. There was no explaining it, death, and there was no question why God took her so soon. Her beliefs told her not to question God's way. But it wasn't the same for Omar.

The more tears he wiped away, the harder they came. His mournful demeanor was perpetual, and at that moment, he wished he were dead too.

"She's home now, Omar. She's with the Lord," said Kizzie.

He remained silent, still holding his mother's hand and gazing at her body.

"Whatever you need, I'm here for you, Omar. Just ask me, okay? She was like a mother to me too," Kizzie continued.

Omar remained silent. He heard her, but he was in too much pain to respond. His mind was elsewhere. It was a yearning that it was still yesterday where his mother was cooking one of her special meals for him, singing to him or soothing him when things became heavy and harsh. She was his rock, always his foundation. And to think that her body would soon be lying in some cold morgue on some cold slab and some strange man cutting open her body, it was disheartening to him.

"I need some air," said Omar, pivoting from his mother's body and marching out of the room.

Kizzie decided not to follow him. She knew he needed some time and some space. So instead, she too went closer to the body, kissed Ms. Richard's forehead, and proclaimed to her how she would be deeply missed, knowing she was now in heaven.

Omar stared up at the bright full moon and frowned. Hours after her death, things still felt unreal. The tears had finally stopped, but that ache and sadness were still embedded in him, and it wasn't going away anytime soon. He stood on the rooftop like a statue—like a lost soul, feeling almost suicidal and pondering about his future. It wasn't until he heard the door to the rooftop open that he moved and turned his head to see who was joining him. It was Kizzie. Somehow, she knew where he would be so late. She knew her friend well.

"I figured you would be up here," she said.

"What do you want, Kizzie?" he asked indifferently.

"I wanted to see how you're doing."

"How do you think I'm doing? My mother is dead, and she's not coming back."

"I know, but remember she's in a better place, Omar. She's with God now."

He chuckled and scoffed. "With God, huh . . .? Why can't she be here with me? *I'm* the one who needs her more than God."

"Omar, you can't question His ways—"

"And why not?" he chided. "Where was God when *I* needed Him? Huh? I can't even afford to bury my mother, Kizzie. Can you believe that? My mother's body is lying in some cold morgue right now, and I don't have a penny to my name to put her to rest. How I'm gonna pay for her funeral? Can you answer me that, Kizzie?"

"I believe it will work out, Omar. Just—"

"Have faith and pray! Is *that* what you were going to say? You want me to pray? I've been having faith and praying since I was knee high with my mother, you, and the pastor. And for what? Look where I'm at now—nowhere! My mother's dead, and I'm still poor, and I'm helpless and got nothing to show for all my praying and faith," he proclaimed expressively.

"Omar—" Kizzie started to say.

"No! I just need time to think and be alone."

"But you're not alone," she said.

"I need to be."

"Jesus said to her, 'I am the resurrection and the life. The one who believes in me will live, even though they die, and whoever lives by believing in me will never die,'" she proclaimed.

"I'm in no mood to hear Bible verses, Kizzie."

"Maybe you need to," she shot back. "Brothers and sisters, we do not want you to be uninformed men about those who sleep in death so that you do not grieve like the rest of mankind, who have no hope. For we believe that Jesus died and rose again, and so we believe that God will bring with Jesus those who have fallen asleep in Him."

"Believe, huh?" Omar uttered, and then he did the unthinkable that frightened Kizzie.

He leaped onto the edge of the rooftop without a second thought, looking like he was ready to jump off and commit suicide. Kizzie was startled by Omar's reckless and terrifying action.

"Omar, are you crazy? What are you doing? Get down from that ledge," she hollered.

"You believe in Him, and you will never die, right?" he exclaimed, mocking the verse. "We shouldn't be afraid of death, right? So why not jump, huh?"

"Omar, just get down from there," she cried out.

"Why?" he screamed. "We all gotta die someday!"

"You know suicide is a sin."

"Everything's a sin! Fuck it! Why do we have to suffer? We do everything right, we try to have faith and keep praying, but everything bad comes our way. Why can a fool like Brice do what the fuck they want to do to people and not suffer? Huh? Why does my mamma have to die, and that fool gets to live and continue to hurt and bully people? But my mother never hurt anyone in her life, and *she* died," he proclaimed gruffly.

"I don't know, Omar. But please, don't do anything stupid. We already lost your mother; I can't afford to lose you too. So please, just get down off that ledge and talk to me," she pleaded. "I know you're hurting, but I'm here for you. I will always be there for you."

He stared at her intensely. All it took was one step backward, and he would plunge eighteen stories to his death. Yet, he remained undaunted, being so close to ending himself. His attitude had changed. Without difficulty, he stared down at the long, harrowing drop and felt nothing—not an ounce of fear of falling was inside of him.

"You think your mother would want this for you?" said Kizzie. "You need to live on for her and become better for her, Omar. Just get down."

He sighed heavily and decided to step down from the ledge, and Kizzie was greatly relieved. However, when his feet touched the gravel, Kizzie angrily pushed him and exclaimed, "What is *wrong* with you, Omar? That was stupid! You scared me half to death."

"I just need to be alone, Kizzie. And I have to figure out a way to bury my mother . . . if God can help me with that," he replied matter-of-factly.

He marched past her and left the rooftop. Kizzie stood there in shock at his behavior, knowing something was wrong with him. She heaved a worried sigh and said a silent prayer for Omar.

"He needs you now more than ever, Lord," she announced.

Once again, Omar found himself gazing at the gun. He was in the privacy of his bedroom, sitting at the foot of his bed. He inspected every inch of the weapon like he was some kind of master of arms. The markings on the .357 were odd but intriguing at the same time. He stood up and walked toward the mirror. He stared at his reflection in the mirror, shirtless and thin, and then he outstretched his arm with the gun at the end of it and pointed the barrel at his reflection. The barrel of the weapon seemed gaping. It almost felt natural in his hand. For a moment, he stood poised in the mirror like he was ready to pull the trigger on himself.

He smiled.

"I like it," he said.

He opened the weapon to check for bullets. It carried six rounds. And strangely, the bullets had the same markings as the gun did. Omar became remarkably familiar with the weapon. It almost felt like the gun were speaking to him and trying to become one with him. He liked how it felt in his hand and how he looked with it in the mirror. It was a beautiful piece of work, and the weapon's designer was exceptionally creative. It all felt priceless.

The sudden knocking at the apartment door snapped Omar out of his trance with the weapon. He groaned with an attitude. He was in no mood to have any company. He placed the gun underneath his pillow and went to see who was visiting him.

Looking through the peephole, he saw Pastor Morgan and his wife standing in the hallway, waiting to be allowed inside. Omar huffed. He wasn't in the mood to be in their presence. He knew why they showed up, to give their condolences regarding his mother. They were faithful church members, and a member's death brought comfort and a spiritual lecture from the pastor. He finally decided to open the door, knowing Pastor Morgan wouldn't go away. When the pastor saw Omar, he threw his arms around the young man and hugged him.

"Your mother was a great woman, Omar. A great woman, and she will be sorely missed," he proclaimed wholeheartedly.

"Thank you."

"She's with the Lord now. She's in peace," he said.

Mrs. Morgan gave Omar a calming hug and offered her condolences. Then the couple stepped into the apartment to spend time with him. They knew he was alone. To them, he was family.

"My Father's house has many rooms; if that were not so, would I have told you that I am going there to prepare a place for you? And if I prepare a place for you, I will come back and take you to be with me that you also may be where I am. You know the way to the place I'm going," Pastor Morgan said, announcing a Bible verse.

The pastor was known for spitting out scripture at the drop of a dime. He knew the good word like the back of his hand.

The couple took a seat on the old couch in the living room. The apartment had seen better days. It was poor and rundown, but it was still home to Omar. Moreover, it was home now more than ever, for memories of his mother were everywhere.

"How are you holding up?" the pastor's wife asked.

"Good days and bad days," he replied feebly.

"If you need anything, just ask us, Omar . . . and come ask the church," said Pastor Morgan. "I know you can't afford to have your mother buried right now; that's why I'm asking for donations from our members to help you."

Omar managed to smile. "Thank you. I appreciate that."

"You are forever in our prayers," said the pastor. "And listen, you are invited into our home anytime. The first lady considered putting together a special dinner to honor your mother. But, of course, now you know my wife and your mother are some of the best cooks in Brooklyn. But boy, I will miss your mother's sweet potato pies."

They all were going to miss her pies.

Pastor Morgan and his wife spent fifteen minutes with Omar inside the apartment. As predicted, the pastor gave him a spiritual lecture about faith, life, death, and hope. He told Omar that God is always in control no matter what happens and will never forsake you.

When they left, Omar felt more lost than ever. The pastor and his wife's visit did more harm to him than good. He thought, *How are they gonna help me bury my mother when the church is so poor?*

The church was already looking for donations to fix the roof. Funerals were expensive; the going cost was three thousand dollars or more. Omar had nowhere that kind of money, not even ten percent of that. And for cremation, it was five hundred. His mother was lying in the hospital morgue. If a funeral director didn't come to pick up the body soon, then she would go "unclaimed," or Omar would have to waive his rights to the body. Unclaimed bodies were treated as "indigent" who died in poverty.

It was a depressing thought for Omar if push comes to shove. Having his mother go unclaimed if the church or he couldn't come through for a funeral was unbearable. He didn't want her to be cremated. He didn't want a fire to touch any part of his mother's remains, knowing her body would be reduced to ashes. She came from the earth, and he wanted her body to be placed back into the ground. It was the Christian way, right?

CHAPTER SIX

PRICE FUNERAL HOME on Mother Gaston Boulevard was quaint, certified, and welcoming. It had been in the neighborhood for ages, and everyone from grandmothers to politicians and gangbangers had been serviced there. It was a family-run business, and their homegoings were extraordinary, something to talk about. They were known for caring for the family and their deceased loved ones—always going the extra mile.

However, Omar couldn't believe the prices they were giving him. He sat there in front of the funeral director, Mr. Williams, stunned by the prices.

"Six to seven thousand to have a funeral for my mother?" he said. "I-I can't afford that, Mr. Williams."

"First off, my condolences to you for your loss. To lose a mother is hard. But that is the average cost, Mr. Omar. And if your mother didn't have any insurance, unfortunately, the family will have to cover the cost," he said. "But our prices include viewing and burial, transporting her remains from the morgue to our funeral home, a casket, embalming, and other preparations."

They didn't have shit!

Omar sighed. It had been three days since her death. He was like a chicken with its head cut off, scrambling about wildly, trying to get his mother's body out of the city morgue and into the ground where she belonged. Each passing day was agony for him, knowing his mother was rotting away in some cold fridge on some cold slab, and the only family she had, was him.

His heart was heavy.

"And what if I can't afford any of that?" he asked.

Mr. Williams had the difficult task of giving him the grim news. "Well, unfortunately, if you simply can't come up with the money to pay for cremation or burial costs, you can sign a release form with the city's coroner's office that says you can't afford to bury her," he informed him.

"A release form?"

"Yes. If you sign the release, the county and state will pitch in to bury or cremate the body," he said. "But it won't be on your terms, and you won't have any say-so on when and where it will happen."

Omar didn't like the sound of that. His mother was a good woman, and she deserved better than to be treated like shit—like she was gum or shit on someone's shoe where they wiped it off and simply threw it away. He was determined to give his mother a proper burial.

He eyed the funeral director with seriousness and said to him, "I'll get you your money to bury my mother."

"I hope so, Mr. Omar. Your mother sounded like she was a good woman."

"She was a great woman. The best," he replied wholeheartedly.

He stood up, shook hands with the man, and left. He had a daunting task to implement, and he wondered how to keep his promise.

He exited the funeral home and marched home with a purpose. But, unfortunately, time wasn't on his side.

It was a stressful walk back, but it was simple, with no difficulties. He didn't run into Brice or any of his cronies. Omar hadn't seen Brice around in days. But when he got to his apartment door, Kizzie's door opened immediately, and she approached Omar with a sense of urgency.

"Omar, ohmygod, I'm glad you're okay," she said.

"Yeah, I'm fine. Why are you asking?"

"I heard that Brice is on a rampage looking for you, asking everyone where your apartment is," she said. "They said you pulled a gun on him the other day. I know that's a lie."

"He's bent on destroying me, Kizzie," said Omar.

"I heard he just got out of jail yesterday."

It explained why Omar hadn't seen him around lately.

"You need to be careful," Kizzie continued. "Maybe you need to just stay home for a few days."

"While my mother's body is still lying and rotting in the morgue?" he uttered. "I need money to bury her, and I don't have a dime to my name."

"I'll help you the best I can," said Kizzie. "I have some money saved up, at least three hundred dollars. You can have it."

Omar smiled. He appreciated it, but it wasn't nearly enough.

"Thank you, Kizzie. But I'll find some way to get the money and bury my mother," he replied coolly.

She smiled. "I know you will. I'm always praying for you."

Omar unlocked his door and went into the apartment. Each day alone inside it, without his mother around, felt surreal. The summer months without an air conditioner or an oscillating fan made the place feel like a sauna. So hot! He went into the bathroom, turned on the faucet, and splashed cold water onto his face, trying to cool off. He then entered his bedroom and removed the gun concealed underneath his pillow. He sat down with the weapon in his hand and stared at it. His thoughts were cultivating into something mischievous and devious. He was desperate.

By any means necessary, he thought to himself—if they *were* his thoughts.

For a long moment, the only thing Omar did was sit on his bed and gaze at the weapon, again transfixed by it. He thought about things, more often than not, *unnatural* things. At one moment, he felt odd. He'd lost track of time with the .357. Nightfall now covered the city, and he had wasted time. He stood up and went to the window. Like a harmful habit in the community, the evening hour brought about several illicit activities. Omar watched from his bedroom window the night owls of the neighborhood conduct drug transactions with the drug users. The fiends were like roaches in the night, scattered and hidden but everywhere. He sighed. It had been a long day, and he needed some sleep. Peeling away from his clothing and being in his boxers, he held the gun in his hand again for one last time, and he felt this sudden urge—the urge to covet. He was craving something, but he didn't know what exactly. It was an ambiguous and lingering longing. One that he felt wasn't so easy to satisfy. Finally, he placed the gun underneath his pillow and climbed into bed.

Tomorrow would be another day—an innovative day to raise money to bury his mother.

The bedroom was dark, and it was still. It was after three a.m., and Omar was sound asleep, out like a newborn baby. A police siren wailed from the city street. The blaring noise traveled to his open window, which quickly grew fainter the farther the police car traveled. It was the devil's hour; some would call it . . . the witching hour. It was a time of night associated with supernatural events. When the devil, sin, and demonic creatures appeared, they were believed to be their most potent at this hour. It was deemed a time of the peak of supernatural activity due to the absence of prayers.

For a moment, Omar twisted and turned on his bed. He was dreaming. The room grew darker, nearly becoming pitch black. The door that had been slightly ajar suddenly closed silently without any help, and everything felt at a standstill. Even the noise from outside seeping through his window had suddenly subsided and stopped. It was sheer solitude inside the dark room. It was almost suffocating.

Omar slept on his back, and he snored a little. He seemed dead to the world, and sleeping was the only time he had absolute peace. The only thing desirable for him was forty winks. But there was a sudden presence with him, an apparition. The air in the room became thick, and some invading entity hovered over Omar, moving closer to him while he slept.

Omar's heart started to pound fast as he lay still, and while asleep, he grew an unexpected erection. It appeared through the slit of his boxers, and it seemed that some entity was seducing him in his sleep. First, he breathed as if receiving some oral pleasure—a blow job. Then, eyes closed and asleep, he clutched the sheets tightly and squirmed while huffing with delight.

"*Soon!*" he heard it say.

In the middle of the sexual climax, he woke suddenly and glimpsed a succubus as she was vanishing. Startled, Omar shot up from the bed and dashed to turn on the lights, but nothing appeared amiss. He was convinced that it was no dream; it was real. His genitals were throbbing and hot. He knew he had to experience an orgasm—but from whom and why.

He wandered into the bathroom to have a look in the mirror. He was shocked.

"What the hell?" he uttered.

His eyes were completely bloodshot and red.

"Let me get two," the young fiend quickly said to the crack dealer lingering in the ghetto lobby.

"C'mon," he said to her.

She followed him into the deepness of the inner-city stairwell, yearning for her treat. The youthful drug dealer reached into his stash and removed two crack vials to serve the user. Money and drugs were hurriedly exchanged, and the drug user pivoted shrilly and marched away from him, ready to shoot up and get high like the sky. She urgently disappeared into the dimness of the building. At the same time, the dealer added her cash to his growing stack of hard currency. He carried a small wad of bills that he placed inside his jacket. He returned to his position in the lobby, waiting for his next customer to arrive.

Unbeknownst to him, he was being watched.

It didn't take long for his next customer to appear. The business was moving and continuously rotating his way like a revolving door. His clientele knew his location in the building, and they regularly came to receive their daily fix. It was a stream, forever flowing and lucrative. And both the seller and the buyer have an identical way of life. The fiend is addicted to the product, and the dealer is addicted to the cash. Finally, an aged male approached the dealer with his weathered-looking face and worn clothing. He carried two wrinkled twenty-dollar bills in his hand, money he received from panhandling on the streets or implementing a petty but illicit activity.

"Youngblood, let me get four," said the user.

Repeating the same activity, the user followed him into the stairwell where the transaction happened. It was always brisk, with the dealer's head on a swivel. He took the cash and stashed it away as he handed the user four vials. The young hustler once again took his position in the building lobby. His attention was on the outside, with his pistol tucked and concealed into the waistband of his jeans. Never before had he needed to use it. The crew he was with, the organization he worked for, was notorious and feared. Therefore, he felt comfortable conducting business in the troubled housing project, one of the most infamous and dangerous places in Brooklyn and Brownsville.

For an hour, things were good; business was brisk, and his money piled up. The hour of the night was late, but it was a 24-hour grind in the game. Then another customer approached another familiar user; the routine was natural. He wanted one. He got it and left. The dealer lingered in the stairwell and counted his money—today's take. He was happy.

And then, things weren't good.

He was still being watched, and he didn't see it coming. And then it happened. Quickly looming from the shadows was a hooded stranger, and the gun was thrust into the dealer's face.

"Shit!" he exclaimed.

Omar was a nervous wreck, but he needed to do this. He needed to do something before it was too late. The money was out there, and he needed to build up enough courage to take it—by any means necessary, he kept telling himself. He galvanized himself to do the unthinkable—rob someone—rob a drug dealer. But with the .357 in his hand, that courage to do it came unexpectedly. He stood in his bedroom, clad in an old black hoodie that he'd found in his closet, and eyed himself in the mirror. The gun was at his side, and it was an awkward transformation for him. He sighed. It was now or never.

Leaving the apartment, he hurried away from his residence, not wanting his neighbors to see him looking like a thug—especially Kizzie. Once he entered the stairway, he threw the hoodie over his face. He tightened the strings, making the hoodie scrunched around his face so he was not easily identifiable.

He had been watching the young dealer for a while now. He knew his place of business, and it was the perfect target for Omar.

He was young and somewhat careless. The dealer had a routine that anyone could follow and map out. He kept money and drugs on him, and he'd gotten comfortable with his position in the drug crew, believing he was untouchable. Tonight, he would be proven wrong.

From afar, Omar watched him serve one drug user after another. Then with the .357 tucked into his waistband, he moved closer to observe the dealer. Omar's heart beat thunderously, knowing he was about to do something way out of his league and character. But he felt it would be worth it after witnessing the money the dealer made. His footsteps paced toward his objective. He entered the back of the building via the maintenance entrance and approached the lobby. He stayed in the shadows and carefully observed his mark from a short distance. He didn't know the guy's name, nor did he want to. And it wasn't personal; it was survival.

Omar watched the dealer make a few hand-to-hand transactions, and he told himself he would make his move after the next one. He removed the gun from his waistband and gripped it nervously. His heart continued to beat like thunder was booming inside his chest. But something changed in him once he held that gun in his hand. He stood erect and alert in his hiding place, and his senses sharpened, and he became keen to carry out the robbery. A boost of confidence engorged him to go through with it. It was almost like he predicted the outcome and saw things happening in his favor.

"*You got this*," a voice or something spoke to him.

He gripped the weapon securely and never took his eyes off the dealer. Instead, he watched him serve the umpteenth user for the night. After that transaction, the dealer counted his earnings in the dimmed stairwell, believing he was alone.

Now! Omar strongly felt.

Omar hurdled himself from the shadows with the drug dealer distracted by his earnings and attacked. The dealer looked up and suddenly found himself staring down the gaping barrel of the .357.

"Shit!" he exclaimed.

"Turn around," Omar instructed him.

Having no choice, the man reluctantly did so at Omar's behest.

"Put your damn hands on the wall," said Omar.

The dealer followed the instructions. But he frowned, being angry, and he made it a point to say, "Nigga, you know who you stealing from? You know who I'm connected to?"

Omar remained silent as he quickly rummaged through the dealer's pockets and removed several wads of cash. The dealer's money was now becoming his money.

"When my peoples find out who you are, you gonna wish you were never born, fo' real, nigga! You fucked up!"

Omar remained silent. He didn't want or feared that the dealer might recognize his voice. Pocketing the money, Omar lingered behind the young dealer and thrust the gun against the back of his victim's head. He cocked it back. The dealer now knew the gravity of the situation, and his arrogant attitude shifted into nearly begging for mercy.

"Look, don't do this, man. I got a little girl; she's two," he uttered submissively. "You already got the cash, nigga. Just don't kill me."

An impulse was building inside Omar—a thirst he'd never felt before. It was strong. It was the power he felt—and control—and something else—something a lot more sinister. He kept the gun against the back of the dealer's head with his finger on the trigger, and all it took was a short squeeze, and Omar felt that would finally quench the thirst.

"*Do it!*" he felt. "*Feel that power!*"

"Please, man, just don't kill me! I ain't see your face," continued the dealer.

He kept the .357 trained on his victim. There was almost a hunger to kill him, but Omar couldn't bring himself to take the man's life, fortunately for the dealer. All he wanted was the cash. He wasn't a murderer.

"Get on your knees, close your eyes, and count to fifty," Omar instructed him.

Quickly, the dealer dropped to his knees and closed his eyes. He started to count.

"One, two, three, four, five, six, seven, eight . . ."

When he got to twenty-five, he stopped. He looked behind him and saw his attacker was gone. The dealer sighed with relief. But he had pissed on himself. Something about the presence behind him had him unexpectedly spooked. But now, he had another problem . . . explaining the robbery to his crew and his leader.

"Fuck!" he muttered to himself.

CHAPTER SEVEN

OMAR COUNTED $875. It was a lot by his standards, but it wasn't enough. Still, it was money he could give to the funeral director, a down payment to help pay for his mother's funeral. He still couldn't believe that he'd gotten away with it. The adrenaline rushed during the robbery; it was a phenomenal feeling, something he had never experienced. What he felt having that gun in his hand and control over someone and someone fearing him for once was all he could think about.

He stood by the bedroom mirror shirtless with the gun in his hand and held it by his side. He smiled at himself. *Wow!* he thought. Feeling that high still, he raised the gun and aimed it at himself, trying to make his image look terrifying. The way that dealer begged for his life and cried out for mercy made him feel almost godlike. And he made nearly nine hundred dollars in a split second. Money like that he could never make at the supermarket, bagging groceries, cleaning, and stocking shelves. It would have taken him almost a month to make that amount. But the power of the gun brought him instant wealth and value.

He smiled. He stood with desire and want and a frightening thought to continue to use the .357 for his benefit. He needed to come up with three thousand dollars or more to give his mother the proper burial she deserved. And he wasn't going to let her down.

The knock at the front door interrupted his moment of wonder and contemplation. He placed the gun inside the dresser drawer, threw on a shirt, and went to answer the door. Looking through the peephole, he saw that it was Kizzie. He sighed. He wasn't in the mood to see her right now, but Kizzie wouldn't go away.

"Omar, open the door. I know you're home," she said.

"What, Kizzie?"

"Open the door, Omar. So, what? We're not friends anymore? But look, I have something for you, and I think you'll like it."

He opened the door, and Kizzie stood there smiling at him with her long hair styled into a ponytail. She stepped into the apartment, and he closed the door behind her.

"Look, you don't have to close yourself in, Omar. You don't always have to be alone. I'm right next door," she said.

"I know."

"So why don't you just come over, chill, and talk to me? My grandmother and I are worried about you. You can even stay the night if you want. I'm sure my grandmother won't mind," she said.

"I'm okay, Kizzie. This is home, even with her not here anymore."

"It is, but you're family, Omar." She smiled.

"I know. You said that you had something for me," he reminded her.

"Oh, yes!" Kizzie uttered with some excitement. She reached into her back pocket, removed a white envelope, and handed it to him. "Look inside."

He did. Cash was inside: fifties, twenties, fives, and tens. He was shocked. "What's this?"

Her smile brightened. "I helped raise some money for you to bury your mother. Five hundred dollars is inside there, Omar. I went to the church and your job and started a collection, and many folks care about you, and they wanna help have a funeral and burial for your mother."

"Wow! Um . . . I don't know what to say. Thank you."

"You're welcome. I told you I got your back and am here for you. And I know it's not nearly enough to pay for an entire funeral. But it's a start, right?"

"Yeah. It is."

"See, God is good, right?"

"Yeah, he is," he replied halfheartedly.

"Are you coming to church tomorrow?" she asked him.

"Um . . . I don't know. There's still a lot to do, Kizzie, and I need some time," he replied ambiguously.

"I know. But everyone misses you there. They want to see you and pray for you, Omar."

"I'll come to church next week. I promise."

"You promise?"

He nodded.

Kizzie smiled. "If you're hungry, my grandmother cooked. Come by and eat something," she offered.

"I'll think about it."

She sucked her teeth and affably replied, "Omar, stop playing! Boy, you know you're hungry and starving like Marvin. You ain't gotta starve yourself too. Grieving folks gotta eat too."

He chuckled. "Yeah, you're right. But I just wanna chill for a moment alone, Kizzie, and think about some things and pray. You understand?"

She did. "Cool. How about I'll bring you a plate by then? You cool with that?"

He smiled again. "I would appreciate that."

"I know you would, acting like I'm your maid. But you got special privileges for now," she joked and smiled.

Before her exit, she hugged him. "Godspeed," she said to him.

He opened the envelope again and removed the cash. Within twenty-four hours, he'd made nearly fifteen hundred dollars. It was impressive. He never made that much money so quickly and fast. Things were looking copasetic for now, but there was still a lot of work to do.

"You let some bitch-ass nigga take eight hundred from you?" Science shouted to his young worker.

"He had a gun, Science. What could I do?" the young dealer replied with fear.

"I don't give a fuck if the muthafucka had *two* guns on you; you always protect what's mine, nigga!" shouted Science. "You know that, muthafucka!"

"I . . . I'll pay it back. I-I swear!" he stammered.

"Damn right you gonna pay it back to me, and with interest, nigga," uttered Science with contempt in his voice. "Twenty-five percent interest."

The young dealer nodded.

"You a stupid muthafucka!" shouted Science. "Do you even *know* what the nigga looks like? Huh? So, we can go out there and get some payback and take back what the fuck some clown-ass nigga stole from me?"

"No. I don't. I'm sorry."

"Yeah, you sorry, nigga. So, my eight hundred is in the wind, right?"

"I'm gonna pay it back wit' interest, Science. I know, I know, I fucked up," uttered the dealer with shakiness in his tone.

"Yeah, you fucked up all right," repeated Science.

Science stood fearfully close to his young crack dealer. His action and response to the loss of cash were unpredictable. He stood six-two with a lean body, a narrow face, intense eyes, and tattoos up and down his tank-topped arms. He was known for his frosty temperament and violent ways. He'd killed, beaten, and brutally injured men and women. He even destroyed families to protect what is his and sent a frightful message in the streets—don't mess with me or mine. There was a chilling story about how he took a wire hanger, uncoiled it, heated the tip with a blow torch, and then gouged out a man's eye. It was done because the man disrespected him by staring at his woman too long.

There were many horror stories about Science and his appalling methods, and the streets of Brooklyn heard every last one of them.

Science kept his cold, black eyes on the young dealer. He was dissatisfied with him. A punishment needed to be handed down to teach him a lesson and send a harsh message to his other workers to protect what is his by any means necessary. He wasn't running a day care. He was running a business.

Science glanced at his right-hand man, Ray, and they both shared an agreeing stare. It needed to be done. Science gave the head nod to a half-dozen young thugs standing around. No words were uttered; they already knew what it meant.

They all surrounded the young dealer in a daunting manner. Science stood in the background and told the dealer, "You lost eight hundred of my fuckin' money, nigga. That's an eight-minute beat-down, nigga . . . no remorse. You survive, then you're tougher than you look."

The second he stopped talking, the first punches were thrown at the dealer, and he quickly became overwhelmed with a brutal beating. Half a dozen goons were all over him like stink on shit, wildly punching and kicking him everywhere. It was a frenzy of assault. And he had folded himself into the fetal position to protect his most important area.

"Fuck that nigga up!" someone shouted.

Eight minutes seemed a lifetime away. The young dealer was a bloody pulp three minutes into the vicious beating. He seemed like a rag doll being kicked and punched, and none of the six men were letting up on him until they were told to by Science. Science stood there fixed on the attack, not wincing from what he saw because he had done seen a lot worse. Teeth were kicked out, the young dealer's right eye was puffed up and completely closed, and his head had swollen grotesquely. They were going to kill him soon if they did not stop.

Science and Ray watch with apathy. And then, four minutes in, Science gave the order. "A'ight, y'all niggas, stop."

All six goons stopped their assault on the drop of a dime at his behest. What was sprawled out on the ground was a critical mess—an unconscious and dying man, if not quickly rushed to the hospital and treated for his serious internal injuries. Science walked over to him and crouched near the beaten victim; if he could hear him or not, it didn't matter. He still spoke.

"This is what happens when a nigga don't protect what is mines thoroughly . . . when a nigga is caught slippin' out there. And God help the muthafucka that ever steals from me," uttered Science with conviction.

He stood up and continued. "Take this nigga to the fuckin' hospital and tell him to keep his fuckin' mouth shut."

They did what they were told. Each man picked up the dealer from the ground, leaving behind a pool of his blood, and they carried him away. Science was pleased with the punishment bestowed on one of his workers. They needed to learn, and they needed to keep fearing him—weakness was a curse.

He and Ray left the room and the building, and they climbed into a black Escalade, Ray being the driver. The moment they drove off, Science said to him, "I want that muthafucka found. ASAP!"

"You already know I'm on it, Science," Ray replied.

"It ain't just 'bout the fuckin' money, but some fool out there had the audacity to steal from one of my workers. You know what I'm ready to do to this fuckin' fool," Science exclaimed with scorn dripping from his voice. "This faggot-ass thief must be on a suicide mission to take from me and mines."

"He gon' get got," assured Ray.

"Fo' sure, my nigga. You hungry?"

"You already know I am, Science."

"I feel like some soul food. What 'bout you?" asked Science.

"My nigga, you reading my mind right now. What 'bout that spot in Bed-Stuy?" Ray suggested.

"You mean Ma-N-Pop Soul food on Lewis Avenue?"

"Yeah," Ray smiled. "That joint was bumpin' the last time we were there. The macaroni and cheese and fried chicken damn near made me come on myself," he joked.

Science laughed. "You a fool, my nigga. But you right; that's the spot right there," Science replied. "Let's bounce over there."

The two men headed to the soul food location in Bedford-Stuyvesant. Ray put on some rap music to listen to, Jay-Z preferably. They leaned back in their seats, talked like good friends, and looked like two ordinary people riding through the streets of Brooklyn rather than two ruthless drug kingpins.

But unbeknownst to Science and Ray, their troubles were just starting. Warring with their rivals over territory and control would be the least of their worries.

CHAPTER EIGHT

OMAR HAD PLUNGED into a deep sleep again. He was on his back, clad in his boxer shorts, and shirtless. It was another hot summer night; the temperature and the humidity were high. Once again, the city was sweltering with a lingering heat wave, which made life in the inner city nearly crippling and unbearable. Sweat poured from Omar's pores as he slept. And once again, the bedroom grew jarringly dark, and the door silently closed by itself. The room grew still. Sounds from the outside came to an abrupt halt.

An apparition floated over the sleeping Omar, bringing itself down upon him. It sexually united against his flesh, stirring an erection for it to devour. Omar moaned and groaned pleasingly in his sleep. Once more, he found himself entirely stimulated by oral pleasure from some unknown entity. Several days had passed since he last felt that equivalent and a strong feeling of bliss. His breathing became ragged, and his chest heaved up and down. He slowly opened his eyes and found a strange sexual being on top of him, taking him into its mouth. This time, it didn't vanish suddenly but showed its actual presence. She was beautiful—her face nearly angelic. Omar became in awe of her.

Her skin was black, silky, and glistening, but her eyes were white like snow and hypnotic. Her beautiful face was surrounded by straight but still gorgeous, shiny-black tresses. The hair flowed freely and framed her face and head perfectly. Showing against the black veil of the hair, a slender neck led from the base of the skull to a pair of bare shoulders. She was a sultry being—a succubus—a mythical female demon that visits its lovers in their dreams and has carnal relations with them.

It continued to please Omar with her full, sensual lips. Omar just moaned and squirmed from the intense and pleasing feeling.

"What . . . What are you?" he faintly asked as his physical continued to be thrust into an overwhelming sexual enjoyment.

It didn't answer him but continued to consume his erection. Then it mounted him with its sensual body slowly twisting absolute pleasure through all his body. Omar felt nearly paralyzed by it. The feeling he felt—it was perverted. He was a virgin, and he felt frozen in place. She pressed her utterly nude body against his hot flesh and continued to please him in ways he'd never felt before. Her touch felt ubiquitous, and everywhere she touched him felt better than it ever had before. Each contact was like the touch of every woman in the world. Each caress was the most sensual caress that he could imagine. Omar had unexpectedly been thrust into a cyclone of bliss. It continued to ride him—devour his being, the suction between her legs bringing Omar closer to the unbelievable. He looked nervous, as he was about to explode.

"*Trust me*," she cooed.

He felt his cum simmering inside his balls, screaming for a way out. But she surprisingly denied his release. And just when he was about to release, it announced once again, "*Soon*," clawing at his chest. She or it vanished from his sight within the blink of an eye, leaving Omar highly aroused and stimulated.

Omar awoke from his deep sleep, covered in sweat. He was breathing hoarsely and looked confused for a moment. *Damn!* he thought. It or she seemed so natural, so real. He knew she was real. Omar had awoken with an erection so rigid that it was painful. But then he touched his chest and felt blood against his skin. He leaped from the bed and dashed into the bathroom, speedily turning on the lights and looking into the mirror. He saw the scratch or mark she'd left on his chest there. Omar was baffled.

"Oh shit!" he uttered.

He didn't know what to think of it. It worried him, but at the same time, he was wound up by the intense and stimulating pleasure she'd bestowed on him. Whatever it was that came to see him in his sleep, he hoped it returned to him soon.

The darkness was like a shroud in his room. And the stillness was a quench to an unnatural desire that had started developing inside him. Omar sat silently at the foot of his bed, the .357 by his side. He was contemplating his next move, but he couldn't stop thinking about it—or her—the nightly visit from the succubus, the female demon. She was beautiful and enticing, and he intensely desired to experience that feeling again. It was pure lust. It was an intense desire. He was a virgin, but this entity made him feel wanted and free. It made him feel vigorous and potent.

He remembered it speaking to him, saying, "Soon," and he wondered what it meant by that.

Once again, he donned the black hoodie and tightened the strings to prevent his identity from being seen. He needed more. He needed to go out and repeat his actions from the other night. This time, he carried inside of him a bit more confidence. He was motivated to accomplish one final thing for his mother—to give her an eternal resting place. And it took him to become something he never thought he would become—a stickup kid.

He moved through the hallway and descended the concrete stairway. Clad in black, Omar moved stealthily through the building and out into the project. The summer night was late. The inner-city streets were still bustling, becoming a cocoon of leisure and painting the town red for so many looking to escape their troubles and the outside world for a night. The clubs and lounges were operating at full throttle, and the ladies came out dressed in their finest outfits, catching the attention they sought.

One particular location Omar had on his mind was a nearby local lounge named "Fun Times" on Rockaway Avenue. It was known to have the local drug dealers, pimps, whores, thugs, and other unworldly types frequenting the place daily. There were always a few nice cars parked in front of the site and regular fights. It was the last place Omar would be caught dead at, not hanging around it at all and not lingering on the outside of it. But strangely, he was attracted to it now. He remained across the street from the place, watching folks come or go from the lounge. They were having another busy night.

He focused on the front entrance, observing and watching the foot traffic. His instincts were looking for the right one. He soon found his mark; a hustler named Anton exited the lounge alone. Omar had seen him numerous times, driving around in a dark blue BMW and making his rounds on the block. He was connected to BMC, Brooklyn Mafia Crew. This organized and ruthless drug crew dominated most of the drug trade in Brooklyn and other tristate areas.

Anton was dressed nicely and was respected. It would be riskier to take him down than the young drug dealer in the lobby. Anton was older, feared, and wouldn't hesitate to kill anyone that tried to rob him. However, Omar found the risk of stealing from someone like him unexpectedly alluring. The challenge was exciting. His heart beat rapidly as he gripped the gun in his right hand and paid attention to Anton's every move. Anton walked with authority. These were his blocks, his hood, and the reputation that preceded him. Who would come at him when he was the boogieman himself?

He would soon find out.

Omar followed him closely but kept his distance innocuously and not alarming. He didn't want Anton to know that he was being followed. He walked half a block until Anton pressed the alarm to deactivate the Beamer nearby. The lights flickered quickly, indicating the location of the car. It would be a mistake. Omar quickly moved toward the parked Beamer, ahead of Anton, who was busy with his smartphone conversing with someone.

When Anton put his hand on the door handle, Omar appeared out of nowhere and struck. Swiftly, he placed the .357 against the back of Anton's head and cocked it back, indicating to Anton that he was serious. Anton halted his conversation, taken aback by the sudden confrontation. But he seemed undaunted by the threat.

"I don't want this to get ugly," said Omar.

Anton scoffed at him. "Nigga, you got to be shittin' me right now. But, look, I'm gonna be generous and allow you the opportunity to walk away. Walk away, muthafucka. Walk away," he growled with intensity in his tone.

Omar's heart continued to race. His arm remained outstretched with the gun against the back of Anton's skull. His adrenaline was pumping, and he felt some animation from the threat. He wasn't going to walk away. He needed the money.

"I'm afraid I can't do that," Omar countered.

"Then you're one stupid muthafucka," Anton retorted.

"You know what I want. On your knees."

"Fuck you!"

Omar saw that he was going to be difficult. He sighed. Anton wanted to make it ugly for him. Omar didn't want to make things ugly.

"I ain't gettin' down on my knees for you or no nigga. So, you might as well shoot me now, nigga, cuz I ain't giving up a muthafuckin' thing," Anton exclaimed with disdain.

Things started to become intense. Omar was on a public street with a loaded gun committing an armed robbery of a well-known drug dealer. The situation could become chaotic for him in a heartbeat. But Omar remained persistent. He frowned. He decided to make it where he came out the victor and not have a loss—and not lose his life. Yet again, something unnatural and ominous flowed through him that he couldn't shake off. Power. Control. Maybe killing?

"I can't," he shouted to himself. "No!"

Anton remained still and calm, looking away from Omar with his hands coolly by his side. He was craving to strike back. He wanted to reach for the pistol tucked in his waistband and end this foolishness—kill this fool for the disrespect. It was apparent that Omar was an amateur who needed to be taught a lethal lesson.

Discreetly, he reached for his concealed weapon while it seemed like Omar was going through a bipolar moment.

"It's not me," Omar uttered to someone who wasn't there, maybe to himself.

"You crazy muthafucka! You fucked up, nigga!" Anton mocked. "You ever done this shit before? I guarantee you this will be your first and last."

Anton covertly placed his hand on the butt of his pistol, ready to react with lightning speed, and put a bullet in the assailant's face. But before he could do so, Omar fired.

Boom!

Anton went down, but he was still alive. Omar shot out the back of his knee, and Anton collapsed in severe pain. His screaming and hollering echoed through the street, and the gunshot was loud like thunder. Omar reacted while Anton was distracted with pain. He hurriedly rummaged through the man's pockets and removed a wad of cash, taking his diamond watch too.

"Muthafucka! Aaaah! Oh shit, you shot me!" Anton hollered, squirming around on the ground in pain and clutching his bleeding leg.

The commotion caught the attention as several patrons, including two of Anton's goons, exited the lounge to see what was happening. They saw a hollering and injured Anton and an unknown male in black running away from the scene. They hurried toward Anton to aid their friend and execute revenge against the culprit. But it was too late. Omar was long gone.

CHAPTER NINE

OMAR FELT RELIEF as the cemetery workers lowered his mother into the ground. He'd done it. He'd given his mother a proper burial. It was cheap, and it came with him committing several crimes and risking his life, but it had been accomplished. The funeral was affordable and simplified, from the low-grade casket to the mundane service. And he couldn't afford to give his mother a headstone right away. Still, he felt proud that she would be laid to rest in the earth and her body not cremated or that he didn't have to release her body to the coroner's office. He was determined, and it paid off.

The attendance at the burial was small. Kizzie and her grandmother were there, along with Pastor Morgan, his wife, and a handful of church members showing their support and condolences.

As the cemetery workers lowered Ms. Richards into the ground, Pastor Morgan preached wholeheartedly about the dearly departed. He was sad about her passing but excited to know that she was with the Lord now.

"But our citizenship is in heaven. And we eagerly await a Savior from there, the Lord Jesus Christ, who by the power that enables Him to bring everything under His control, will transform our lowly bodies so that they will be like His glorious body," he preached.

Kizzie stood by Omar's side, being a good friend to him—ready to hold her friend in her arms and console him if he needed it. She knew it had to be hard to watch his mother being buried. She dealt with her own burdens and troubles from her past; the only family she had left was her grandmother.

"And in answering questions about life after death," Pastor Morgan continued, "we are left with only two sources to consult. And I say this, and I say it with authority; either we turn to human experience, or we turn to the word of God. And you know what? If we turn to human experience, what are we going to find . . . What are we going to find? I tell you what we're going to find. Too many guesses, and too many ideas, and too many theories . . . but no sure answers. No human being has a sure answer. The only people who have the answer are dead! So, what does that leave us with? I will tell you what it leaves us with. It leaves us with the word of God. In God's word, we find sufficient and abundant answers. God who knows the future knows what happens when we die, and He hasn't left us to wonder about it."

Omar stood there aloof and unmoved by the pastor's words. It was his mother's burial, the one he risked life and death for, and he stood there a few feet from his mother's grave showing apathy. He was clad in all back, wearing dark shades to hide his eyes or emotions, if there were any. Kizzie wiped away the few tears that trickled from her eyes. She was grieving like it was her mother. She tried to take Omar's hand, but he slightly opposed her.

"Are you okay, Omar?" she asked him.

"I'm fine," he replied with nonchalance.

With his mother's casket now in the ground, he was ready to pivot and leave the area. He didn't want to stick around. It was painful. Now in the dirt, her body indicated that she was truly gone, and he would never see her physically again. It was a daunting thought that Omar wanted to vanquish, but it was nearly impossible not to think about someone who constantly meant the world to you. Omar sighed.

"Brother Omar," the pastor cried out to him, "you will always be family to us. And you will always be welcomed in my home and the church, for you are loved. For God loves you, and we love you. And as it says in the Bible, 'Do not be amazed at this, for a time is coming when all who are in their graves will hear His voice and come out . . . Those who have done what is good will rise, and those who have done what is evil will rise to be condemned.'"

Omar heard him, but he wasn't listening or attentive to the pastor's words. Instead, he felt bitterness and betrayal. He thought about what he had to do to bury his mother. He wanted to know where God's help was when he needed to rob drug dealers to raise money.

"You will always be in our prayers, Omar. And I hope to see you in church this Sunday," said the pastor.

"I just need some time to myself, Pastor," Omar replied casually.

"I understand. But you keep God close always. Do you hear me, Omar? Keep Him in your heart and in everything you do. Be strong and courageous. Do not fear or be in dread of them, for it is the Lord your God who goes with you. He will not leave you or forsake you," the pastor proclaimed.

Omar remained silent. He grew tired of the pastor's encouraging words and random Bible verses. Finally, he pivoted and walked away. Regarding attending church on Sunday, he already decided that he wasn't going this Sunday, next Sunday, or any other Sunday after that. The church was gradually fading from his life. He remembered attending church faithfully every Sunday with his mother, and their lives always remained the same—fucked up! Where were the blessings that were promised to him—his family? He remembered his mother always praying, believing in God, and having unwavering faith. Yet, she died a poor and sick woman. And he was constantly bullied and made ashamed.

Omar felt that the Lord had already left and forsaken him.

He and Kizzie left the cemetery. He refused a ride home from friends because he wanted to take public transportation and walk. He needed to think and wanted to be alone, but Kizzie refused to let him wander off by himself in the state that he was in. She was adamant about keeping him company to ensure her friend was safe.

Although it was a sad day for Omar and Kizzie, Brownsville was bustling with folks. A sea of people headed in different directions, businesses were swimming with customers, and traffic cluttered the streets. The sunny day and the clear blue skies made the Ville look like a festival was happening. The shoppers on Pitkin Avenue swarmed the stores with their credit and debit cards, eager to spend and treat themselves to various consumer goods. And by night, the atmosphere shifted where the streets belonged to the pimps and drug dealers.

Omar remained silent from the cemetery to the neighborhood. He had a lot on his mind. The other night he'd shot someone of great street magnitude and clout. He was shocked that he pulled the trigger and crippled a man—a dangerous gangster, no less. It happened unexpectedly. Omar reacted without hesitation when Anton showed resistance, and to see Anton weaken and whimper from the bullet was a thing to see. He was impressed with himself. He wanted to take his life, but Omar fought that sudden urge and injured the man instead.

"Are you hungry?" Kizzie asked him.

"No. I'm good."

"Are you coming to church Sunday?"

He sighed. He shot a dubious stare her way, where Kizzie deduced that he planned on skipping Sunday service for the third time.

"Omar, you can't keep yourself locked inside your apartment daily and mope. You need to get out and talk to people. It would help if you kept yourself active. It really helps," she said.

"How do you know what fuckin' helps, Kizzie?" he somewhat snapped back.

"Look, don't be snapping and cursing at me, Omar. I know you're angry and frustrated, but you don't need to become rude and make it seem like I'm hindering you more than helping you," she returned. "I'm just trying to be a friend right now . . . something that you need. So, stop pushing me away."

"I'm sorry, Kizzie. I just got a lot on my mind," he apologized wholeheartedly.

"It's cool. Like I'm always telling you, I'm right here if you need someone to talk to or a shoulder to lean on. I'm not going to let you go through this alone."

"I know. And I do appreciate it."

They continued to walk, approaching the projects. Ahead, some police activity was happening. Walking closer to the action, Omar and Kizzie saw several young men harassed by four plainclothes officers implementing a stop-and-frisk. The officers had the young thugs lying face down on the pavement. Their arms were spread like wings against the burning ground as the cops went rummaging through their pockets and belongings, searching for weapons or drugs.

"Yo, this some bullshit! I thought stop and frisk were illegal and shit," cursed one of the thugs.

"I said shut up and turn the fuck around. So, what you know what's legal and not?" retorted one of the cops.

"I swear I hate the fuckin' police!" uttered another young male.

Omar got the pleasure of seeing that Brice was one of the men detained by the officers. Brice scowled and cursed. For once, the bully was bullied by the NYPD—and he was helpless and vulnerable. Omar locked eyes with Brice, and it was a delight to see the ignorant thug become humiliated and embarrassed. Omar kept his eyes on Brice for a moment, smirking at the bully, and Brice frowned so hard that it looked like his face was about to crack open. Omar chuckled at the incident and mouthed to Brice, "*Bang! Bang!*"

Omar did a bold thing, taunting Brice while he was detained and being ridiculed by the officers. But Omar didn't care. He was fed up, and though it wasn't physical payback, it was fun to see Brice face down on the ground in the middle of the day and maybe on his way to jail.

"C'mon, Omar, we don't need to be around this," Kizzie said, taking him by the arm and rushing him away.

Brice, however, glared at Omar and Kizzie leaving the scene. He fumed so intensely and became so heated that he could have set himself on fire lying against the hot summer concrete. First, Omar pulls out a gun on him and then mocks him in the presence of the NYPD; Brice was ready to rip him apart right there. His number one priority was finding Omar and fucking him up so bad that he would wish that he was buried with his mother.

"You ain't got a good look at the nigga, yo?" asked Thomas, one of Anton's goons.

"If I did, that nigga wouldn't be alive right now," Anton said.

"How much he took from you?"

"Eighteen hundred . . . and my fuckin' diamond watch," Anton replied.

"Damn."

"But I want you to put the word out, five grand on that fool's identity. I want him got like yesterday; you hear me, nigga?" said Anton.

"No doubt. I'm on it. We gonna sniff that nigga out and handle it."

"Nigga got the balls to steal from me and shoot me. Look at me; they say I might never walk right again," Anton griped.

"When we catch this fool, he gonna get a lot worse," said Thomas.

Anton's entire right leg was in a white cast. He was immobile and in pain. The bullet tore straight through his kneecap and exited through the side of his knee, completely shattering his bones and devastating the structure of his leg. The joints that connected his femur to his shin had disintegrated, making him immediately collapse to one side. And though the threat of death was relatively low with no vitals, the wound could have been powerful enough to rupture his femoral artery. Doctors told him he was fortunate and that the recovery time for a complete kneecap replacement with bolts and titanium plates would likely take a full year. However, he most likely would feel discomfort his entire life.

"I don't care how it gets done, but get it done, Thomas. Fuck it; make it ten grand on that nigga that shot me. And if possible, I want that fool barely alive, so I can holler at him and torture him myself before I kill him," Anton proclaimed through his clenched teeth.

Thomas nodded and replied, "Considered it done, my nigga."

He gave Anton dap, turned, and left the room to execute his orders from Anton. As he left the hospital room, two detectives entered to speak with Anton about the shooting. The moment

Anton saw them, he frowned, indicating that he wasn't a fan of the police.

"I ain't got shit to say to y'all fools," Anton uttered contemptuously.

"Too bad. I thought we were friends, Anton," replied Detective Bunk Foster. He was a slightly stout Black man with a robust appearance, dogmatic attitude, and nearly two decades on the police force.

Anton scoffed their way.

"We came here for your benefit, Anton. Are you going to tell us what happened? Who shot you?" asked Detective Danny Greene.

"Fuck y'all," cursed Anton.

"No snitching, huh? Some fool damn near took your right knee off, and you have nothing to say to us?" said Danny coolly.

"Yeah, I don't. I don't know why you two faggots even wasted y'all time coming up here to see me."

"Yeah, well, maybe next time we'll come to see your dumb ass in the city morgue, right?" retorted Foster.

"Are you threatening me, Officer?"

"Just a possible prediction," replied Foster.

"We're just doing our jobs, Anton. That's all. You get shot, we like to know what happened," chimed Danny.

Danny Greene was a clean-cut, all-American-looking Black male with a cool fade. He was handsome and had a pristine background coming from the military. He carried an impartial attitude with folks from the streets to his brothers in blue. He believed in justice and equality and opposed his partner's tyrannical demeanor.

"You know my position in these streets. I can handle my own, Officer, and I don't need any help from some bitches in blue," Anton replied sarcastically. "You understand me?"

Foster chuckled at the mockery. "That's 'Detective,'" he corrected. "And all you niggas out there in the streets are fools . . . killing each other over territory and blocks that y'all don't own. So, if it was up to me, fuck it. Go ahead, y'all niggas can shoot each other to the death as long as that blood doesn't get spilled onto the innocent and hardworking folks in the neighborhood," Foster proclaimed. "But my superiors have other alternatives for y'all idiots."

"Look, we don't need you going out there and carrying out your own revenge. You know what they say. You go looking for revenge, then you best dig two graves," Danny mentioned.

"I don't need no damn preaching from y'all about handling my business," Anton gruffly replied. "Matter of fact, get the fuck out my room, cuz I'm done talkin' to y'all."

"Like I said, fool, we'll see you soon in the city morgue," Detective Foster chided. "That's where all niggas like you need to be at. Dead."

Anton scowled at his disparaging comment. "Fuck you!"

Foster exited the room. Greene lingered there for a moment, not upset with Anton's comment. On the contrary, he felt sorrier for the man than anything. Men like him were trapped, he felt. He wanted to help, but Anton was already seasoned with his criminal ways and hatred for the police. Danny Greene nimbly dug into his inner suit jacket and pulled out his card. He placed it on the stand near Anton and said, "That's for you in case you change your mind about things. And I'm not like my partner. I believe everybody has a chance to change. But, of course, you must want to do it."

Anton scoffed at the remark. "That's some pussy shit!"

Danny shrugged off the rude reply. It didn't bother him. He reached out the best he could, and that's all he could do. He left the room, leaving Anton in his thuggish ways.

CHAPTER TEN

THE NIGHT SEEMED too long and endless for Omar. He couldn't sleep. He tossed and turned on his bed for nearly two hours, sweating and overheating from the summer's heat and becoming apprehensive and restless. It was midnight, and the night was still young. Yet, he couldn't stop thinking about it or her. The thing that had been coming to visit him at night, in his sleep—in his dreams. The she-demon or succubus had gripped his mind and sentiment. The feeling it brought out, Omar wanted to feel that blissful sensation again and again. The sexual desires it instigated had latched onto Omar like his skin inside. He desired and longed for it as a fiend did for its drugs. It had been days since he experienced that strong, sexual feeling. It almost felt like he was in withdrawal.

He wanted to know its name.

He fussed, removed himself from the bed, and went to the bedroom window. He peered out at the project below. It was a calm and quiet night. He sighed heavily. Alongside feeling such a domineering sexual desire, he was inclined to leave the apartment and commit another crime with the .357. He was amped. He was charged up like a battery and ready to feel that rush again. It was a high that he didn't want to come down from. The yearning to be out there, in control, feared and commanding stimulated him in ways he did not understand. He could no longer use the excuse of robbing dealers to help bury his mother. She was already in the ground. Now, it was a rush that he yearned personally. It was whirling wildly inside of him, uncultivated, and it was ready to be released like a tornado touching the ground and creating havoc and chaos wherever it went.

Once again, Omar donned the black hoodie and black jeans. Then he left the apartment with the .357 tucked into his waistband. He hit the concrete jungle with a mission to find another victim to take down. He moved through the projects and inner city in contrast to his earlier self. Whereas before, he walked timidly, now, he moved with aggression and hunger—a hunger to hunt for the next high to fulfill for a payoff. But the night was slow, and movement was scattered. Since Anton got shot, the word was out. Some fool in black was robbing drug dealers, and a ten-thousand-dollar contract was placed on finding his identity.

He was frustrated that the streets of Brownsville were jarringly quiet and slow. He walked back to his building and went onto the rooftop. There, he gazed at the full moon glimmering above, but it also played peek-a-boo, weaving in and out of ribbons of black clouds scudding across the sky.

It was Wednesday night, which meant Bible study night at the church for Kizzie and her group. A group of eight folks, men and women, led by the pastor's wife, sat around in a circle in the church's basement with their Bibles opened to a particular verse. They were discussing the story of Job. Their discussion was intense and full of zeal about a wealthy man named Job living in a land called Uz with his large family and extensive flock. He was blameless and upright, always careful to avoid doing evil.

However, God allowed Satan to torment Job to test his bold claim, but He forbids Satan to take Job's life in the process.

"The book of Job focuses on questions about God's justice and why good people suffer," the pastor's wife said.

"At the same time, it also asks the question we rarely think to ask: why don't good people prosper?" a church member replied.

Throughout the book, Job, his wife, and his friends speculate on why he, an upright man, suffers. Job accuses God of being unjust and not operating in the world according to the principles of justice, and his friends believe that Job's sin caused his suffering. Finally, Job decides to talk directly to God.

Kizzie believed Job's story emulated Omar's in a way. Omar was a righteous man who was in pain and suffering. He was having a hard time, and he started questioning his faith in the Lord.

The pastor's wife continued. "Job's friends tried to console him, but they soon started to blame him for his own trouble, inferring that he must have sinned for all these trials to come upon him."

"That is something that is far too easy for believers to do," uttered Deacon Fry. "When they see a Christian suffer, they unfairly assume that there must be sin in that believer's life. But I believe that suffering is not always a result of sin, as we see with Job. In my opinion, and in many cases that I see, those who are sinners suffer little while those who are saints suffer much."

"And do you feel that many people see that as a stumbling block for Christianity and ask why God allows suffering? Instead of asking 'why,' they might be better off asking 'what' . . . What is God up to?" the pastor's wife said.

"Like the refiner's fire, God often uses suffering to produce righteous character in believers," uttered Sister Josephine. "Sometimes He wants those who suffer to be more dependent upon Him. It may be that He is trying to get our attention. And

God always has a way of getting our attention. We might even sin; however, we cannot always equate suffering with sin in a believer's life as we see with Job's experience."

"Well, God reminds Job that the world has order and beauty, but it is also wild and dangerous. So, while we do not always know why we suffer, we can bring our pain and grief to God and trust that He is wise and knows what He's doing," Kizzie chimed.

It was an intriguing and intellectual conversation and one that lasted two hours. Unfortunately, the group had lost track of time. It had gotten late, and it was time to make their exit from the church and go home. They stood up, held hands in a circle, and said a prayer before departing.

"It's late. Do you want me to walk you home, Kizzie?" Deacon Fry asked her.

"No. I'll be fine, Deacon. I'm only a few blocks away."

"Okay. Get home safe," he said.

Kizzie smiled, grabbed her things, and walked out of the corner church with her head held high and feeling inspired. She enjoyed the discussion tonight at Bible study. It opened her eyes to Omar's situation. She thought he was like Job going through his trials and tribulations, minus the wealth. He was suffering. But her life wasn't peaches and cream either. She'd been through her troubles, losing her parents early and living with Lupus.

The inner-city streets were quiet tonight. Kizzie crossed Livonia Avenue, entering the towering ghetto buildings. She walked at a steady pace, eager to get home and get some sleep. But she couldn't stop thinking about Omar, wishing he had come to Bible study tonight. She figured he needed to hear tonight's discussion about the book of Job. But lately, Omar had been making himself absent from church, and it seemed like he was absent from the word of God too.

She heaved a worried sigh at the thought of Omar's sudden behavior change. In the past week or two, her friend had changed in ways she didn't like. He was becoming aloof to her and the church. And his attire seemed to darken. He started to wear more black and talk disparagingly about life and faith. It made her nervous, and she continued to pray for him.

Kizzie crossed the courtyard that was littered with trash and discarded drug paraphernalia. In doing so, she passed a shifty-looking man lingering in the playground area who was almost invisible. The sight of him made Kizzie uncomfortable. He gazed her way, and Kizzie put an extra pep in her step. She wanted to put enough distance between her and him, whoever he was. His presence sent chills through her being. But when he shifted and started to follow her, she became nervous. It was late, and the projects were unnaturally quiet and still. She felt alone, so she hurried to her building, already reaching for her keys.

When Kizzie neared the entrance to the building, she noticed that he was still following her, and he wasn't alone. Shockingly, Brice and several others appeared in her view too. Brice was smirking at her and uncouthly catcalling her way, "What's up, bitch? Let me holla at you!"

She knew they were up to no good. She hurried to get inside the lobby to rush to safety. Still, Brice and his boorish cohorts eagerly gave chase. They caught up to her before Kizzie could escape inside the elevator or the stairway. Brice angrily grabbed her with intensity, roughed her up, and wrapped his thick hand around her neck, slamming her against the wall with brute force. Kizzie shrieked and tried to fight him off, but his strength was animalistic.

Seething and through his clenched teeth, choking her heatedly, he growled, "Where ya fuckin' boy at? Huh? Where dat nigga at? He thinks he can fuckin' mock me n' not get fucked up!"

"Leave me alone!" she cried out.

Brice's crew circled Kizzie like a pack of wolves about to feast. She was cute. And each man glared at her with no good intentions on their minds.

"What apartment dat nigga live in?" Brice asked her.

Kizzie refused to tell him anything about Omar. Then frowning, she daringly stared at him and boldly replied, "I'm not telling you anything about Omar. Just leave him alone! He's been through enough!"

"Bitch, you think I'm playin' games wit' you? Fuck you think this is?! Either you tell me where dat nigga stay at, or we gon' fuck you up, and I don't care if you a bitch."

She struggled with him, but Brice's hold around her was like vise grips, clamping against her body sternly. He continued to hold her against the wall, his fingers digging into the skin of her neck.

"Yo, Brice, c'mon. Let's just do this bitch already," said Chuck with a thirsty and sinister purpose.

Brice grinned. "Yeah. Bitch, you either give up your boy now, or you gon' see what we about. And it ain't gon' be pretty, bitch."

She remained stubborn. Omar was her best friend, and she wanted to protect him. However, her stubbornness felt like gold to Brice's crew. It was on. Brice punched her in the face, and a sharp pain shot through Kizzie like lightning had struck her. Brice and Tip forcefully grabbed a resisting Kizzie and dragged her into the poorly lit stairwell. Kizzie continued to holler and fight, knowing what their intentions were.

"No! No! Get off me! No! Someone help me! Please! Help me!" she screamed at the top of her lungs.

Unfortunately, no one was around to hear her cries for help—or if they'd heard, they were most likely too scared to get involved. The door to the stairwell closed, and the men were like savages around Kizzie. The looks on their faces were treacherous and gleaming with perversion. Brice struck her again in the face for good measure, and Kizzie's face started swelling up like a balloon. Blood trickled from her lips. Her clothing became disheveled and torn. They forced her against the dirty, concrete floor, on her back, with her still kicking and fighting.

"Hold that bitch down!" Brice instructed them.

They did, and while holding her down, they forcefully pulled off her pants, ripped off her panties, and sexually assaulted her. Brice hastily undid his jeans and eagerly dropped between her legs, forced open, and his jeans around his ankles. He wanted to go first. He didn't hesitate to force himself inside her while the others held her down. Kizzie continued to fight. But once she felt him thrust inside of her, she felt defeated and cried a river from her eyes. Her eyes became swathed with tears, and her face covered with absolute anguish. This wasn't happening. No! She was a virgin, and Brice had sadistically taken what was pure and sacred from her. He grunted against her and orgasmed quickly while inside her, not having the decency to pull out.

He laughed when he finally pulled out and zipped up his jeans, uttering, "Damn, that bitch is tight."

"I got next," uttered the next man.

Kizzie wanted the nightmare to end. The next man hurriedly climbed over her and forced himself inside her. She'd stopped struggling, and every second that passed felt like an hour to her—excruciating hours believed, but only several minutes. It felt like her soul was being murdered. They laughed and slapped each other fives after they were done with her like she was some toy they were passing for their sick amusement. She felt paralyzed; her arms, legs, voice . . . everything becoming useless. Her body didn't belong to her anymore; it belonged to them. And each hard thrust inside her and each enjoyable groan released were ripping something away from her. Kizzie felt as if they all had reached inside her soul and forced it slowly to die.

She could not do anything but wait until they were all finished.

When it was finally over, Kizzie felt like she was a foreigner in her skin. She felt shattered and contaminated. *Why?* she thought. *Why did this happen to me?*

CHAPTER ELEVEN

HE HEARD "RAPE" and "Kizzie," and Omar fumed. It was early morning when he got the tragic news about his friend. He didn't want to believe it at first. It was hard for him to swallow the information of Kizzie being raped in the building stairwell last night. How did it happen? And why did it happen?

And most importantly, who did the shit? he asked himself. Right away, he hurried to visit her at Brookdale Hospital on Linden Blvd.

The car ride there was agonizing and slow for Omar. Traffic was thick. And Brooklyn was too congested. It took up too much of his time to travel to the hospital. He wanted to be there for Kizzie immediately—be by her side during such a harrowing and traumatic experience. The only thing he could think about was Kizzie, and he asked why God would allow something like that to happen to a good and faithful girl like her. He didn't know the extent of her injuries, but he knew they were ghastly for her to be rushed to the hospital and treated in ICU. And rape was an ugly crime that Omar could never forgive.

Omar put together his list of suspects. One man or monster he knew could commit such an appalling and audacious crime to his close friend in their building. *Brice*, he thought. Brice was a sexual pervert—evil in the neighborhood that needed to be put down. The rape of his friend had spread throughout the community, and the residents were shocked by it too. Kizzie kept to herself. She went to church, school, work, and home. She didn't bother anybody, but she always was a helping hand when it was needed. The detectives were investigating the incident. But Omar couldn't stop wondering why bad things happen to good people.

The cab came to a stop outside the entrance to Brookdale. Omar paid the fare and rushed from the backseat to the front door. His mind and thoughts were clouded entirely with worries and anger. He hoped she was okay.

While trying to hurry to visit Kizzie, he accidentally stumbled and bumped into a man pushing his friend through the lobby in a wheelchair. Thomas pushed Anton, who had been discharged from the hospital with his right leg still in a giant cast.

"Oh. I'm sorry," Omar apologized to the man in the wheelchair.

"Nah, you good," Anton replied.

Omar caught his footing and hurried off, but Anton kept his eyes on Omar for some reason, watching him hurry down the hallway.

"What's up, Anton? You know that nigga?" asked Thomas.

"Nah. But something just feel off about him," said Anton.

"Like what?"

"Don't know. Fuck it, just get me the fuck outta here; I'm tired of this place," he said.

Thomas continued to wheel him out of the hospital. On the outside was an idling black Yukon waiting for them and a few homies to welcome Anton back.

Omar took a deep breath, feeling somewhat ambivalent about seeing Kizzie's grave condition. He'd lost his mother the last time he was in the same hospital. He didn't want to lose his friend too. He took another deep breath and walked into the area where Kizzie was being treated. Her grandmother was present. The seventy-year-old woman sat by Kizzie's side, her head slightly bowed in silent prayer. She appeared to be concerned about her granddaughter's condition. When Omar stepped into the area, the grandmother smiled and looked up at him. And he wondered how she could smile at him at a time like this.

The sight of Kizzie was disturbing. Immediately, her beaten and battered face stood out. Her face was swollen, disfigured, and nearly unrecognizable. She was asleep but in bad shape.

"How is she?" he asked the grandmother.

"In bad shape, Omar. Doctors say that she has extensive vaginal tearing, and they're trying to maintain her swelling." She stood and hugged him. "I'm glad you came to see her."

"Of course. She's family to me . . . y'all both are," he said.

The sight of Kizzie made Omar cringe. His attention lingered on her swollen eyes and busted lips.

"What kind of animal could do this to a woman . . . to Kizzie?" he asked rhetorically.

"I don't know. But I'm praying for her," replied the grandmother.

Praying?

Omar refused to pray. What he wanted was revenge. He felt there was more power with the gun than in prayer. What they did to Kizzie couldn't go unpunished or unchecked. He knew Brice and his goons were the culprits. It was bad enough that they attacked and bullied him; now, they came after his best friend.

"I'll be back, Omar. I need to use the bathroom. I've been here since last night," said the grandmother. "Just keep her in your prayers for me, Omar. But I know you will."

He didn't respond.

She left the area, leaving Omar alone with Kizzie and his disturbing thoughts. He clenched his fists with the damning thought of Brice violating Kizzie in the foulest way, taking something away from her that could never be replaced. It angered him that he wasn't there to help her when she needed him the most. Now the only thing he could do was vow vengeance against those who had attacked her—make it right by any means necessary. Strike with a vengeance like he was the Lord Almighty Himself.

Pray? No. Now it was time to act.

Omar moved closer to Kizzie with sadness and contempt—and hatred. Then with a glaring look masking his face, he made a promise to her. "I'm gonna make them all pay for this, Kizzie. I promise you that," he expressed with conviction. "This ain't right. You didn't deserve this."

He fumed. He could no longer look at her; it was too disturbing to see her like that.

He turned and marched out of the room. He could no longer suffer to see his friend in such a broken and distressing condition. He departed the room and left the hospital lobby filled with a whirlwind of emotions—ready to ignite and explode disastrously like TNT. Lingering outside the exit, Omar removed a cigarette from the pack of Newports and lit one. When did he start smoking? It just happened. Out of the blue, he had a nicotine addiction and a craving for a cigarette. He lit the cigarette and took a few needed drags as he stood on the sidewalk, looking contemptuously at the world around him.

Finally, he decided to walk home and smoke his cigarette.

He also decided never to feel weak again or become a victim.

His anger, hatred, and rage for Brice attracted her that night—the succubus. The room became eerily dark and still. Then, from out of nowhere, it came to him again and latched its dark, sultry, shimmering form against Omar enticingly. The longing he felt for it—to see it again, to feel its presence and immoral contact against his skin—his beseeching flesh. It was perverted and uncanny. He knew it would return to him, and he wanted it to stay this time. He wanted the perversion it bestowed on him to last. He didn't want it to vanish suddenly and deprive him of the sexual pleasure it perpetually implemented. He wanted to feel an orgasm inside of it. He wanted to feel the power it created. It was a being unexplained but alluring.

It gripped his hard dick and started to stroke it up and down, creating a harmonious and pleasurable hum from him. Omar cooed from the sensation, knowing it was only the beginning of better things to come. She twisted her darkish being around him and allowed him to penetrate her with his fingers. She right away bent in half, pulling her nether lips away from Omar's quizzical fingers, and her mouth latched onto the tip of his dick. He spicily felt her tongue swirl around the tip as a hot suction excited him. Omar groaned with the sudden jolt of pleasure and felt his hips press upward to her siphoning lips as she curved even further to take more of his manhood into her mouth. She added a tinge of vibration to his balls, making Omar squirm fervently.

As he latched onto her nearest breast, her eyes smoldered with lust and a carnivore's hunger for him. Their mouths hungrily devoured each other's lips—and a jolt of electricity passed between them. He felt her lustful hunger fill his body with its power. Omar shivered nearly witlessly as his erection thrust into her slippery silken inner walls, and her gyrating movement became delicious to his flesh. He groaned with a satisfying intent, feeling the heat of her sex rising and falling ubiquitously, all while feeling trapped against and inside her pussy.

With each deep penetration, he felt her jerk around his erection, and the sensation was beyond arousing. It felt like a vacuum of pleasure between her legs as it continued to latch onto him intensely. Her eternal suction and quivery heated velvet walls were too much for Omar to bear. He bellowed with obsession as he felt his balls contract and release his seed deep into the demonic woman straddling him. He huffed and puffed. He didn't want it to leave. He wanted to know its name. He wanted the gratifying feeling to continue.

"What . . . what is . . .?"

"Malaka," it spoke. She spoke. Her voice sounded radiant to him.

It lingered on top of Omar, uncovered, and stared down into his eyes, becoming captivating and nearly hypnotic to his soul. It spoke with its eyes. It demanded something from him, which was unequivocal about what it wanted.

Revolution! Chaos! Murder!

Brice climbed out of the idling cab cursing the driver.

"Fuck you!" shouted Brice. "I don't owe you shit!"

"You pay! You pay me what you owe!" retorted the cabdriver.

The driver, an older Hindu male with thick facial hair, jumped out of his cab, looking ready to confront Brice. Still, he thought against it, for Brice was a solid-looking thug and troublemaker. However, the driver was upset with Brice for the unpaid fare. He had driven him ten miles to the Ville and wanted what was owed to him.

Brice spun around with his fists clamped together tightly; he was ready for a confrontation with the shorter man.

"What you gon' do, bitch? You gon' try n' take it from me? C'mon, nigga, try n' take ya fare from me and see what happens," exclaimed Brice, daring him.

"I call the police," the man responded.

The mention of the police infuriated Brice. He charged at the man and swung madly, knocking the driver out. The cabdriver lay flat on his back, exposed like he'd gotten knocked out by Mike Tyson. Brice hurriedly rummaged through his pockets and stole a small amount of cash. He then speedily poked around the front seat of the man's cab and snatched his cell phone from the dashboard. Then he took off running, leaving the driver unconscious.

Brice continued living up to his reputation as a menace to society. Knocking out the driver after stiffing him of a cab fare and robbing him, it's who he was—a violent thug. He walked around feeling like he was untouchable. Then he hurried away from the incident he had created and disappeared into the folds of the building project. He would be far away from the ugly doing by the time any police came to the crime scene.

He walked into his building, counting the stolen money from the driver. It was only forty-eight dollars—that was it! Still, easy money. While distracted by the cash and the man's cell phone in his hands, he wasn't aware he was being followed. Since he entered the crinkles of the housing project and moved meaninglessly, he was being watched and not careful. But he had no reason to be cautious while walking around in his domain. After all, he was the king of the concrete, the urban jungle, and he believed no one had the audacity or balls to rob or try him. His reputation preceded him.

He took the elevator to the fifth floor. It had been a long day for him, and he was ready to call it quits for the night. He was high and a bit tipsy. He'd spent nearly all day at a friend's place in Crown Heights drinking, smoking, and having sex with several young girls before returning home for the night.

Satisfied!

After one in the early morning, the hallways and the entire building were surprisingly calm and quiet. But that peaceful and serene atmosphere was about to be interrupted.

The moment the elevator doors opened on his designated floor, Brice was shocked at what he saw awaiting him . . . a figure in a dark hoodie with his arm outstretched and aiming a .357 at him.

"What the fuck!" he growled. "You here to rob me, nigga?"

The sinister figure stared at him attentively—in silence—intimidatingly. Brice couldn't make out who was behind the hoodie. But whoever it was, he was ready to kill him.

Brice scowled while being trapped inside the elevator at gunpoint. He tried to hold his own and remained undaunted by the sight of a gun, but he was vulnerable and caught off guard. He glared at the man with the gun, hoping he didn't have the gallant attitude to take his life.

"Who you, nigga?" asked Brice. "What the fuck you want?"

The figure decided to reveal itself. It pulled back the hoodie from his face revealing to Brice that Omar held him at gunpoint. Brice was more outraged than shocked—and he wasn't scared.

"You muthafucka! Nigga, you don't fuckin' learn, do you, you bitch-ass nigga?" Brice shouted and mocked. "I swear I fucked that bitch you like, and I swear I'm gonna do you so much worse—"

Boom!

The gun exploded in Omar's hand, and a bullet tore through Brice's chest and plunged him backward against the elevator walls.

Boom!

Omar fired again, and another bullet from the .357 left another gaping hole in Brice's chest. Shock and fear suddenly registered on Brice's face as he frightfully clutched his bleeding chest and collapsed. Barely alive, he stared up at Omar, now towering over him with the smoking gun. He didn't know the fool had it in him—to kill him. He coughed up blood and was dying.

Omar had no choice words for Brice, nothing to say. He was there to do one thing—carry out a murder. But he wasn't done with Brice yet. He aimed the gun at a particular place, his genitals, and fired three more shots.

Boom! Boom . . . Boom!

The rounds from the gun mutilated Brice's private parts, and the final round was lodged into his forehead. Brice's bullet-riddled body lay contorted inside the elevator, blood pooling everywhere. Omar stood near the body, nearly appearing transfixed by what he'd done. But, instead, he smirked, pivoted, and coolly walked away from the scene.

It needed to be done.

One down and several others to go.

PART TWO

Life hurts a lot, more than death.

CHAPTER TWELVE

THE BLACK CROWN Vic stopped at the concrete curb leading to the Tilden homes in the Ville. The driver killed the engine and exhaled. It nearly reached the morning, dawn an hour or two away, but the activity outside a particular building was already bright and bustling. A few residents gathered around the entrance to the building lobby. They all were inquiring about the shooting that happened not too long ago. They wondered who it was that'd gotten killed inside the building. The lobby to the fifth floor was buzzing and crawling with police activity. It was a circus, and the detective was about to jump into one of the rings and put into action his performance.

Danny Greene exhaled with a job to do, and he coolly climbed out of the Crown Vic. His brown shoes touched the aging concrete, and he stood tall and meaningful outside the towering projects. Then he walked toward the crime scene ahead; his stride was genuine and urgent with his tunnel vision on—another shooting—another murder—another case.

He took the foul-smelling concrete stairs to the fifth floor instead of the elevator. The elevator was inoperative; it had become his crime scene to investigate—a bullet-riddled body sprawled across the grimy floor. Another homicide in the Ville was like another THOT getting pregnant—natural and expected.

The second Danny stepped onto the fifth floor, a wave of uniformed cops greeted him. CSI snapped pictures and dusted for fingerprints, and other detectives flooded the narrow, urban hallway. It was tight and congested with police movement, but it was big enough for him to squeeze his way toward the crime. Foster was already present and throwing out his off-putting opinion and two cents about the homicide and the victim.

"What we got here, Bunk?" asked Danny coolly.

"Another nigga dead . . . shot to shit like he was target practice," uttered Bunk with recklessness.

Danny shot him a slightly sour look like *enough with the antics and negativity.* "Jesus, Bunk, this is someone's child."

Bunk laughed. "Child? You're not familiar with the deceased . . . our newly departed. The one with his dick shot off and a hole in his head the size of a golf ball."

Now wearing latex gloves, Danny carefully moved closer to the body. He crouched toward it for closer inspection—examining the dead from head to toe. It was a gruesome sight. It was death—an appalling reality of human cruelty he'd seen countless times. Blood was everywhere, and the victim's genitals were shot to shit.

"This was personal," said Danny.

"Yeah. It most likely was with that fool. His name was Brice Patterson . . . a nasty fuck, a true menace to the society around these parts, and the nigga had a rap sheet longer than my big dick," Bunk said to his partner.

Danny ignored the latter Bunk's statement. Instead, he stood and took in the scene from different angles. His eyes shifted everywhere, trying to deduce what happened.

"The shooter either knew his location beforehand or followed him home and opened fire the moment the doors to the elevator opened," said Danny. "And by the two shots to his genitals . . . maybe a female or something to do with a woman."

"Yeah, you're the regular Sherlock Holmes, Danny," Bunk joked.

Danny didn't laugh.

"This entire fuckin' neighborhood is going to shit. But I tell you this, that fuck nuts Brice won't be missed at all. And far as suspects go, try all of Brooklyn. Who didn't hate this muthafucka and wished to see him dead?" said Bunk callously.

Danny sighed. "Still, we have a job to do."

"It's going to be like damn near trying to breathe in space . . . fuckin' impossible. He was hated, Danny. He was a lowlife that was into everything . . . you name it. The way I see it, it was bound to happen to this muthafucka sooner or later," Bunk said. "I wouldn't even waste my breath or time on this one."

Danny was agitated by his partner's lack of interest in the case. They were the primary, and despite the victim's troubling past, it was still a murder that needed to be investigated and likely solved. But Bunk pranced around the crime scene with apathy—with judgment for the deceased.

"Who was the officer first on the scene?" Danny asked a cop nearby.

The officer told him, Manton. Danny went into investigation mode despite his partner's indifference to the victim.

"I want to start knocking on doors to see if there were any witnesses to the shooting," Danny told the cop.

The officer nodded.

"An uphill battle in this neighborhood," Bunk chimed. "You already know people don't talk to police around here."

"We at least are going to try."

"Waste of time and manpower to me," uttered Bunk with distaste.

Danny shot his partner another glaring and disapproving gaze. He wondered why he became a cop or a detective. Detectives were meant to be impartial to all victims, not only those they liked or believed were law-abiding citizens.

"What, you have a problem with me and my fucked-up choice of words for that piece of shit?" Bunk exclaimed.

"He's a victim, and that's all that matters," Danny returned sharply.

"And because of that shit there," Bunk pointed at the dead. "How many fuckin' victims do you think he left behind during his pathetic and useless years on this earth? Whoever shot him to shit like that did us and everyone in this forsaken neighborhood a fuckin' favor."

Bunk pivoted and marched away with agitation in his steps. Danny released another taxing sigh and continued with his work. He felt that Bunk possibly had a personal incident or clashed with the deceased. He'd never seen his partner so worked up before. Still, he was a homicide detective, and murder had been committed. His duty was to roll up his sleeves, have a soft eye at the crime scene, and get to work putting the pieces together. It didn't matter what kind of ugly reputation Brice had for Danny. What mattered was solving another murder.

It was the job.

Residents on the streets of Brownsville heard about the murder of Brice, and they all were reluctant to speak with the police. Instead, they reacted with widened eyes and furrowed brows and usually ended politely but guardedly, "No, thank you."

The NYPD was like a plague in their community. Some people felt the cops were worse than the gangs and the drugs. So, when interrupted or stopped by an officer, a few residents just kept walking or interrupted with a question of their own, "What do you want?"

Danny tried to interview residents and folks and got nowhere. Then finally, the news of Brice's demise spread quickly like wildfire. It wasn't a shock to many, but it was a relief that the man was dead to many. He was twenty-three years old and considered a terror.

But Brice's murder was only a tiny drop in an overspilling bucket. There was a drug war between three different crews. The bloodshed was spreading throughout the city like cancer.

The NYPD had their hands full. And it seemed like Brownsville was becoming ground zero for the city's violence and carnage.

Detective Danny Greene climbed back into his Crown Vic. The sun was now blazing in the sprawling blue sky, shining fiercely down at the Ville, indicating that it would be another hot day. He momentarily lingered behind the car's wheel, gathering or collecting his thoughts. He'd been a homicide detective for two years and had seen his fair share of carnage and horror in the streets of Brooklyn. He compared the violence in the Ville to having done two tours in Iraq, and the two places were indistinguishable.

CHAPTER THIRTEEN

KIZZIE MANAGED TO smile at Omar. But Omar didn't smile back. Instead, he thought, *What is there to smile about? You were beaten and raped.* She was awake, somewhat conversing, and she was, to some extent, functioning. She seemed to be okay, but Omar knew she'd been through a traumatic experience, and the road to recovery would most likely be long and trying. Still, he wanted to be there for her.

"How you holding up, Kizzie?" he asked.

"I'm . . . I'm okay," she replied, her speech a bit slurred.

Her swelling had gone down. The doctors had given her some antibiotics and implemented a rape kit to collect hair, semen, clothing fibers, and other evidence of the attackers' identity. However, the horror and realization came when the staff treated or checked her for sexually transmitted diseases. She was given emergency birth control. It was important for Kizzie to receive birth control and treatment for any STDs within 72 hours of the assault for maximum effectiveness. The horror of becoming pregnant from the rape or getting any STD would become a nightmare—especially when she was a virgin before the incident.

The sex crime unit had visited Kizzie in the hospital several times to take down her statement. They wanted to know what happened. *Who did this to you?*

She didn't say anything to them. Brice had warned her if she said anything to the police about it, he would kill Omar without any hesitation. Therefore, she had remained silent, pretending to have amnesia about the incident. Everything happened so fast; it was a blur to her. The statement she gave to the police was she'd entered her building and was grabbed from behind by someone. She was forced into the stairwell, where she was raped and attacked. The detectives wanted to find the culprits and put them behind bars. But bizarrely, their only witness wasn't cooperative. They asked many questions about how many were there, if their faces were covered, etc. It was overwhelming for Kizzie, and the nurse had to escort the detectives out of the room.

"She needs her rest," said the nurse.

But Omar knew who they were. Deep in his gut, he knew it was Brice and his goons. And he wondered why Kizzie wasn't telling the police about it.

"Why you not saying anything, Kizzie?" he asked. "It was Brice that raped you, right? Just tell the truth. You don't need to protect that monster from me! He threatened you to keep quiet about it, right?"

More questions from a friend.

"I want to forget about it, Omar. Please," she begged.

"Forget?" he replied, bewildered by her statement. "How can you forget something like that? Look at what they did to you . . . to your face. They all need to pay."

"And they will!" spat Kizzie.

"What . . . by God's justice, huh? That's what you believe, Kizzie, that God will take care of it . . . punish these fools by His hands?"

"It is not for us to be vengeful," she replied.

Omar glared at Kizzie, upset. "Are you kidding me?! They attacked you, spread your damn legs, and raped you. They took something precious from you, and you fuckin' lie there and want to remain passive and humble about this shit?" Omar exclaimed, upset.

Kizzie started to cry. Then he knew he had pushed things too far with her. She had been through a lot and was still recuperating and healing from the incident. Omar spun her way with a change of emotions. He had "I'm sorry" screaming in his eyes, and they soon spilled out from his mouth. "I'm sorry, Kizzie. I didn't mean to go off on you like that. It's just I care about you."

He pulled her into his arms and hugged her. It was a lingering hug that Kizzie strongly needed and felt, and as she buried her face in his chest, she continued to explode with tears. She erupted with emotions and sentiment. She wanted to be strong but broke down like a collapsing structure. And as Omar held her in his arms, he could feel her tremble. It was as if she were reliving the horrific ordeal all over again. Her eyes were closed, and her tears continued to wet his shirt.

"I wish I were there for you, Kizzie. I wish I were there to stop it. But I'm going to handle it. They're gonna pay for what they did to you," he spoke with conviction.

He didn't want to let her go. He wanted to make her pain go away, but he couldn't. He couldn't rewind the past. The damage had already been done.

Knock! Knock!

Omar looked up and saw the pastor and his wife standing at the door's threshold. They'd brought Kizzie some flowers and interrupted a private moment between them. Kizzie pulled her face from Omar's chest and wiped away the tears pouring out like a running faucet. The couple stepped into the hospital room with looks of compassion and concern for Kizzie. Omar stood from the bed and greeted the pastor with a handshake.

"I knew you would be here with her, Omar. Always. You are such a great friend," said Pastor Morgan.

"I just wished I was with her that night," Omar replied.

"We all do," returned the pastor.

"We brought you some flowers, Kizzie," chimed the pastor's wife. "I feel so horrible that this happened to you. I shouldn't have let you walk home alone that night."

"I'm okay, Sister Morgan, and it's not your fault."

"No. You're a young and pretty girl, and you should have had an escort walking you home that night," Sister Morgan uttered with regret. "It was late, and the kind of neighborhood we live in . . ." Her voice trailed off, and she became teary-eyed.

"I'm still here. God still has me here with y'all no matter what," Kizzie said modestly.

"And an Amen to that," the pastor bellowed.

Omar wanted to cringe. He didn't want to hear it right now—about God and to turn the other cheek. But what he did the other night, killing Brice in cold blood, was an awe-inspiring feeling that he couldn't stop thinking about. The image of Brice's bullet-riddled body sprawled across that elevator floor by his doing was something magnificent glued to his memory. It was power! It was supremacy! It felt something had finally been quenched in his soul.

Murder got it . . . got *her* excited.

Malaka paid him another visit the following night and bestowed him what felt like a hundred orgasms. The pleasurable feeling made him growl and almost feral. The blissfulness felt endless and enduring, and she collected much semen from him. She continued to contort his soul and influence him.

"*More . . .*" It had spoken to him.

"Let us pray," said Pastor Morgan. He attempted to grab Omar's hand, but there was some slight resistance.

Why pray? he felt. *Why believe?*

"You okay, Omar?" the pastor asked him.

"Yeah. I'm . . . I'm just still upset that this happened to her," he said.

"We all are upset, Omar. But this is the time we need to continue to show strength and support," the pastor replied.

Omar sighed, and he gave in. He didn't want anyone asking him questions. So, instead, he took the pastor's hand into his left and his wife's hand into his right, forming a semicircle around Kizzie's bed, and they all bowed their heads in prayer. Omar wanted to get it over with. But before the pastor could start his prayer, there was another knock at the door interrupting their ritual.

Everyone turned to see two detectives entering the room from the sex crime unit. Detective Roughan and Detective Ellison. Man and woman.

"We're sorry to interrupt things," Ellison spoke; she was a tall, leggy Black woman with short-cropped hair and wore a dark pantsuit.

"No, Detectives, we were about to go into a prayer for Kizzie, but that can wait," the pastor said. "Is this important?"

"Yes. We know you been through a lot, Kizzie," Detective Roughan uttered. He matched the same height as his female partner with a bald head and grayish goatee and wore a dark blue suit. "We just want to show you a picture of someone . . . a person of interest to your case."

Kizzie heaved a troubled sigh but nodded. She wanted to forget, but the sexual assault wasn't something to forget quickly and take lightly. And the SVU was adamant about finding the culprit(s) but tried to tread gently with the victim—not wanting to push her too hard in remembering something so horrible.

It was a delicate situation for them.

Detective Ellison opened a black folder and removed a glossy photo from it. She approached Kizzie gently, not wanting to spark a relapse with her. She was awake, functioning, and seemed to be relaxed around her peers and talking. They figured now would be the best time for questions and identifying an attacker.

Ellison showed Kizzie a mug shot photo of Brice. Even in his picture, he seemed terrifying. The moment Kizzie saw the photo, she started to hyperventilate. Glancing at the picture had stirred or triggered some negative reaction in her, indicating to the detectives that they most likely were on the right man.

"His name is—"

"Brice," the pastor interrupted her. "Yes. We're familiar with him, Detective. Is he the one that raped Kizzie?"

"He has a long criminal record, including sexual assault and battery," answered Ellison. "And he was a person of interest."

"Was . . .?" inquired Pastor Morgan.

After a brief pause, Roughan answered, "He was shot and killed the other night inside the elevator of his building."

"Ohmygod," Mrs. Morgan gasped, her hands covering her mouth, shocked.

Kizzie was shocked too. "He's dead?"

"Still, with his demise, we need to know, was he the one that raped you?" asked Ellison.

Becoming teary-eyed again, Kizzie softly nodded and whimpered, "Yes."

"Oh God," Mrs. Morgan spewed.

The detectives continued to tread lightly with their questions and the situation. Kizzie was still fragile. But now that she'd confirmed that Brice was one of the men that raped her, they were determined to continue their investigation in hunting down and arresting the others responsible.

Omar remained cold toward the news. Brice was dead, and he smirked at the information. While the others were shocked and entertaining the detectives, Omar became aloof. He retreated into his mind—his subconscious. The vision to him was still clear as day . . . Brice dying, choking on his own blood, and lying in a pool of it. The shock on Brice's face when he pulled that trigger and took him down thrilled Omar. He wished he could have done it several more times—but unfortunately, you can only kill a person once.

"May God has mercy on his soul," the pastor uttered.

Hearing that snapped Omar heatedly away from his musing, and he shot the pastor a foul stare.

"Say what, Pastor Morgan . . .?" he started to gripe. "May God has mercy on his soul? Are you serious after what he did to Kizzie? He raped and beat her . . .and me, what he did to me and others in this neighborhood. He terrorized everything he came in contact with. He was the devil himself and didn't deserve any Got-damn mercy. He deserves to burn in hell forever! Fuck him! I hated him, and I hope he's rotting and burning in hell right now."

Omar stormed out of the hospital room. Pastor Morgan appeared dumbfounded by the impulsive outburst—and others too.

Wow!

"I'll go talk to him," Mrs. Morgan said. She tried to chase after Omar, but she was too slow. Omar was gone by the time she made it halfway down the hallway. He ran down the stairs like a bat out of hell and emerged into the lobby. He didn't want to be bothered. He wanted to be alone.

Pray for his soul. And forgiveness. He wanted none of that for Brice.

CHAPTER FOURTEEN

There's a war going outside no man is safe from
You could run, but you can't hide forever
From these streets that we done took
You walkin' witcha head down scared to look . . .

THE MOBB DEEP lyrics blared from the moving Honda Accord on Sutter Avenue. It was a late summer night, and a loaded clip slammed into the butt of a .9 mm Beretta. It was ready for war—death. The gun was in the hands of a known killer named Bookie—a notorious hitter for the Brooklyn Mafia Crew. He was nineteen with three homicides to his name. And he'd already seen things that would scar and scare any man. His eyes and heart were cold like winter frost.

Bookie took a pull from the burning cannabis. He was sitting in the front passenger seat, nodding to the rap tunes and staring out the window, looking for something—looking for trouble, always trouble.

Driving the dark green Accord was Bookie's friend, T.T. And together, both men carried a fierce reputation in the Ville, one that reached far beyond the streets of the Ville. Belonging to the BMC, one of the most sinful and violent drug crews in Brooklyn, they intentionally drove into rival territory looking for trouble—searching for rivals to take down. Their rivals were niggas from the Boss Crew, who ran the Howard homes between Pitkin and

East New York Avenue and the towers between Belmont and Pitkin. BMC and Boss Crew had been fighting each other for years, but the internal beef inside Sean Black's drug organization, BMC, was raging out of control. A civil war between Anton and an ambitious young gangster named Kenya had ensued. Both men despised each other. Sean Black's sudden demise left a gaping beef between the two, who wanted control over the lucrative drug organization. It controlled movement and product in the Tilden homes and Van Dyke homes and the surrounding streets.

Bookie was Anton's leading man and his go-to shooter. Not only was Bookie in charge of finding the hooded stranger in black that'd shot and crippled Anton, but he was the Grim Reaper on the streets, ready to kill anything that threatened Anton and the organization, including fellow BMC members. Brooklyn was his home, and the gang was his loyalty.

Bookie took another pull from the blunt and kept his eyes on the streets. He had a keen eye for spotting things that didn't want to be spotted.

For months, three violent drug crews fought over territory and control in Brownsville. And civilians and residents found themselves in the middle of World War 3 with fledging gangsters and gangs trying to make their way up the ladder and trying to solidify their position on the streets and in the drug trade. As a result, violence and bloodshed became a regular on the Brooklyn streets. And the Ville was beginning to look like Baghdad.

"Yo, slow down," Bookie told T.T.

Bookie had spotted something in the distance. T.T. slowed the Accord as it bent the corner of Rockaway Avenue.

"Yeah, that's that muthafucka right there . . . fuckin' Bobby," said Bookie, staring frantically ahead. Focused.

Bookie cocked back the Beretta. No fear. His attention was keen on Bobby and another young male coming out of a Crown

Fried Chicken on the corner with their food in hand. Bookie watched Bobby sink his teeth into a crispy chicken leg and laugh with his friend. The streetlights lit up the avenue with an orange glow, but the late hour made the area sparse of people and traffic. Stores were closed. Police weren't around at the moment, and they were alone with an opportunity that didn't come often.

"Yo, I'ma fuck dis nigga up right now," Bookie uttered colorfully, gun in his hand.

T.T. drove the Accord closer. Bookie poised himself for action in the passenger seat, the window coming down. Bobby and his friend paid no attention to the approaching Honda Accord as they walked toward a parked Mercedes-Benz. The Accord moved closer, and Bookie wanted to get at them upfront and close. There would be no drive-by—it wasn't his style.

T.T. brought the car to a slow crawl where Bookie could jump out with his gun and hastily move toward the duo. They had their backs turned and were almost near the Benz when he called out, "Yo, Bobby . . ."

Bobby and his friend turned toward the threat and caught a fleeting glance at Bookie coming at them with the rising pistol and a steely glare. He didn't falter and squeezed robotically, continuing his violent reputation.

Bak! Bak! Bak! Bak! Bak! Bak!

Both men went down in a hail of gunfire, their food spilling everywhere on the sidewalk. Bookie hit both of them at point-blank range. Then to make sure they were dead, he stood over them both, fired several additional rounds into their bleeding frames, and marched away coldheartedly. T.T. brought the car to a stop. Bookie quickly jumped back into the passenger seat, and it sped off, leaving two dead men from Boss's Crew sprawled on the street.

"Say that again," uttered Danny Greene to the medical examiner, Lenny Diaz.

"There were no bullets recovered from the victim . . . from the body at all, I'm afraid," Diaz said, indicating an anomaly. Brice's cold, naked body was displayed on the cold slab in the examination room for the detective to see. "Not a single one."

Greene was shocked.

What?

"How is that possible?" asked Danny. "He was shot multiple times right there on the scene. I am counting more than four holes in him myself, and since we didn't recover any shell casings at the scene, I assume a revolver killed him."

"Yes, that is true. A revolver killed him, and from the measurements I've taken myself of the multiple entry wounds, I say maybe from a .357 Magnum. But when I thoroughly examined the body, the wounds were there, indicating the victim died from gunfire, but the rounds weren't. And there are no signs of any exit wounds."

"Are you telling me that somehow the ammunition that killed my victim is no longer present? Gone?"

"Unfortunately, yes."

"And is that even possible?"

"Unfortunately, this isn't the first victim I've seen this with. Two gunshot victims came into the morgue with similar damages a year ago. Whatever killed him, like the others, the rounds just vanished. Dissolved inside of him," said Diaz. "And this has been a mystery to me since I started working here."

Danny wanted to shout out, "*You're fucking with me, right?*" but the look on the examiner's face showed he was just as confused as Danny.

Lenny Diaz had reached out to Danny personally, telling him that he needed to see him immediately. It was important.

Danny expected to recover several rounds for ballistics. But instead, he was hit with the unthinkable: no bullets to match a gun—a revolver. It was crucial evidence to his case, but there was no telling what caliber was used without the dispensed rounds.

Greene's investigation was going nowhere fast so far. Everything was leading to a dead end for the detective. There were no witness statements, not even a witness. Everyone refused to speak to him or the police. There were no video recordings of anyone coming or going from the building—not even one of the victims. The ghetto—grimy, crime-ridden Brooklyn projects sprawling with violence and any surveillance in the area was either nonexistent or temporarily not working—destroyed by the hands of young kids. And now, Diaz was telling him that somehow whatever bullets killed his victim had dissolved inside the body.

Fuck!

"I've been doing this for two years, Detective. And I've seen my fair share of almost everything from gruesome, weird, outlandish, and crazy in this line of work, but this has truly stumped me since the first time it came to my attention. Again, I thoroughly examined the deceased and figured I would find something hidden in the victim's organs this time. But it's like . . . he was killed by something unknown . . . unquestionably shot, but shot with what . . . nothing?" said Diaz. "And there's something else that I found strange," Diaz added.

"What is that?"

"Like some other victims a year ago, some of his organs and insides were completely charred."

"Charred? You mean like burnt?" Danny asked doubtfully.

"Yes. Like they'd been set on fire," Diaz added. "I'm sure other detectives in your precinct have mentioned this before. This isn't my first report."

"This is new to me," said Danny.

Danny was becoming far from befuddled. Instead, he was becoming overwhelmed with the unbelievable. "Set on fire? Could a bullet have done that?" he asked.

"In all my years of implementing autopsies, I've never seen any bullet cause anyone's organs or insides to burn like that or even explode completely."

"So, I have a body, but no shell casings, no bullets, no suspects, no witnesses, and charred organs," uttered Danny with displeasure.

"Maybe you can check with the ATF, see if there's some kind of new high-end weaponry out there that can implement this kind of damage," Diaz suggested.

"With a .357 . . . ? You assume that was the weapon used, right?"

"They are powerful guns."

"Yeah, they are. But not that powerful to make someone's insides crispy, right?" Danny replied.

"This victim isn't the first; I fear he will not be the last. I wish I had an explanation, but I don't. I suggest you reach out to your peers on the job about any old cases with similar injuries," Diaz said.

Danny turned and left the examination room, looking overcome. He sighed heavily. It was one of those "*What the fuck!*" moments, and it felt like something out of one of Stephen King's novels. Bullets were dissolving, hypothetically—and organs were charred.

Leaving the examiner's office, he climbed into his Crown Vic, started the ignition, and sat inside the idling vehicle, his thoughts and investigation going haywire. Bunk had warned him that this investigation would be an uphill battle. And it was. Danny had recorded every step of his research and tried to create a timeline for Brice. He tried learning everything about his victim, putting together his final days. And Bunk was right again; the man was feared and hated. No one wanted to get involved with his case, and not too many people had love and respect for Brice.

But there was his crew.

Danny knew that a good investigator gets to know the victim, their habits, friends, and hobbies.

He would go after Brice's crew either by force or cooperation. But of course, one, maybe all of them, had a criminal background he could use as leverage. Or maybe one or all of them were on some parole or probation that he could use to his advantage. Greene was the type not to give up, no matter what. Many hated and despised the victim, but someone out there would help him break open his case—and speak for Brice, he believed. He told himself sometimes, you need to take a few steps back to see the entire picture. And in his gut, he knew there was something that he was missing. Something that he wasn't seeing.

He huffed. To ease his baffled mind, he sifted through his minor music selection inside the car and pushed a Mos Def CD into the CD drive. He skipped several songs until it landed on one of his favorite songs recorded by Mos Def. "Umi Says" started to play inside the car. Danny let the music take over for him. He closed his eyes and listened intently to the lyrics, regarding Mos Def as a musical genius.

He hummed along with the tuneful beat. Then he started to sing along with the song. "*Tomorrow may never come for you, Umi. Life is not promised. Tomorrow may never show up . . .*"

It was therapeutic for him—music. When the world around him was going crazy, there was music. When investigating, the dead became overwhelming, or a case seemed like a dead end, there was music. When he felt he was drowning in homicides and police politics, there was music. Danny Greene was a fan of Hip-Hop, Rap, R&B, and Reggae; he loved it all. Before the police academy, before the gun and shield, before the streets, he played the piano and the guitar—was once in a group named "Way Down We Go." They'd achieved some notoriety in the early

2000s, and then egos and greed got in the way. Like a cliché in a VH1 reality show, arguments abounded, and the subsequent breakup of the group followed. Then a year later, Danny found his calling with the NYPD.

Danny sighed after the song ended. Just like writing songs and playing instruments was an art, he saw solving homicides as an art too. It took particular skill, patience, and a keen eye to investigate and solve homicides. Something he was becoming good at doing.

He shifted the vehicle into drive and drove away from the parking spot. It had been a long day. The last thing he wanted to do tonight was go home, unwind with a shot of gin and a cigar, and put on some old records.

CHAPTER FIFTEEN

THE ROOFTOP WAS where Omar found some comfort and solitude. It was hours into darkness—late. He jumped onto the edge of the rooftop like an agile cat, becoming undaunted and perched on the ledge, which was twelve stories high. He took a long gaze at a wide-ranging Brooklyn. It was another hot summer night, but the streets grew hotter by the day. Violence had exploded throughout the borough, especially in Brownsville. Omar stood exceptionally high and just a step away from falling and death. He saw flashing blue and red lights from afar, indicating a heavy police presence, possibly another shooting—another murder.

His eyes stayed fixed that way, thinking and contemplating. The Ville was jumping off badly with a drug war happening.

Omar lit a cigarette and took a few pulls from it. Smoking had become habitual for him. The feel of the nicotine coursing through his body became necessary. He stood perched on the ledge like Batman, watching and patrolling the city from high above. But he was no Batman—far from being a vigilante. Instead, his mind became cluttered with implementing revenge. It became filled with darkness and rage. Killing Brice wasn't enough. Others needed to be punished and taken care of. They also raped Kizzie, and they also took something away from her. And they also brutalized and bullied him for years.

He felt trapped in the night. He felt trapped in anger and betrayal. He felt trapped in lies from those he trusted. He felt trapped in Bible verses he thought would help.

He remembered something from Deathlike Silence Productions, lyrics he had once heard. Lyrics he remembered for some strange reason years ago.

"Trapped in the Night."

He took another drag from the cancer stick and shouted, "*He runs alone with nothing there to help him, to guide him. The stars are lost amongst the clouds; their light won't find him. Oh, how he cries, tears in his eyes. His innocence will come to harm. Only thirteen, there's no escaping, no flight. He runs painlessly, trapped in the night. Fleeing from monsters and murderous wights. The trees around her are malevolent beings, fiends who'll hunt her down. The ground painted red with his blood . . .*"

He flicked away the cigarette into the night and stood aimlessly. Those lyrics from Deathlike Silence Productions nearly described his entire life.

He removed the .357 tucked into his waistband and held it with a purpose. He was proud to have it, to own it. It gave him life. It'd awoken him, and now, it was time to take advantage of the power he had—that it offered him. And while the pastor and Kizzie wanted to pray and forgive, they wanted to continuously turn the other cheek, forget, and continue to be stepped on and look and feel weak, he would show everyone what power felt like and what it was to be genuinely feared.

Omar continued to gaze over the edge, his eyes hooked on the long drop down. For a moment, he wanted to step farther, step ahead with a feeling like he was Superman. Bizarrely, he felt untouchable. He could do whatever he wanted and not be touched.

He grinned.

No more Mr. Nice Guy.

Lingering on the edge for a moment, thinking and gawking—and seething, he finally turned from the sprawling view of Brooklyn. He hopped down from the edge, his feet landing on the gravel. Then he walked away with determination. He felt the night was still young, and there was still time to hunt—to seek and to kill.

Prime Time was a local nightclub on the Brownsville corner near Linden Blvd. It thrived with rap acts, gamblers, dancers, heavy drinkers, hustlers, and shot callers from Tuesday night to Sunday night. It was a place where the street wolves felt comfortable because the owner was an ex-drug kingpin with a pedigree that equaled Supreme of the Supreme team. He'd been home from prison three years now after doing ten years in the Feds. Instead of returning to the streets, he put his money into nightclubs and promoted rap acts and significant events. Tonight, a local rap group was performing on the makeshift stage. They rhymed about the streets and from experience. They had the crowd amped. And the hustlers and dealers were nodding knowingly to the fire they spit.

"For real, dawg, it should be no beef money, just respect what's mine and know not to cross that line so I won't have to come out of line and clap you wit' my nine. I could love you like a brother or hate you like any other. It could be peace, or do I have to prepare my dawgs fo' war, gonna say in preparation for any fuckin' situation . . ."

The girls were dancing, the men were flirting with them a great deal, and the shot callers shouted, "Drinks on me."

Mo, a young goon that roamed with Brice's crew, was mixed in with the excitement and the revelers. He was nineteen, nappy-headed, short, and Black, and he was a reckless young thug—a young Black male that didn't give a fuck! He was on a straight path to either prison or death. Which one would find him sooner, only time would tell.

Mo threw back a shot of Quavo and grinned at the brown-skinned, big-booty girl next to him. She was dancing nimbly to the blaring rap music, being in her own world, enjoying the scene around her. Mo licked his lips and moved closer to her with a purpose, having something naughty on his mind. He admired the girl's short dress, which revealed more flesh and cleavage than it covered. She looked good, and Mo had his eyes on her for a while now.

He was antsy. Horny. The last time he had pussy was when he'd participated in that violent rape with Brice and the others. It was a glorious moment for him that he continued to laugh about and communicate with the others. Though his action was quick inside the girl, it was good for him. He didn't know her name, but he remembered what she felt like when he was inside of her.

Now with Brice gone, Mo felt somewhat dissociated from everyone else. Brice took him under his wing awhile back, and Mo would follow Brice around like a stray puppy. Whatever Brice did, Mo involved himself too, yearning to impress his sadistic mentor. His thinking imitated Brice's thinking. Brice became a bully, and Mo became a bully.

Mo downed another shot of Quavo and displayed a chilling grin her way.

"What's ya name, shorty?" he asked her. "Yo, let me buy you a drink. Whatever you want, I got you tonight. Ya know what I'm sayin'? But you lookin' good in that dress, shorty."

His approach was jagged and arduous. She scoffed his way. Not interested. It made him upset to be dissed by her but more determined. He was a young goon with raging hormones, and the skin she was in, he was ready to peel it back and fuck.

"Oh word, so you playin' it like that shorty," he continued, becoming relentless. Finally, he placed his hand on her side without her invitation.

She reacted harshly. She quickly jerked away from him and scolded, "Nigga, don't be putting your fuckin' hands on me. You fuckin' crazy? I'm not fuckin' interested! Bye!"

"Yo, shorty, why you actin' like that? I'm here tryin' to be nice and shit!"

"Fuck off!" she rebuked.

"What, bitch?"

"Bitch . . .? Your fuckin' mama is a fuckin' bitch!" she retorted.

Mo was known to be temperamental. She embarrassed him in front of a crowd with people looking his way, laughing and mocking him. He hated the feeling. His eyes shifted into narrow and angry slits. He clenched his fists and churned with resentment for her now.

He heatedly stepped closer to her, ready to become highly belligerent and hostile. "You fuckin' dumb-ass cunt bitch," he shouted, creating a scene inside the place.

She wasn't scared of him, and she wasn't backing down either. Instead, the young girl continued to assault him with sarcasm and scornful words—words and statements that were an anomaly to his vocabulary. She was hood, but she was educated. And Mo was two seconds from punching her in the face.

"Bitch, you don't fuckin' know me!"

"And I'm so glad I don't and don't want to. What girl would want to know you, stupid?" she scoffed and countered with dripping sarcasm.

Before Mo could react by bashing her face in and before their argument escalated, someone firmly placed a hand on his shoulder, which carried some weight behind it.

"Chill, nigga, not in here," said a man from behind. "You know better."

Mo spun around. It was the bouncer intervening in the quarrel between them. The man towered over Mo like a skyscraper and outweighed him by over a hundred pounds.

"That bitch being rude," Mo spat.

"I don't care what she is. You know whose place this is, and you already know he don't want any trouble inside of here," the bouncer replied.

Mo frowned. He didn't have a choice. It was either play nice or don't play at all.

"You understand me?" the bouncer asked with sternness in his deep tone.

"Yeah. I'm good," Mo uttered halfheartedly.

"You sure?"

Mo nodded. "Yeah."

"Don't have me come back over here, little nigga. You don't want any problems tonight. Ayyite?"

"Yeah. Whatever!"

The young girl sneered at the bouncer's remarks, slightly enjoying Mo's humiliation. Tonight wasn't his night. She walked away, leaving Mo fuming by the bar. He was angry and frustrated. His friend was dead, and the police didn't know who had killed him. He needed another drink, something more potent. He briskly signaled for the bartender with his two fingers and hollered, "Yo, I need another drink."

He didn't want to wait.

"What can I get you?" asked the bartender.

"Get me a black Russian," Mo uttered tersely.

The bartender's right eyebrow became askew when hearing Mo's drink demand. It was an odd drink for someone like him to order.

"Black Russian, huh?"

"Nigga, did I fuckin' stutter?"

"Nah. Coming right up."

Mo sighed deeply. It had been a rough week for him. He eyed the bartender mixing his drink, a vodka and coffee liqueur cocktail. His subsequent attention shifted across the room and through the thick crowd, where his eyes became locked on the young girl that'd embarrassed him. She was now laughing and partying with her lady friends and two hustlers who had the girls' undivided attention. Jealousy stirred inside of Mo.

"That's twelve," said the bartender, interrupting Mo's fixed stare on the girls.

Mo reached into his pocket, removed a few crumpled twenty-dollar bills, and handed the bartender one of them. The look he gave the bartender indicated that he wanted his change back. And he did; eight dollars was placed on the bar counter for Mo to snatch up.

Cheap bastard! mouthed the bartender.

Mo consumed the drink speedily. It was a strong drink, and he was pretty drunk.

"Yo, make me one more," Mo hollered.

It became late. Mo staggered out of the club and into an urban cityscape, where the streets were filled with junkies, whores, pimps, and hustlers. They roamed the sidewalks, the roads, and the boulevard as if it were daytime anywhere else.

Mo staggered by a group of fiends. Their eyes were yearning and sullen—hopeless and hopeful. It was time for their routine dosage of "Get right," which they were pining to slam into their veins or inhale into their system. Before long, Mo staggered by a cluster of whores on the block. Each one was less scantily clad than the other. Mo smiled their way, and he couldn't help himself. The liquor had him antsy and fired up. And eyeing the whores' teasing flesh ignited an excitement inside of him. He had money to burn on a pleasurable desire. Pussy. He wobbled their way with a lecherous grin splashed across his face. He approached a pretty young thing named Flavor while digging into his pockets, reaching for whatever cash he had left that he didn't spend inside the nightclub.

"Shorty . . . How much?" he asked frankly.

She gave him the once-over. His clothing was subpar—no kind of flash or style to him. And his being tipsy was palpable. He flashed her a few twenties and asked again, "Shorty . . . I said how much?"

She debated if he would be worth it. She was pricey.

"A hundred to suck your dick and one-fifty to fuck," she told him.

"Damn, shorty . . . I'm sayin', I can't get a fuckin discount? Shit!" he fretted.

"Go fuck with one of those crack whores down the way if you want a discount," she sighed and sucked her teeth. Already, he was wasting her time. "Nigga, just go that way!"

"I'm sayin', shorty, you out here lookin' all fine and—"

Boom!

It seemed to happen out of nowhere. His head and face exploded. Mo's brain matter and blood unexpectedly sprayed all over the young whore. His body dropped at her feet with a gaping hole in the side of his head. Her screaming became piercing—like a banshee. It echoed through the street. Disturbing. Standing over Mo's body, clad in a black hoodie, was Omar. The .357 was smoking in his hand like an erupted volcano. He didn't flinch. He showed complete apathy for his murderous action. He silently pointed the gun at the girl, and she was beside herself.

"Please, don't kill me! Please! I'll fuck you for free!" she frantically pleaded.

He remained silent. Unruffled. He lowered the gun from the girl's face. He'd already accomplished his mission. He glanced down at Mo's contorted body as it lay in a thick, crimson blood pool. Death wasn't kind. The bullet entered his flesh as if he were nothing, just meat. He was there, and then he was gone.

Omar stepped over the body like it was trash and hurried away, leaving the young whore stunned at what she'd witnessed. She couldn't stop trembling. She had seen death—the Grim Reaper, a personified force up close and personal. Mo's blood and brains were stained against her clothing and face—forever tainting her well-being.

CHAPTER SIXTEEN

"HOW ARE YOU holding up, Kizzie? You okay?" Omar asked.

"I'm fine," she replied.

"If you need anything, I got you."

She weakly smiled. "I know. I just want to relax and get some rest," she replied.

Kizzie was home. She was healing. She was praying and wanted to try to forget the entire ordeal. But it was harder said than done. Omar loitered by her bedroom window. He would regularly stare out of it, looking below, gazing at people and traffic—nothing in particular. It was something for him to do. What he did the other night didn't bother or disturb him. He remained cool like a cucumber.

Kizzie's bedroom was neat and nicely decorated. The walls were deep blue, sprinkled with posters mostly of gospel singers like Kirk Franklin, Yolanda Adams, Kim Burrell, Marin Sapp, and others. A desk stood in one corner. It was littered with a large Bible and wadded-up pieces of paper and pen. A few shelves were pushed against the walls and filled with books. It indicated that she was a voracious reader. A closed laptop and another Bible were placed on her comforter. Kizzie sat propped against the headboard. Her bruises were healing; her spirit hadn't been entirely broken but somewhat fractured. It was a long road to recovery—not physically, but mentally and emotionally.

They both could smell her grandmother's cooking coming from the kitchen into the bedroom. She was making fried fish and grits with garlic bread. It was one of Kizzie's favorites.

"Omar, come from that window and sit with me. Talk. Why are you standing by the window?" she asked.

"I'm just thinking, that's all, Kizzie," he replied solemnly.

"Thinking about what?"

"Just about life," he replied, still gazing out the window. He then turned to her and fixed his eyes on his best friend. "What do you think death feels like? What is dying like?"

It was a question out of the blue. Kizzie was somewhat taken aback by the question. She didn't know how to reply to it.

"Why are you asking about death?"

He shrugged. "Don't know. It's just came across my mind."

"How does something like that cross your mind?"

"I've been thinking about many things lately, Kizzie," he replied.

"Well, you know to die is for us to be with the Lord in heaven finally . . . and Jesus Christ Himself," she stated.

Omar didn't want to hear about that. He frowned slightly. He asked about death, not about heaven. Kizzie picked up on his pessimistic reaction and responded with, "What is going on with you, Omar? Lately, you've been aloof . . . from church, the word, me. Every time someone mentions God, the word, or prayer, you get upset and cringe. Why's that? I know you've just lost your mother, but there is this change in you."

"Change?" he chuckled. "I'm still the same me. I just see some things a bit differently."

"And what is different?" she wanted to know.

Before he could answer, someone knocked rapidly at the door, and then Kizzie's grandmother pushed it open. She came into the bedroom to join the two. She softly smiled at Kizzie and Omar.

"Is everything okay in here?" she asked.

"Yes, Grandma. We're fine. We were just talking."

"Well, dinner is almost ready," she said. Then she turned to Omar and asked, "Omar, are you staying for dinner? There's plenty to go around."

"I'm not that hungry," he replied.

"Not hungry? Boy, it would be best if you started eating something. You're starting to become . . . what they call it . . . rail thin, looking like some skeleton in my home . . . and you were already a skinny boy in the first place, Omar," she joked.

He smiled.

"Listen, you stay and eat something tonight. And I'm not accepting no for an answer. There's no rush to leave here; you know that. You're family, and your mother would want that. And besides, I will need help caring for Kizzie," she said. "She's been through a lot these days, and I'm gonna need double the prayers around here. Do you understand me, chile?"

"Tell him, Grandma," Kizzie chimed.

Omar felt he didn't have a choice. The aged woman was relentless, and Omar thought he had no other option but to relent to her asking—dinner it was. Ms. Jones was a kind and loving woman. She was a spiritual woman with a dogmatic personality, and she was a retired schoolteacher. She was a strong Black woman with Southern ties to the South—coming from Alabama. But unfortunately, she came up in an era where Black life was cheap and expendable. White men could get away with crimes committed against Black people—even raping a Black woman.

"I guess set a plate for me too, then," said Omar halfheartedly.

"Good," said the grandmother. She was about to depart from the bedroom when she turned around with an afterthought for Omar. She fixed her eyes on him and said, "The two of you will need each other during these trying times. You hear me? Omar, you look after Kizzie, okay? And the Lord Almighty will continue to look after all of you. He always does. And, Omar, I love you just as much as I love my granddaughter. So don't you dare start to become a stranger in this home. Do you understand? You are *always* welcome here. I just wanted to let you know."

She smiled softly them, and then she finally left the room, leaving some words of wisdom for them to soak in.

When the door closed behind the grandmother, Kizzie said, "She's right, Omar . . . you're family . . . my family, and whatever is bothering you, let me know. I'm here for you."

"There you go again, Kizzie," uttered Omar with some contempt.

"What did I do?"

"That righteousness!" he exclaimed. "You're making it about me when it should be about you. *You* were raped and beaten and damn near left for dead, and you're worried about *my* well-being. What about *yours*? Huh? I wish you would stop trying to be perfect and just get mad and selfish . . . and want revenge," he griped.

"Omar, you know that isn't me, and it shouldn't be you, either."

But it was. He was angry inside. Killing Brice and Mo wasn't enough. It didn't quench his thirst for justice and bloodshed. Omar felt that more needed to be done. Everyone needed to pay, and there wasn't any room inside his heart for forgiveness and moving on. So instead, what he felt was contempt.

"This world . . . This place is ugly, and there isn't any room in it for the weak," he spewed.

"But we don't have to become ugly with it," replied Kizzie.

"How can we not become ugly with it? Huh? How can we live in such a vile and corrupted place and *not* become corrupted by it too just to survive? This shit, the horror out there, it's there, Kizzie. Permanently! It's everywhere, infectious like a damn epidemic . . . like a plague, a foul disease sickening and destroying everything it touches. Men like Brice get to do whatever they want and get away with whatever they want because they drive fear into people. And the cops, what good are they, huh? They're too busy belittling and killing us than doing their damn jobs. How many Black men were killed by white cops and received no jail time? Where's the justice in that, huh? So how can you not become infected by it, the ugly that's out there taking over?"

Kizzie could see the hate in his eyes as he spoke. They lit up with rage and disgust, and she didn't like his speech. It was hateful and negative. It was scary.

"I believe everything happens for a reason, Omar," was her feeble reply.

That remark enraged him. "What? Are you serious? So, a bunch of lust-crazed niggas attacking you and raping you in a dirty stairwell happened for a reason? So you believe that's God's doing? Savage fools that took away your virginity?"

Once again, Omar's remark stirred up some hurt and pain inside Kizzie. He couldn't help himself. He was tired of being weak—of her being vulnerable, and he wanted Kizzie to see the truth—that it would take more than faith and prayer to change anything. It was ineffective in his eyes, and he felt he had wasted enough years in both. He believed it took action and violence to earn respect and live the life many dreamed of living.

"Omar, I don't know what's going on with you . . . this change, but I don't like it," said Kizzie.

"Sometimes change is needed to survive . . . to thrive," he replied.

"No, not that kind of change, Omar. Not hate and anger," she hit back. "That kind of change, wanting revenge and retribution, is hell-driven. And besides, we do not heal the past by dwelling in hate and anger. We heal the past by living fully in the present and forgiveness . . . and faith."

There was that word again—*forgiveness*. Omar was tired of hearing it. The sound of it was weak and agonizing. It created a seething mood inside of him.

"Well, I'm glad he's dead. Brice," he proclaimed wholeheartedly. "And I hope they all die painfully . . . get what they all fuckin' deserve, to burn in hell. Fuck 'em all!"

Kizzie was shocked by his cursing and his reaction. "Omar! Don't be using that kind of language here. What is *wrong* with you?"

"You know what . . ." he started, still seething. "Fuck it! I'm out of here, Kizzie. I ain't got time for this shit. Tell your grandmother I said thanks for the invite to dinner, but no thanks."

Before she could get a word out, Omar stormed out of the bedroom, marched down the hallway, and moved past the kitchen and the grandmother like a gust of wind, and he quickly left the apartment.

Kizzie was taken aback by his outburst and outlandish departure. She was hurt and shocked. It wounded her that she was losing her best friend. It hurt and cut deeply more than being raped. Omar was someone special to her—a true friend she could always depend on. However, the change in him was unambiguous. With the loss of his mother and her being raped, she figured he too had taken on a lot. She sat there in her bedroom in tears, crying. It didn't take long for her grandmother to enter her bedroom with a quizzical gaze.

"What is going on, Kizzie? Where did Omar go?" she asked. "He's not staying to eat?"

"I don't know, Grandma. He just left. Upset."

"Upset? What is he upset about?"

"I wish I knew, Grandma. But something is going on with him, and he's not telling me anything," said Kizzie with grief in her voice. "He's just becoming different."

Her grandmother sighed. And then she said, "We just have to pray for him."

CHAPTER SEVENTEEN

A BLACK CADILLAC DEVILLE was parked on the Brooklyn street in front of a low-grade strip club in Flatbush, and Foster was seated in the driver's seat. He sat alone. Pensive. He sighed heavily and leaned toward the vehicle's passenger seat, opening the glove compartment and removing a sliver flask. Untwisting the top, he took a few swallows of some brown juice. He needed the taste of alcohol in his system. Then he twisted the lid back on and placed the flask back into the glove compartment—a hidden treasure for him.

Another heavy sigh spewed from his lips as Foster seemed like a man with much on his mind. He gazed at the substandard strip club nestled on the inner-city block between several commercial businesses. The foot traffic in the area was sparse because of the late hour.

Clad in a dull black suit and gray tie, with his Glock 19 holstered at his side and badge on the opposite side, he climbed out of the Cadillac and moved toward the solid black door. With the bottom of his fist, he repeatedly banged against the door to get their attention on the other side, and it soon opened with a slender male looming into the detective's view. As the thin male was familiar with the detective, he spoke no words, merely opening the door wider to allow Foster access inside.

Bunk Foster entered the seedy and dimly lit club with rap music blaring. Inside, he wasn't in Kansas anymore. There was the smell of cheap perfume and cigarette smoke. The place was crowded with naked whores and lusting men. The lights were dimmed enough to hide stretch marks, as the talent pool wasn't deep. Lining one section of the club was ripped and stained velour booths and chairs for the customers' pleasure. And on the wide makeshift stage were two butt-naked and voluptuous strippers in stilettos dancing seductively against each other as several men tossed cash their way.

It was voyeurism and debauchery at its finest.

Detective Foster moved through the club with aloofness. He was unmoved by all the pussy in the place. Several ladies lured horny men into covert areas of the club where they could experience their supreme desire orally or sexually for the right price.

Bunk moved through a narrow passage to an area that bisects that passageway. A guard stood by a black door. Bunk was expected. The guard opened the door, and Bunk descended the concrete stairs into the basement. Surprisingly, the basement was lavishly decorated with stylish furniture and a 60-inch plasma TV mounted on the wall—the best that money could buy. Unlike the raunchy activity upstairs, it was laid-back and neat—a complete anomaly for the downgraded club.

It was nothing new to Bunk. He was used to seeing the irregularity—from the streets to this place of business. It seemed heaven was down there while a nightmare was above.

Several nude ladies in stilettos and Red Bottoms pranced around the area. They were beautiful and pristine—well put-together. And the men seated on the stylish furniture accompanying the ladies looked like they belonged on Wall Street or owned Fortune 500 companies. It looked like they were a long way from home in Brooklyn. Still, then again, they looked comfortable in the pleasant environment. A few lovely, naked girls sat on the men's laps and flirted with them. There was laughter and small talk—and cheap feels. And unlike upstairs, there were blissful-looking private rooms with leather couches and lush, high-back chairs for the girls to entertain their VIP clientele.

It was a buffet of some of the finest pussy in town for the men to pick from.

Bunk took in the area with a straight-faced gaze even though a few ladies smiled his way and flirted with him. But he wasn't there for pleasure. It was business.

Emerging from a backroom—a private office—was Anton. He was shirtless with an athletic build but disabled. He walked slowly with crutches and a limp; his leg was still in a cast. Flanking him was a nude blonde—Karen. She was his support. Anton and Bunk looked at each other with indifference. And then Anton said, "Let's talk in my office."

Bunk followed behind a slow-moving Anton. They entered an adequate-sized office, and Anton sat in a high-back chair behind a black desk and placed his crutches to the side.

"You don't know if you want to be a pimp or a drug dealer, do you?" Bunk mocked.

"Why not have the best of both worlds?"

"The best of both worlds, huh . . .?"

"Pussy sells, and drugs sell too, and a smart man knows how to capitalize on both," said Anton. "You know the difference between them bitches upstairs and the ones I have down here. I mean, pussy is pussy, right? No matter if you're young, old, rich, poor, Black, white. It's still gonna be fucked, either way, right? That shit is inevitable. But the difference between them bitches up there and the ones down here is that these here know their fuckin' worth. They know the difference between turning tricks and having clientele. They know the difference between making a few dollars for spreading their legs to making a few hundred or thousands of dollars for doing the same thing. If you're gonna get fucked, then know your worth. So, Detective, know your fuckin' worth," Anton proclaimed.

Bunk smiled.

"Now you're trying to add a philosopher to your hustle," Bunk scoffed. "How's the leg?"

"Fuck you think . . . I'm still fucked up by this shit, and you see me still on fuckin' crutches. Niggas ain't caught that fool yet. Shit, we don't even have that nigga's identity . . . and it's been over a fuckin' month," Anton griped.

"You think it was a hit from Science or Kenya?"

"Muthafucka, if it was a hit, then my crippled ass wouldn't be sittin' here talking to your ass, would I . . .? They would have put two in the back of my head. That's it! Not leave me behind like this," Anton retorted. "Anyway, you got that for me?"

Bunk reached into his pocket and removed a piece of paper. He handed it to Anton.

"The info's good?" asked Anton.

"It's always good."

"A'ight, I'm gonna get my peoples on it and make this move."

"I appreciate the overtime I'm receiving because of your troubles with other rivals. But do me a favor, and do things smoothly, Anton."

Anton chuckled. "Smoothly . . .? What the fuck do you think this is? I'm at war, muthafucka. Ain't no 'smooth' to this shit; there's sending a fuckin' message and wiping out the competition."

"Yeah, but the murders are becoming too much, even for a veteran detective like myself. This is Brooklyn, not Iraq."

"Listen, nigga, I ain't making no promises. You do your job like you feel fit, and I'll do mine," Anton replied.

"Well, I just want to make sure I'm playing for a winning team," Bunk said.

"Consider us Jordan and the ninety-three Bulls."

Anton reached into his desk drawer, removed a white envelope filled with cash, and tossed it the detective's way. Bunk picked up the payment and peeked at the hundred-dollar bills inside. He was content.

"It's always good doing business with you," said Bunk.

Detective Foster was ready to leave the room. But Anton uttered to him, "Well, I got more business coming your way, Detective."

"Like what?"

"The nigga that shot me, I want him found."

"Don't you have your people on that?"

"Well, at the moment, unfortunately, my niggas are caught up in this fuckin' war with these two idiots. And I ain't got that many bodies to spare to look for this nigga. I want him got, Bunk. I want him found, and I want him to pay for what he did to me. And I'm willing to pay—whatever!"

Bunk sighed. "I'll see what I can do."

"Do it, and I'll make it worth your trouble and time," said Anton. "And one more thing . . ."

Bunk looked like he was growing impatient with Anton's requests. "What the fuck you think this is, the fuckin' Jeffersons, and I'm fuckin' Florence Henderson?"

"Funny. But I heard they ain't found my cousin's gun yet . . . that .357 Magnum."

"And that's your concern because . . .?"

"I want it. I want that gun," Anton said seriously.

"Are you shitting me?"

"No. I'm not. I want that gun found, and I want it in my possession. There was something about that gun that my cousin loved. Like, it had him possessed or something. Nigga didn't go anywhere without that .357 on him. It changed him. And I swear I used to hear that fool talk to it like it was his bitch. Shit, I remember when that nigga was a nobody from Queens.

He came to Brooklyn to live with me, a pussy nigga, and then it seemed like overnight, he became this coldhearted muthafucka, not giving a fuck and taking extreme risks, killing niggas out here like he was some fuckin' gladiator and becoming feared out of the blue. I won't lie; Sean Black had shit on lock on these streets."

"You're the one that set him up and brought the DEA to his front door," Detective Foster reminded Anton.

"You think I don't fuckin' know that? It needed to be done! Muthafucka was going crazy. Insane!" he shouted. "And I've been in these streets since I was ten years old, and my fuckin' cousin comes along and builds in three years what I've been trying to do since I was sixteen. He gets more respect than me . . . a nigga from Queens. Fuck him! I'm glad he's dead because it's *my* time to shine. And now Science and Kenya want to take that away from me. It ain't happening. I'll burn this fuckin' city to the fuckin' ground before they can take anything from me."

Anton seethed. Bunk stood there and listened.

Anton continued, "I'll give you ten stacks for that gun, Detective. I know it's out there, and I want it."

"I'll see what I can do," Bunk nonchalantly replied.

"Don't *see*. *Do*. Listen, I'm not paying for a service; I'm paying for results . . . nothing less," said Anton with gravity and emotions.

CHAPTER EIGHTEEN

"YO, CRANE, SPIT that fire shit, my nigga," said Grind. "I've been tellin' niggas about you all da fuckin' time . . . Let these niggas out here know dat they ain't fuckin' wit' you, my nigga!"

Grind took a few pulls from the potent weed called AK-47—a hybrid strain with a rich genetic heritage and bold, mood-brightening effects. It was from South America. And it created a relaxed and mellow feel inside the apartment.

Crane smiled, snatched the cannabis from Grind's hand, and indulged in the potent strain that left a pungent and lingering scent throughout the place. Then Crane thrust himself into the creative mood to spit one of his infamous rhymes for everyone to hear.

Apartment 4C was lit with the hustler's ambition. The money-counting machines regularly went off, totaling cash from the streets into the tens of thousands. Next to it, several ten-thousand-dollar bundles. It was a hustler's paradise inside the two-bedroom, smoke-filled, bustling apartment. It was a stash house for Science and the organization. And that night, the place was swarming with nearly a hundred thousand dollars and still counting. Two men sat at the folding table in the kitchen, jotting down numbers and figures, hood-certified accountants. In the next room was the muscle. Three men, including Crane and Grind, played *Call of Duty* on the Xbox 360. They passed a blunt between them and stopped playing Xbox briefly. Grind went into a musical mode, rhythmically banging his fists against the coffee table, creating an impromptu beat for Crane to rhyme to.

Crane was ready. The AK-47 was rousing him into inventiveness—a final pull from the blunt, and it was showtime.

Crane spit out, "*Nigga . . . Nigga, weak-ass nigga, fuck what now, nigga, what you gonna do when these streets become too much fo' you? Too real for you, every movement got you flinching, actin' like a fool. Got ya boyz askin' what's up wit' you, nigga pussy, nigga who? Yes, you! Frontin', that's really you; you done did so many wrong, now niggas are comin' back strong, put a bullet in your lungs, mark fo' death is under your tongue. Now these streets got ya eyes in tears, mind in fears, spines in chills, watchin' ya back; you ready to spill. Shit is real; who the fuck cares, nigga? Death is near . . . Nigga, now who's sincere? Spread ya last tears cuz no one cares. That Glock cocked back, feelin' ya screwed, lookin' down that fuckin' barrel wit' that bullet ready to blast into you. Now I see the pussy in you. Ya weak, ya eyes look in desperate need. Now you coppin' pleads. Damn, nigga, straight character, holdin' props like amateur . . . Scandals, fool, now it's lights out fo' you and ya pussy-ass crew . . .*"

Grind jumped up excitedly and gave his friend an animated dap. He then exclaimed, "What I tell you? My nigga is fuckin' nice!"

Grind snatched the blunt back from Crane and continued to get high.

"Y'all muthafuckas ain't got nuthin' better to do than sing in here like bitches," griped James, one of Science's lieutenants, coming out of one of the bedrooms.

"C'mon, James, we just having some fun," replied Grind.

"Fun . . .?" James spewed out with his face twisted into a frown. "Y'all niggas need to be on top of shit. Y'all heard what happened to Bobby the other night, right?"

They all heard.

"Nigga got gunned down out there on the streets being stupid . . . not being cautious. Y'all niggas know we at war out here," continued James. "All this fuckin' money and product we got in here, and y'all niggas wanna play video games and act like this is fuckin' Def Jam. Fuck is wrong wit' y'all niggas?!"

It was a scolding they listened to. The room fell silent—knowing James was right. Grind took a final pull from the blunt and extinguished it against the coffee table. He stood up, picked up his .45 from the table, stuffed it in his waistband, and said to James, "I'm making a store run. You cool wit' that?"

He wasn't asking.

James remained silent, gawking at Grind with seriousness. It was known in the room that the two men had their differences.

"Bring me back a pack of Newports," said Crane.

"I got you, my nigga."

"Nigga, get some more White Owls, too," uttered someone else.

Grind mentally noted their orders and exited the secured apartment/stash house with his .45 tucked and concealed. He needed some air—meaning a timeout from James's authority. One guard unlocked the heavy steel door, and Grind made his exit. He removed his last cigarette from the pack in the hallway and lit one up. He needed the nicotine; it was a stressful situation for everyone—including him. He was close with Bobby, and that was his second friend that'd been murdered this year.

Grind walked toward the elevator and sent for it, puffing on the cancer stick. It was a half-minute wait until the bell chimed and the elevator door slid open. He stepped foot into the foul-smelling elevator and pushed for the ground floor. Alone, he continued to puff on the cancer stick as it descended toward the lobby. It was a quick descent to the entrance, and when the rickety elevator door slid back into the wall . . . Grind got the shock of his life.

It was an ambush. Several goons abruptly attacked him, shoving a Glock into his face and someone yelling, "Ask me if it's loaded, bitch!"

There was a slight skirmish at the threshold of the elevator with Grind yelling out, "Fuck y'all niggas!" and the Glock went across Grind's head, dazing him. Outnumbered and unmatched, his knees hit the elevator floor, and his attackers rowdily crowded around him. Another attacker shoved a cell phone into his face with a woman's picture and exclaimed, "That's ya baby mama, right, bitch? Guess what? We got two big-dick goon niggas outside her front door right now. We make the call, that bitch is raped and dead in a heartbeat, and ya daughter gonna be in fuckin' foster care."

It wasn't an idle threat.

"You know what we want," said the man holding the Glock in Grind's face. "Make this shit soft and easy like baby shit."

Grind grimaced and huffed. He was trapped in a corner with no way out. He counted four shooters, and from experience, he knew they weren't amateurs. Instead, they were lying in the cut—in the shadows, waiting for their opportunity to strike, and they created one by going after him and his baby mama.

"Yeah, nigga, you fucked up. And fuck wit' us, bitch. I'm dying to make that call, fo' real, nigga," uttered the man with the cell phone.

Grind continued to pout and gripe. But he relented. "Apartment 4C," he uttered while being accosted.

One pushed for number four on the panel, and the door closed with them inside and Grind still on his knees.

Stealthy and cautiously, the four gunmen moved down the narrow hallway with Grind as their captive. They strategically positioned themselves at apartment 4C, purposely out of view from anyone looking out through the peephole in the apartment.

Grind stood at the door with guns still trained on him. Yet, he appeared relaxed and calm.

He knocked twice and then shouted out, "Yo, it's me, Grind. Open the fuckin' door; I forgot sumthin'."

He was believable.

More than a few locks could be heard opening from the other side, and a lean, jewelry-clad teenager said, "Damn, nigga, you always forgetting something."

The fortified door finally opened with the teenager continuing with, "I'm ready to sm—"

Before he finished his sentence, the four hidden gunmen rapidly made themselves known and violently forced their way into the apartment. Immediately, chaos ensued. Two men inside seated on the couch hurriedly reached for their weapons nearby, seeing the intruders, but were immediately cut down by gunfire coming from a sawed-off shotgun and .9 mm Berretta.

The continuous crackling of gunfire echoed inside. The four men moved through the apartment like a SWAT team—in union and with skills. Whatever became a threat to them, they swiftly cut down and killed. The hood-certified accountant in the kitchen took a bullet to his head. And the other took a shot in his leg. He was left alive for a reason. Crane took a shotgun blast to his chest and was sprawled across the floor in a pond of blood, and Grind took three hot rounds in the back of his head. James was mowed down with gunfire in the hallway as he tried to react with violence himself with a MAC-10. It was pure bloodshed inside the apartment.

Swiftly, the men maneuvered from room to room, tossing stacks of money into a black garbage bag. Finally, one of the shooters brutally interrogated the last man still alive. He pistol-whipped him and threatened to press his face against the hot stove if he didn't tell them where the kilos were stashed. An inside source told them about a recent shipment. The last man standing quickly talked.

"The shit's in the bottom cabinet in the kitchen, underneath a false bottom," he sang to them like a canary.

They hastily rummaged through the kitchen, and the product was where he said it was—five kilos of uncut heroin—that nasty, black gold.

It was a sloppy operation inside, having money and drugs in the same location. Bookie and his men had hit payday. They were ruthless and fierce. It was ugly—meant to be ugly, and it sent a message to everyone—there was a new boogeyman in town, Bookie, and Anton had him on his payroll.

A black Range Rover with tinted windows stopped outside an auto body garage on Cropsey Avenue in Coney Island, Brooklyn. The doors opened, and Science, Ray, and one of their henchmen climbed out of the vehicle. Science walked to the rear of the SUV, lifted the latch, and removed his precious American Pit Bull Terrier from the back. This purebred dog weighed about 55 pounds. Around the terrier's neck were heavy chains. Science gripped the dog tightly by its leash, and the men entered the body garage. Inside were many men, some owners, and other dogs—fighting dogs ready and prepared to battle it out inside the pit for enormous sums of cash.

Science was immediately recognized and respected. His terrier, named Smash, was the reigning champion in the pit. Unfortunately, it had battle scars to show. The dog's ears were cropped, and its tail docked close to its body to limit areas that another dog could grab during a fight. Along with the crude and inhumane technique, Science also conditioned his dog to fight with anabolic steroids to enhance muscle mass and encourage aggressiveness.

Smash's opponent was another terrier named Killer, who was undefeated. Vast sums of money were placed on tonight's match—over a hundred thousand dollars.

The fight would occur in a 14 by 20 square foot pit designed with plywood to contain the animals. The floor was stained carpet, and the spectators anticipated seeing a good fight. Science rudely tugged the dog by its collar, and then he crouched low to gaze strongly at his dog.

"You gonna do this for me tonight, right, Smash . . . right? We gonna get this fuckin' money!" he uttered, still rudely tugging the dog's leash and collar to stir up aggression in the animal.

Smash growled and snarled, teeth showing in a hostile way.

It was ready.

Science had a hundred large for his dog to win. And others put ample cash up in favor of Smash. So first, the dogs were weighed to ensure they were approximately the same weight. Next, their handlers washed and examined the opponent's dog to remove any toxic substance that could have been placed on the fur in an attempt to deter or harm the opposing dog. Afterward, the animals were placed inside the pit on opposite corners.

The referee for the fighting dogs stood in the middle, his attention shifting back and forth to both animals. Science gripped Smash's leash as the dog was ready to be set free and perform—execute what he was bred and trained for—maim and kill.

"Don't disappoint me, Smash . . . Get this fuckin' money for me, and tear that fuckin' bitch apart," Science said with animation.

Ray's cell phone rang while the dogs were ready to be released, tearing into each other, fur and flesh. He answered the call and listened. The caller informed him about the tragedy. "We got hit tonight!"

"What . . .?" Ray replied, taken aback. "What the fuck you talkin' about, nigga?"

"They ran up in the spot and fucked us, Ray! Niggas is dead!"

Ray heard him correctly. He frowned. He knew Science was going to go ape-shit crazy over the news. He put his eyes back on Science just in time to see him release Smash from his leash, where both dogs met in the middle, wrestling fiercely to get a hold of the opponent. Smash was in perfect form, trying to inflict maximal damage on his canine opponent.

It was a five-minute match in which Smash became the victor. Science was beside himself with joy and jubilation. The opponent was lying on its side, suffering from lacerations and other crushing injuries implemented by Smash.

"Yeah, muthafucka!" Science hollered. "That's what the fuck I'm talkin' about!"

But his joy would become short-lived. Ray approached him with the grim news. "Yo, we got hit tonight."

Science's expression transitioned from joy to upset in a heartbeat. "What?"

CHAPTER NINETEEN

THE FLASH EXPLOSION from the camera went off several times, capturing the dead—multiple bodies sprawled out in the living room and elsewhere. The crime scene photographer had his work cut out for him; so did the detectives and forensics. It was a bloody mess inside apartment 4C. The photographer twisted and turned his camera haphazardly. He was freezing time—creating a supposedly incontestable record of the chaos inside the living room, kitchen, and hallway—among other areas. The photographer was methodical in his work. He couldn't afford to leave out an essential piece of evidence or produce photographs that could be considered misleading in court.

As the camera continued to flash, several detectives gazed at the horror.

"I swear to you, I fuckin' love this fuckin' borough," uttered Detective Foster. "These animals never leave things boring, do they? Shit. This here, I don't know what the fuck to call it."

Detective Greene and Detective John were impassive but also in awe. They'd seen their fair share of carnage, but things were worsening in Brooklyn. Bodies and blood were everywhere, and dispensed shells, guns, and the smell of a bloodbath and death. It was sickening. It was easy to piece together what'd happened—an invasion and robbery from a rival crew. They had forced their way into the apartment, most likely with a captive, and came in shooting. The dead in the living attempted to fight the invaders off but were ineffective.

"I can tell you this. I can identify at least two pieces of shit right away," continued Foster. "This muthafucka right here by the door with the three holes in the back of his head, his name is Grind . . . a hitter for Boss Crew, and this other muthafucka on the floor with his chest ripped opened, that's Crane . . . fuckin' Beavis and Butt-Head we have here."

Foster knew the players in the game and on the streets. But Greene was still disturbed at how his partner mocked the dead.

The chaotic and bloody events in the apartment had traveled through the hood like wildfire. It seemed like everyone that lived in the building was crowding the hallway, the stairs, and outside. They were in shock and taken aback.

"Damn. How many dead?" one spectator asked someone.

"Shit, I heard like a dozen niggas are dead up in there," someone replied, amplifying the details.

Controlling and securing the crime scene became the detectives' and the officers' priority. Residents wanted to know who had gotten killed. So, the officers cordoned off the area and prohibited entry to anyone. And they'd closed the door to the apartment. It wasn't a pretty sight for any local to get a glance at. And then, the detectives took steps to protect any evidence.

The media was posted outside the building looking for access to the carnage inside. They felt the murders of several Black drug dealers were a juicy story—*if it bleeds, it leads*. And several men shot dead in a violent home invasion were primetime news.

One reporter exclaimed, "It's the public's right to know!"

But officers kept them at bay.

And it didn't take long for friends and family members of the deceased to hear about the tragedy. Nearly a dozen men and women hurried to the scene—brothers, sisters, mothers, cousins, friends, and fathers of the dead inside charged that way like a bull seeing red—but besieged with concern. Hearing about it, they were all torn to pieces and heartbroken.

"My son is in there! No, my baby is in that apartment," a mother screamed. "Oh God!"

"Yo, my cousin too. They say he shot dead in there," a young male hollered.

They were kept behind the barricade, but a few officers treated them with compassion, knowing it must have been a hard loss for each of them.

Watching the tragic spectacle unfold from a distance—across the street in the front passenger seat of the Range Rover was Science. He frowned. He was tightly seething. His spot had been hit, assaulted, merchandise and money had been taken, and his men were dead.

"Muthafuckas," Science growled. "Muthafuckas got the audacity to come at me like this."

"You know who's behind this shit, right?" said Ray.

"Yeah . . . that bitch-ass nigga Anton. He wants the crown, and he gonna end up like his fuckin' cousin, no doubt."

"Word is, he got that young goon doin' much of his dirty work . . . young nigga named Bookie."

"Fuck this nigga; I'm gonna body that nigga like the police did his fuckin' cousin. I swear, fuck with my business and my money. Yo, these niggas gotta get got, and they gotta get hit fuckin' hard, Ray. I want everyone involved with this shit . . . their balls cut the fuck off and their tongues at the bottom of my fuckin' boot," griped Science.

"I'm on it, Science; best believe it. We gonna fuck these niggas up," replied Ray with conviction.

Science sighed heavily. "Get me the fuck outta here, man. I'm sick of seeing this shit," he said in disgust.

The Range Rover peeled away from the curb and headed north. Unfortunately, it passed another dark soul watching the spectacle from a reasonable distance.

Omar's eyes were fixed on the spectacle—the blaring police lights, the growing crowd outside the building, the media, and the local thugs posted nearby, grieving their dead friends. He stood there like a statue, unassuming, waiting. He watched as the coroners carried one body bag after another out of the lobby and loaded it into the meat wagon—what the locals called it.

Omar's heart started to beat fast. He could smell it—smell them—their souls, their torture and pain. Ironically, he felt rejuvenated. His senses felt heightened. Their core was fresh. Once again, there was this thirst—this bloodthirsty hunger. Seeing multiple bodies carried out excited him. His heart rate continued to increase. And his hormones increased too. But what got him truly going and excited was seeing the two men mixed in the crowd of spectators—Tip and Chuck, two men from Brice's crew. Omar's attention remained fixed on them. The two men stood among the onlookers like they were innocent—harmless.

Omar fumed.

The audacity of them, he thought, remembering what they did to Kizzie. They were next on his list. And Omar couldn't resist. This rage bubbled inside him, and with his eyes fixed on the two men standing amongst the others, he marched their way like he was in a robotic-like trance. The .357 was tucked in his waistband. He reached for it. He gripped the gun firmly, his index finger already against the trigger, and felt invincible. He wanted to see them suffer—murdered. And he wanted to taste and smell their souls being ripped apart as he snatched their lives. The killing started to give him pleasure—something of an orgasm. It had become fulfilling; he wanted to please and satisfy it—her, his demonic muse. It was the only way she came to him—via murders and mayhem and gave him what he needed: unadulterated bliss and contentment. He already missed its touch and the sensation it brought him—the power he felt when it came around. Its darkness was uplifting and stimulating.

Omar yearned for it tonight—to be thrust into wicked fornication with what he vigorously desired. But first, he had to implement his revenge and continued massacre of the damned.

He neared his targets, ready to execute them in public, in front of dozens of witnesses and the police. He felt he could do it quickly because Malaka protected him. It had promised him power, revenge, and fortune. It had pledged to him a desirable and pleasing future.

His heart continued to beat fast, like drums banging against his chest. He felt impervious and determined. He was death. Not once did his attention divert from the two men as they stood in the crowd, watching. So, all eyes were transfixed by the carnage inside the building. Not one eye was on him approaching the group with malicious intent. He was set to destroy, to kill. He was about to lift his hand with the pistol and kill them both. But then something happened; a fight broke out in the crowd and with the police. It was an inconsolable individual, a male that had taken the news of his brother's murder extremely hard. He ranted and cursed.

"That's my fuckin' brother, yo! I swear to God, whoever did this shit is fuckin' dead. Get the fuck off me. Get off me!" he screamed out. "Yo, I don't give a fuck! Man, fuck the police! Fo' real, niggas is fuckin' dead out here!"

He wrestled with the police and was quickly subdued and then handcuffed. The distraction altered the moment. Omar looked back and saw Tip and Chuck walking off, both men going their separate ways. He didn't want to lose out on the chance. *Which one to follow? Who is next?* He made his decision, and he followed Chuck. It would be Tip's lucky day—for now.

He pursued Chuck for two blocks in the night, yearning to fulfill the bloodthirsty desire gnawing at him. Omar wanted to murder him for his and its satisfaction, to appease the succubus—and curb his perpetual hunger and lustfulness.

Chuck moved through the courtyard of the projects, relaxed like he didn't have a care in the world, and did not know that he was being followed. The police activity a few blocks away drew a large crowd. But on the other hand, it made his journey through one of the most notorious New York projects calm.

He reached the door to the lobby but stopped suddenly, and that relaxed feeling disappeared when he turned around. He felt something. Suddenly, a deep chill shot through his body, and he looked behind him but saw nothing. He waved it off as imagination and continued inside the building. He chose to take the stairs instead of the elevator. But then, it felt like he was being followed. When he entered the stairway, he heard the squeaking doors to the lobby open, indicating someone else had come right behind him. Chuck felt that his imagination was getting the best of him. He removed his pistol and paused by the stairwell door, hoping whoever it was would come his way. Chuck was ready to react, poised by the door with his gun in hand. And he had the right to be worried. Within two weeks, Brice and Mo were killed, and Chuck felt it wasn't a coincidence.

He remained poised by the stairway entrance, ready to respond with violence. But instead, he grew nervous and edgy. The body count was rising in the Ville, and he didn't plan on becoming another statistic.

He could hear whoever entered behind him approaching, so he cocked back his gun and took a deep breath. His eyes stayed on the stairway entrance, where he tried to remain hidden and could hear either his foe or whoever was approaching. When the door opened, Chuck immediately pounced on who entered the stairway. He thrust his gun into the person's face and was seconds away from pulling the trigger, igniting his survival. But when he saw who it was, he instantly lowered the gun and threw out his apologies.

"Oh shit, my bad, Mr. Timmons. I thought you were someone else," he said.

Mr. Timmons was his neighbor down the hall. He was a pleasant man in his early forties with three kids. The look on the man's face was fear.

"Boy, you damn near made me piss on myself," Mr. Timmons replied. "You're making enemies that strongly out here that you were about to shoot me for mistaken identity."

"You know how it is out here," said Chuck. "I'm just watching my back."

"Yeah, I do . . . that's why I hardly go out. I'm out now because I was coming from my girlfriend's place . . . and getting a piece of pussy tonight damn near got me shot by my own neighbor."

"You good?" asked Chuck.

"Yeah, I am now. Are *you* good?"

Chuck sighed. "Yeah, I'm good."

"Take your butt home, Chuck, and stay there for a while," Mr. Timmons said. "Whatever is out there that has you jumpy like this . . . then you need to leave it alone and find Jesus, boy. Please do."

Mr. Timmons climbed the stairs, leaving Chuck to think about what had happened. He felt that maybe he had become a bit paranoid. He exhaled, tried to collect himself, and went up the stairs a minute later after his neighbor. When he reached the third floor and exited the stairway into the hallway, the first thing he saw was the barrel of the .357 that looked the size of the Holland Tunnel. The hooded stranger and the gun seemed to come out of nowhere.

Chuck reacted before Omar could strike. He swung his right fist and slammed it into Omar's jaw. Omar stumbled, but he didn't go down.

"You here for me, muthafucka?" Chuck shouted.

Chuck wasn't doing down without a fight. He gave Omar a few sharp punches to the chin and face—surprisingly, Omar grinned. He took the hits to him like they were paper thin. Chuck was not expecting that kind of reaction. This wasn't the same scared boy they had cornered in the back street a few weeks ago. He was different.

"What the fuck?" Chuck exclaimed, breathless.

He continued to wrestle with Omar on the stairway. He grabbed Omar's wrist with his left hand and held Omar's gun against his chest, the gun caught under the jacket. Chuck hit him twice more with his right, square in the nose. But Omar didn't budge or flinch from the blow. Instead, he seemed determined to end Chuck's life. Finally, Omar seized the upper hand, and with sudden brute strength, he shoved Chuck down the concrete stairs. Chuck was dazed and dumbfounded by the attack; his skull vibrated painfully.

Chuck was defeated and shocked. Omar approached him with the .357 in full view of him.

"Fuck you!" Chuck managed to stand up and curse right before . . .

Boom!

The bullet destroyed the right side of his face at close range, from his eye to his chin. The gunshot propelled him against the wall, spraying the walls with his blood and some brain matter. Yet, shockingly, Chuck was still alive—barely. He was sprawled against the ground at Omar's feet. He was conscious and barely breathing. Omar ominously stood over him, aiming the demonic weapon at his foe, and he fired again—*Boom! Boom! Boom!*

It was the end of Chuck.

Omar spun and hurried away. He disappeared from the carnage as neighbors had been jolted and awakened yet again by the sound of gunfire.

CHAPTER TWENTY

KIZZIE AWOKE FROM her sleep abruptly. She had been jolted awake in the middle of the night by another nightmare. She shot upright against the headboard, breathing sharply and looking worried. It had been her eighth nightmare in the past week. Her breathing remained heavy, and her mind was spinning with fear. The room was dark, so she quickly reached over and turned on the small lamp on the nightstand near the bed. Her eyes danced around the room, frantically looking for an intruder inside her bedroom, but she was alone.

It felt like she was being attacked again, and it felt like they were inside of her. Her disturbed sleep was becoming a problem and occurring more frequently. Memories of the assault were returning to her like lightning strikes inside her mind—without warning. The flashbacks of the attack were becoming so vivid it felt like she was reliving the experience of the assault.

A few tears trickled from her eyes as Kizzie felt scared and alone. She wanted to close her eyes and pray but feared seeing their faces again. She stressed over the experience of her attackers wickedly thrusting themselves inside of her and assaulting her, all while laughing. She often felt dirty, ashamed, and weak.

For a moment, she experienced a period of emotional numbness. But she was drowning in emotions inside.

"God, please help me," she cried out. "Make me strong and make me whole again. I'm begging you. I need your help to get through this, Lord."

Sleep wasn't happening anytime soon for her. She was fully awake, wanting to pray, and she wanted the nightmares to stop. She didn't want to become angry, scared, bitter, and a recluse.

She removed herself from the bed and walked to the window. She wiped away the tears that fell from her eyes and breathed out. Her room felt stuffy. She opened the window to allow some air into the bedroom. She gazed outside into the balmy night and felt somewhat uneasy. The Ville had been her home for years. Now, she felt like a victim and a casualty in her own neighborhood. She wanted to believe that she was OK—that she was strong and in control of the situation, especially around her family and friends. She tried to put up a front line of defense against the overwhelming feelings and reality that she had been brutally raped and assaulted. But at night, she was falling apart with nightmares, anxiety, flashbacks, guilt, fear, and so many other feelings.

From her bedroom window, Kizzie fixed her attention on a figure approaching her building, a man in a black hoodie moving with obscurity and coolness. She couldn't distinguish the face from her viewpoint, but something about him seemed familiar. He walked with his hands in the front pockets of the hoodie as if he were clutching something inside. His eyes were glued below, not once looking up. And he moved quickly.

She watched him come near the building. And in the distance, she could hear police sirens blaring, indicating another crime had been committed in the area.

The figure stopped unexpectedly, and then his attention shot upward to where Kizzie was gawking at him from the above window. It seemed like he knew she was watching him—maybe he felt her presence. And when she finally saw his face and saw that it was Omar lurking in the night, she was shocked. However, their attention on each other was fleeting. Omar shot his head back down and moved robotically into the lobby. Kizzie wanted to call out to him, but her voice became mute. However, there was something about him that continued to disturb her. It gave her a cold chill when she caught his attention.

She removed herself from the window and hurried to grab her robe from the closet to cover her indecency. Though she was going through her own issues and problems, she needed to see Omar. It had been days since he left her bedroom, ranting and griping about the world being ugly, and it seemed like he'd disappeared. It seemed like her best friend was becoming the recluse instead of her.

Kizzie shot out of her bedroom, into the hallway, and toward the front door. The moment she swung it open, Omar already had his apartment door open, and he was ready to step inside.

What is he, the Flash? she wondered.

How did he move so quickly from outside to his front door? Kizzie thought it would be at least another few minutes until he showed up on their floor. But there he was, looking dark, somewhat sickly, and like a mystery to her.

"Omar!" she called out.

He turned around to face her. Unsmiling, he replied, "Hey, Kizzie. How have you been?"

"Where are you coming from so late?" she asked him.

"I went for a walk," he said.

"A walk . . .? It's like two in the morning . . ."

"And what? You're all of a sudden my keeper?" he scoffed.

"I haven't seen you around in a few days. I'm just . . . I just missed you, that's all," she said sincerely.

She didn't get a reaction from him. He remained unaffected.

"I need to go. I'm tired. I'll see you tomorrow, Kizzie. Good night," he replied matter-of-factly.

He stepped into his apartment and closed the door behind him. Kizzie stood there at the threshold of her doorway, looking dumbfounded. He shunned her like she was a stranger to him. She didn't like it. She was having nightmares and flashbacks, and besides her grandmother, Omar was the friend she needed the most to talk to, but he wasn't there.

Sadly, she turned and returned to her apartment with her mind heavy on her best friend. She believed something strange was happening to him and wanted to get to the bottom of it.

Omar entered the dark apartment and refused to turn on the lights. He didn't need them. He knew his way around the area too well. He walked from the living room to his bedroom and closed the door behind him. His bedroom was creepily dark. Blackout curtains covered the windows. There was something in the darkness that was like a vow. The dark and depressing room was like a place out of time—a place to rest without consequences. It became his sanctuary and a place for him to recharge and reform. He welcomed the dark.

He exhaled.

He set the .357 on the dresser, then peeled off his clothing, leaving a small pile near the bed. Naked, he stood still and silent. Omar felt he did well tonight. Another one was down, and there was one left to kill. Tip. Omar's heart started to beat like a wildfire raging through the woods, unstoppable, callous, destroying life and peace as it spread. He thought about his recent victims; their hearts that used to beat now were still. He enjoyed knowing their bodies were now abandoned shells left to rot where they lay. The lights of life were permanently extinguished from their eyes, and their souls were left to be damned. His victims became nothing but another carcass to bury. But he thought, who would bury them and cry tears onto their graves? Who would miss them? Likely, no one at all, he felt.

For a moment, Omar stood in the center of his room in heavy silence, inundated by the dark and stillness. His heart continued to beat tremendously. He needed to see it, to see her tonight. This craving was so intense inside him that it almost became unbearable to his flesh. It had been days since it came—since it cured and appeased his desire or hunger for sexual gratification. He was willing to kill for it—and he did. What it wanted from him, he was unsure. And why did it choose him? He didn't care. The sexual fulfillment that it brought with it and the power it bestowed on him were the only things Omar cared about.

He was falling in love with it, the succubus. He couldn't stop thinking about her. And without its continuous presence, Omar just about felt suicidal.

He moved toward the bed and lay flat on his back. The bedroom was hot and muggy, nearly becoming a breeding ground for something unearthly. Nevertheless, the darkness continued to be his comfort. Omar lay there completely motionless and naked, closing his eyes, and said out loud, "I need you tonight. Please, come to me."

His voice dripped with anguish, and his body was suffocating for a specific need. Omar lay there for what seemed like forever and soon fell into a deep sleep.

The feeling against his bare chest was cold and unpleasant like someone had tossed snow on him. A chill swept through him, and he released a winter's breath from his trembling lips. However, it was a fleeting sensation as that cold, prickly feeling transitioned into the warmth and something pleasurable below. His eyes remained closed as he was now wholly aroused and stimulated. His erection was inside of her—pussy that felt out of this world, and Omar's eyes shot open to see Malaka riding him sweetly. The pleasure was now consuming his entire body. The heat was intense, and he became intoxicated with her scent.

Her dark and smooth flesh glimmered in the shadows, her eyes a soulless black, almost unnatural.

Omar wanted to extend his hands and touch her. He tried to cup her breasts and caress her skin, but her soulless look paralyzed him. He couldn't move at all. He couldn't react. She enveloped him, had him in her spell, and coaxed his orgasm out with her gyrating and stimulating damp walls.

"Ooooh God," he cried out, experiencing his heaven.

The mention of God irritated it. It growled at him. A chilling and demonic sound made Omar's bones vibrate underneath his skin, and the room shuddered. He was fighting a feeling that he couldn't understand. Malaka clamped its clammy hands against the sides of his face, holding Omar's attention firm, and it continued to fuck him intensely. Then finally, it locked eyes with him. Her soulless eyes were hypnotic, and the sensation he continued to feel became indiscernible. It didn't seem to be either pleasurable or unpleasant.

"Speak His name no more . . ." it growled.

It removed its hand from the side of his face, and they became clamped against his chest like magnets. It continued to grind its pussy against him as Omar lay there still and in a deep trance by it. Its sharp nails punctured his skin, drawing blood, and as she fucked him, it dragged its spicy, sharp nails across his chest, leaving a long, bloody claw mark behind. Omar continued to lie there with paralysis. He couldn't move or react to the sudden pain—if it was pain he felt. He felt an orgasm brewing as Malaka continued to milk his hard dick with its pleasing movements. It straddled him, rousing an orgasm, and he exploded into it—like fireworks going off.

Omar lay there momentarily, his sexual hunger temporarily quenched and his chest bleeding.

It was morning, but it was hard to tell that it was morning with the blackout curtains covering the windows. Omar woke up, and immediately, he clutched his chest and felt the blood on his hand. And then a sharp pain shot through him. He became extremely queasy. He leaped from the bed and made a beeline for the bathroom, where he dropped to his knees and started to throw up what seemed like blood. He had no idea what was going on with him. He felt heavy and weighed down. He heaved a deep sigh and remained on his knees for several minutes. Then he stood up and gazed at his reflection in the mirror. The mark was ugly across his chest. It was inches long, bleeding, and painful. His eyes stayed fixed on it, the mark, and then suddenly, he smirked.

CHAPTER TWENTY-ONE

LENNY DIAZ PULLED back the sheet that covered the dead on the cold slab and revealed Chuck's body to Detective Greene. It was a mangled mess with multiple gunshot wounds from the face to his chest.

"Not even his mama would recognize this one," Lenny said.

It was an ugly sight to see. Detective Greene stared at the body without any problems and remained blank. He was a seasoned detective, and he'd seen it all. The city morgue had a strange smell to it. The smell of rotting meat filled his nostrils with death scenting the room. Each body, their deaths, told a story. And this was one body with a story to tell—like the others.

"I did a full autopsy on this one, and it was the same results . . . nothing there. I found no exit wounds or retrieved any ammunition from the body. And his organs were the same, completely charred. And there was another victim brought in here a few days ago killed by a .357 and having charred organs. It's happening again. And I can't come to a rational explanation for why this is happening. How are these men dying without any shells to find inside their bodies? And there is no other indication of death. What is going on out there, Detective?"

asked Lenny with utter bewilderment. "Is there something I need to know about?"

Danny Greene was stumped too. He had no answers for the medical examiner.

"I wish I had the answers myself," said Greene. "But I'm afraid there will be more bodies like this one."

"My hands are tied, Detective. I brought this issue up with my superiors and the NYPD a year ago about these anomalies with the bodies, and yet, no word back from anyone," said Diaz. "I'm starting to feel some kind of cover-up happening here."

Danny sighed. Maybe the man was right.

While conversing, Danny's cell phone rang. It was Bunk calling him, and he answered. "Yeah?"

"We got another multiple shooting," Bunk said.

It was the last thing Detective Greene wanted to hear. He sighed and asked, "Where?"

Bunk gave him the location, uttered, "Prepare yourself for this one," and hung up.

"Another shooting," Greene told the medical examiner.

Lenny Diaz's expression was palpable—*what the fuck!*

Danny Greene arrived at the crime scene on Saratoga Avenue, right off Atlantic Avenue. It was a neighborhood bodega nestled in the middle of the block called Elsa Deli and Grocery, where all the fuss occurred. The one-way street was swamped with police activity—police cars parked askew on the road, and their blaring blue and red lights illuminated the area. It was another circus with homicide detectives and the crime scene unit. Yellow police tape and the looky-loos stood behind the yellow tape, gazing at the scene with curiosity when such attention was unwelcomed.

Greene climbed out of his vehicle and approached the scene with some slight uneasiness. He knew it was going to be ugly. He could sense the horrors already. The look on the beat cops' faces said it all.

Shit!

He ducked underneath the yellow crime scene tape and approached the bodega where the entrance was crowded with cops. One officer couldn't hold in the contents to his stomach. So, he hurried to an unoccupied area on the sidewalk, rapidly hunched over with nausea, and let it all fly out onto the sidewalk, decorating the pavement with his last meal.

"It's fuckin' bad, Detective . . . really bad," another beat cop said.

Greene didn't respond to his statement. Instead, he made his way into the bodega and could already smell death. It hit him in force, the blood—the horrors that men were able to do to each other. The first body was behind the counter. It was the store clerk, a young male in his early twenties. He had been shot in the face, and his body was lying in a pool of blood.

"The real fun is down in the basement," said another detective, examining the clerk's body.

Danny moved through the store toward the rear, and he immediately deduced that it was a front—a drug depot. More security cameras than average were placed throughout the store, and they weren't just watching shoplifters. Its inventory was subpar, and the area was a drug paradise for fiends and dealers. The black steel door was a security partition between the store and the basement. And a security camera was above the steel door, watching everyone's arrival or departure.

Danny Greene took a deep breath, marched forward, and descended into the lower area of the store. It felt as if he were sliding into the pits of hell. He sensed the iniquity he was about to observe. He already saw the first body sprawled out at the foot of the stairs. He had to step over it to enter the basement. The dead man was shot several times in the face and chest, and his blood had pooled so thick that it felt knee-deep if one were to step in it. But that was only the appetizer to the scene. Danny knew there was more to come.

His partner, Bunk, was already on the scene. But, of course, the two weren't the primary detectives. They already had their hands full with several other cases. But this was a situation where they needed many eyes and attention.

"Our boy Science is coming back on Anton in a brutal way," said Foster.

Danny took in the concrete basement with adept attention. Solid, concrete walls with ventilation, more security cameras above believed to be observing the merchandise or workers, and an opened safe—an empty safe. It was a stash house, but there weren't any signs of weapons, cash, or drugs. He believed whatever the place housed was now long gone.

"The real fun is behind door number one," Foster said jokingly.

Detective Greene didn't find anything funny. Two people were dead, and he knew there was more to come. But Danny kept calm and said, "I see lots of cameras . . ."

"No footage, though. They were smart enough to erase or grab the film," another detective said.

It was time for Danny to see the main prize behind the black door. He entered the room, and the smell of blood and death hit him instantly, becoming overwhelming. But what he saw sadistically displayed in front of him . . . What other human beings could do to each other . . . was something that made his seasoned stomach start to churn slightly. He latched his eyes on four bodies sprawled across the floor. Two were hog-tied, feet tied together, naked, and headless—and the other two were also naked with their lower parts stuffed into their mouths and their eyes gouged out. It was a level of violence so brutal it was almost unfathomable. Danny then saw the bloody chainsaw in the corner. It was a no-brainer; each man was brutally tortured and butchered. There was no regard for human life at all.

"This some cartel shit right here," Bunk said.

"What I can't figure out is why cut off two heads instead of four?" asked another detective in the room.

"Maybe they got tired," Bunk chimed lightheartedly.

The Crime Scene Unit was painstakingly processing the scene. And they too were shaken by the sadistic violence. Each man was careful where they stepped. The crimson blood was thick, pooling, and everywhere—along with the victims' heads displayed on a folding table. It was evil on an unspeakable level. It was malevolence at its greatest. And mostly, everyone was utterly shocked. This was Brooklyn—not Tijuana, Mexico.

"If they wanted to send a message, it was definitely sent," said Foster. "Fuck!"

Danny Greene stood in the center of anarchy and impiety—it was a lot to take in, even for a seasoned detective like him, and he thought, *What are we dealing with here?*

The New Life Fellowship Church in Hollis Queens was a place that stood the test of time. The church had been around for decades. It had seen its fair share of trials and tribulations. And it had become a beacon of hope for so many in the neighborhood. Pastor Gregory and his staff had become iconic to so many folks. It was where the misguided, the unfortunate, the sinful, the troubled, and those seeking guidance came. Truly a community-centered church that focuses on relating the word to all walks of life.

It was a place where, if you were looking to feel the love of God, then you would feel great there. And it was a place that Detective Greene had been attending for years, where he too would look for guidance and answers. After what Danny saw the other night, he entered the church with a heavy heart and a lot on his mind. The place was empty and quiet on a Tuesday night. He walked down the aisle, sat in the front pew and stared at the large cross with Jesus' crucifixion suspended on the wall behind the choir's seating and the pastor's podium.

Danny sat there and released a heavy sigh. He closed his eyes and said a silent prayer. It was hard for him to forget those bodies in the bodega's basement. The images were like concrete inside his head—heavy and weighing profusely on him. And although he wasn't the primary detective on what the media was now calling ***"Bloody Brooklyn Friday,"*** he somehow felt that everything was connected. He had seen it all, but that night, those headless and tortured bodies became an unshakable and faintly daunting feeling for him.

He sat quietly and gazed at the large cross, searching for guidance or answers from a higher power. Danny felt he was fighting an uphill battle. Brice's investigation, among others, had reached a dead end for him. There were no witnesses and no hard-core evidence to arrest anyone. But the kicker for him was the bodies in the morgue with charred organs and no bullets recovered from the deceased. Baffled was an understatement.

Danny Greene continued to sit there in grave silence, looking pensive, until he heard, "What's disturbing you, Brother Greene?"

It was Pastor Gregory entering the room and approaching Danny. Danny stared up at the pastor, a man with gray facial hair, dark skin, and short gray hair. He stood six-one—an imposing-looking man with a humble and subservient demeanor. He was a man in his late fifties but looked ten years younger. He was a generous and astute man to talk to.

"It feels like I'm fighting a losing battle, Pastor," said Danny dejectedly.

"With your job or faith?" the pastor asked him.

Danny sighed heavily, "Maybe both," he admitted.

"I see."

The pastor took a seat next to him. Danny gazed ahead, brooding.

"You've been a cop for a long time, Danny . . . and before that, a soldier, so I know you've seen some bothersome things . . . things that maybe the mind finds difficult to cope with," the pastor said.

"What I see happening in Brooklyn, it's . . . It isn't comforting; it's evil, and then there's . . ." Danny paused. He didn't know how to explain it to the pastor. He didn't know how to explain it to himself.

"This is why we have the church, and God, and mentoring, where one could come to exhale, talk, and perhaps recharge his faith."

Danny turned to look at the pastor. There was a certain warmth and paternal feeling that the pastor gave off. His eyes were kind and knowing. He was always willing to listen intently and give the needed advice.

"You see and investigate the iniquities and immorality of man on a daily. And I can only imagine what you've seen as a cop in this city. You take on a lot with your position, Danny. You want justice for those that have been wronged. And I can understand where and why your faith can falter sometimes."

"You know me, Pastor, I don't judge anyone . . . but there's this one case that I'm going nowhere with. The victim wasn't well-liked; in fact, some might say he was the devil himself, causing nothing but misery and harm to his community. Yet, I treat his case like I would if it were an innocent child killed. Murder is murder in my book, no matter what the victim's background may have been," Danny proclaimed.

"Love the sinner, hate the sin," Pastor Gregory uttered.

"Sometimes it becomes difficult to love the sinner after you've heard the horror stories about him," Danny replied. "But still, I have a job to do. And right now, I feel that this man's crew is being hunted down and killed, and these bodies . . ."

Once again, Danny paused. It was hard to fathom the unthinkable—that something supernatural was happening in the Ville—something unexplainable.

His expression became profound.

"Is there something else going on with you besides the job?" the pastor asked him.

"Maybe I need to take a step back . . . Take some time off and look at things from a different perspective. Then hit restart and look at this case with fresher eyes."

"You probably need some balance in your life, Danny," the pastor uttered.

"Balance . . .?"

"Yes, balance. When was the last time you took some time out for yourself to enjoy something? Maybe go out on a date with a beautiful woman?"

"My life is hectic, Pastor."

"No, you make it hectic. You bring the job home with you every day. What's happening out there? Has it become your life night and day? It's gradually eating away at you. And there's no one in your life to help you escape it. You've been divorced what . . . two years now?"

"Three," he corrected. "And I have my music."

"Music is good, but you need equilibrium to help keep you centered. And, yes, God can be our equilibrium, but man was meant to have a wife, a family, people he cares for, and who will care for him," said the pastor.

"Family . . . It's the reason why Patrice and I divorced in the first place. She wanted a family, kids. I didn't. Why bring children into a world like this, Pastor? Why risk it?"

"You're bringing fear of the present to your future," said the pastor.

"It's ugly out there, Pastor Gregory, and the way this world is going, why would I want to bring kids into this . . . start a family?" Danny rebuffed. "Last year, I investigated the death of a thirteen-year-old boy, shot three times because he looked at a gang member wrong . . . because of a look. So, I thought, what if that was my son? What would I have done?"

Pastor Gregory exhaled sharply. He said, "You're a good man, Danny, an intelligent and impartial man. But I see you becoming consumed by fear because of things you've seen as a cop. But as the Lord says, 'Don't fear, for I have redeemed you; I have called you by name; you are mine.' And He knows the enemy uses fear to decrease our hope and limit our victories."

Danny didn't respond but listened.

Pastor Gregory continued, "And family is the foundational institution of society ordained by God. Family is a fundamental institution of human society. If more Black men came from adoring families with strong fathers and doting mothers . . . a solid structure, a home with values and lessons, this world would be a different place. And that's where the devil has attacked us . . . with family, with fatherhood. He created a distraction in so many ways that too many families, especially Black families, are in disarray and confusion. Family is important because it provides love, support, and the formation of values to each of its members. The purpose of it is to give you a safe and supportive base from which to explore the world."

"I hear what you're saying, Pastor, but—"

"There is no but, Danny. You see enough evil out there that you take it home with you, and you've become combative to your own needs and future. You have no one to talk to regularly to help dilute the wickedness and malice you steadily see as a cop. The job has taken a lot from you. And, yes, there is the church, but there also needs to be a private foundation at home. Family time is important because it allows family members to feel loved and secure. Family is the only thing you can rely on in a tough situation. And family is something you can trust with anything and have when you have nothing else. God is family."

Danny's eyes sank to the floor. He was lost in thought—dwelling on something.

"I also sense that something else is truly bothering you," uttered the pastor, reading Danny's body language.

"Do you believe in the supernatural, Pastor?"

"The supernatural . . .? Well, I'm a man of faith, and I have seen some uncanny things in my lifetime," he replied.

Danny looked up from the floor and turned his attention to the pastor. He seriously told him, "I think something evil, foul, and supernatural is happening in my neighborhood, Pastor. Some unspeakable force is taking over, causing unrest and violence."

He said it aloud, which sounded crazy to him, but Danny believed it wholeheartedly.

CHAPTER TWENTY-TWO

KIZZIE TOSSED AND turned in her sleep in a futile attempt to slip away into the depths of unconsciousness. Finally, the darkness inside her room encouraged her to fall deeply asleep. Her room soon became a darkness that robs you of your best sense and replaces it with paralyzing fear. Dawn was many hours away, and the blackness engulfed her thoughts. It stretched out like a map, and the unknown studied her worries. It felt like her muscles were cramped, and she could not move. Her breathing became shallow. Her eyes remained closed until some compelling horror made them spring open. However, she might as well keep them closed because the darkness was strangely copious and frightening. It felt like it overcame any sense of purity and consumed any hope of cleanliness. It had taken a stranglehold around Kizzie, trying to squeeze the life from her. Kizzie knew she was still there, still awake, because she felt herself blink. The darkness started to form some primitive hatred. Something began to seep through the floorboards, and it began to snake itself from dark corners and crevices.

Kizzie felt fear. She knew something was in the bedroom with her. She couldn't see it yet, but she felt its ungodly presence. It was something dark and sinister. She propped herself against the headboard and tried to adjust her eyes to the dark, and the blackness inside the room must have deceived her. Her eyes became confused and dazzled by a sharp glare nearby. For a minute, she could make out nothing at all but the furniture inside her room—the chest of drawers by the wall, her desk, and lamp . . . and then the subsequent low growl. It sounded like some small animal was nearby. Kizzie became more alert—scared. Was she still dreaming? No, she wasn't. She was wide away, and she wasn't having a nightmare.

Her eyes continued to try to adjust to the dark. She attentively stared into that one particular corner where she heard the growl. Suddenly, she saw a mysterious figure. It was perched on her dresser, still like a statue, and watching her. It was a woman—a naked woman, and there was something demonic about her. Her skin was black and gleaming, and her eyes were soulless. She almost looked human, but her feet were like hooves, and horns seemed to protrude from her head. She was perched on her dresser motionless, with her soulless eyes fixed on Kizzie. And it looked like this woman, this demonic creature, was ready to pounce her way. Kizzie couldn't believe her eyes. She had never seen anything like this, not even in her worst nightmares. She couldn't breathe; it started to feel like someone was choking her. Her heart began to race. All Kizzie wanted to do was curl up into a tight ball underneath the covers, pray madly, and hope and wait for someone to rescue her from this demonic entity.

"*Kizzie*," she heard.

Her attention snapped to her left, and there was Omar. He seemed to come out of nowhere, looming into her view with a possessed gaze. He was naked, and blisters, scratches, and scars covered his body. She was shocked.

"Omar . . . What are you doing here? What is happening to you?" she exclaimed with panic. "Help me!"

He didn't respond to her outcry. Instead, he stood there in chilling silence, staring at her oddly. The demonic woman perched on the dresser growled louder. Its sound was frightening. But Omar reacted to it as if he was given a command from it. He leaped Kizzie's way with fearsome speed and started to attack her. Kizzie screamed. Suddenly, her arms became pinned against the bed, and her body became pinned against the mattress. She couldn't move at all. She couldn't fight him off. Once again, she found herself utterly helpless from an attack. The air became stale around her, and she felt her legs forced open. Kizzie screamed heatedly, and she burst into tears and anger. This wasn't happening—not again! Not with Omar. He continued to attack her, and he was trying to rape her.

A choking cry for help forced itself up her throat, and she felt teardrops run down her cheek.

"Nooooo!" she shrieked from the top of her lungs. "Nooooo!"

It seemed like it was the end of the road for her.

And then she woke up screaming. Kizzie nearly hurdled from her bed, jolting awake from the horrific nightmare that she was having. Her breathing was heavy, and it felt like she had a panic attack. It seemed so real. It *was* real, she thought. Her eyes darted around the bedroom, and everything seemed back to normal. It wasn't unnaturally dark, and no demonic entity perched on her dresser. But Omar? *Why did I have that dream about Omar?* she wondered.

She gradually collected herself and her thoughts, becoming rational again. She'd screamed so loud she was surprised it didn't wake her grandmother. But her grandmother always had been a heavy sleeper.

Kizzie glanced at the time and saw that it was 2:00 a.m. She removed herself from the bed and went toward the window. It always felt like something was pulling her to the window. Maybe she needed some fresh air. She opened the window to allow a breeze to sweep through her bedroom. It was summer, and the heat wave had subsided somewhat. She exhaled. She stared out the window and again saw Omar approaching the building at a late hour. It was the same. He was marching toward the lobby routinely in a black hoodie and smoking a cigarette this time. Kizzie was taken aback by his action. She thought, *When did he start smoking?*

This time, she removed herself from the window before he entered the lobby. Kizzie wanted to talk to him. She tried to greet him before he went into his apartment. She threw on a robe and slippers and headed toward the front door. The nightmare she had with him in it was unexplainable. Again, she thought, *Why would Omar try to rape me in my dreams? And who was the strange woman?* But it was something she couldn't dwell on at the moment. She opened her front door with her arms folded across her chest, looking like an irritated mother waiting for her child after their curfew. She stood there waiting for Omar to arrive. She needed to have a serious talk with him.

But he didn't show up. He never arrived at his apartment, and Kizzie thought that was odd. She was sure he had entered the building, and there was nowhere else for him to go—nowhere but—the rooftop. It was one of his favorite places to go. It was where they would talk, think, pray, look out at the city, and dream of a better life for themselves one day. She was certain Omar was there.

Kizzie returned to her apartment, grabbed her keys, and left again. She entered the stairwell and traveled upward. But after a flight up, she stopped sharply and clutched the railing tightly. Her mind became trapped with hallucinations of being angrily grabbed and raped again. She was in the same stairwell where the attack happened. Kizzie stood there frozen for a moment, trying to get her shit together and collect herself. Maybe this was a mistake, she thought. But she thought about Omar, someone she cared for, and he was going through some issues. Bad shit!

"C'mon, Kizzie, get it together," she said with labored breathing.

Her hand continued to clutch the railing tightly. The stairwell was dim and quiet, reeking of urine and foulness. She took a deep breath, said a silent prayer, released her grip from the railing, and continued toward the rooftop.

"God, give me strength," she said to herself. "I know you are there for me."

Omar took another pull from the Newport and kept his gaze ahead at a late-night Brooklyn. The streets were quiet tonight. There were no blaring police sirens, no loud gunshots, and no commotion for blocks. Things were too slow for him. Although he had killed three of Kizzie's attackers, he still seethed that one was still left. He had been looking for Tip for several days, and there had been no sign of him. Omar figured the fool left town, knowing what was best for him. He could run, but he couldn't hide forever. Omar was persistent in finishing his task for Kizzie. No! It was no longer for Kizzie. He wanted to complete the job for it—for Malaka. The bloodshed became enthralling, and the power behind the gun became riveting and absorbing. Murder made things enthralling for him—with it. The energy, the sensation—the relief; the addiction he had for it was crippling and desired.

He took another pull from the cancer stick and breathed in. He stood there with his back turned to the door and his eyes fixed on the night. Cloaked in his black hoodie during a summer night and the .357 tucked in his waistband, his demeanor becoming darker than ever, Omar had become a force to be reckoned with. The streets were talking. It wasn't his name ringing out, for he had remained anonymous, but the image and figure of a black-hooded killer wiping out Brice's crew. The killings were brutal and bold. Dealers and stickup gangs were on the alert. With a drug war tearing apart the neighborhood, now a fierce assassin was running free in the Ville and amplifying the violence.

"Omar," he heard her call out.

He didn't turn around. He knew Kizzie's voice.

"What are you doing up here, Kizzie? I just want to be alone," Omar said indifferently, his eyes still fixed elsewhere.

"I saw you again from my bedroom window coming into the building late. Why are you out so late?" she asked. "Let me guess; you went for another walk."

She moved closer to him, tying her blue robe securely with the gravel crunching underneath her house slippers.

"And when did you start smoking?" she asked him.

"Go back to your apartment and go back to bed, Kizzie. You have nothing to do with what's going on."

"What *is* going on with you?" she demanded to know.

He finally turned to face her, the lit cigarette still in his hand. His eyes were cold and unfeeling. He seemed thinner, almost sickly, and the back of his hands appeared scarred. His face was masked mainly by the black hoodie. He looked like a thug and a drug addict wrapped into one. He was completely different. This wasn't the Omar she knew.

"I want to be left alone, Kizzie. Go, and let me be," he demanded.

"No!" she opposed. "I'm not going anywhere. Look at you. Look at what you're becoming—this thug. You look horrible, Omar. Look at you!"

He looked at her, emotionless from her statement. Her view of him didn't bother him. But Kizzie was upset.

"I'm taking care of something," he replied dryly.

"Taking care of what? What are you doing out there in those streets all night?"

"Just go, Kizzie. I'm asking you as a friend," he said.

"And as a friend, I'm not going to stand by and let you destroy yourself with whatever you're going through . . . or whatever you're on. Are you on drugs, Omar?"

"No."

"Then what . . .?"

He sighed, upset. "As I told you before, this doesn't concern you."

"Yes, it does!" she shouted. "How long have we been friends? Since the second grade. So, you think I'm just going to leave and abandon my best friend, who I've known since the second grade, just like that? No! You need help with whatever you're going through."

He angrily marched closer to her with his fists clenched. "I don't need your damn help!" he retorted.

Kizzie stood her ground. She stood firm, not wavering from his angry approach.

"So, you're going to attack me now? Huh? That's what you want to do to me?" she rebuked and was undaunted.

Omar stood there, fuming.

"What is happening to you, Omar?" she asked softly. "What demons have gotten into you?"

He didn't answer her. Kizzie kept her eyes glaringly on him. Seeing Omar in her dreams or that gripping nightmare flashed inside her head like a sudden lightning strike. She felt something troubling, unsure what it was, but it felt like something was trying to tell her something. His presence felt damaging and disturbed, corrupted by some evil entity.

"Get out my way, Kizzie," he said sternly.

He tried to leave. He tried to push past her, but Kizzie was adamant about knowing the truth. She was angry too. She was mad that she didn't have her best friend anymore. She was mad because she'd become a victim, and almost every night, she could feel her attackers inside her. As a result, she felt fear and weakness and continued asking God for guidance and strength. And though she suffered from her trials and tribulations, she still cared about Omar and his well-being.

Kizzie stood her ground against him, and he attempted to shove past her again. She pushed him back and shouted, "No! Talk to me!" And that's when she felt it; the gun tucked in his waistband.

"Omar, what is that on you?" she asked nervously.

"As I said, it's none of your damn business," he cursed.

"Is that a gun you're concealing?"

He didn't answer her. His look was intemperate, and he was growing impatient with her.

"Why are you carrying a gun on you, Omar?" she asked him. "What is it for?"

Silence. Anger. Edginess. Revenge. Power. Those were the traits Omar manifested. And then he exploded with, "You was going to let them get away with what they did to you!"

"What . . .? What are you talking about?" she responded, and then she was hit with a sudden and shocking realization. "No! No, tell me that it isn't you! Please, Omar . . . Tell me you're not out there doing that! Not murder . . ."

"There's your fuckin' truth, Kizzie," he growled contemptuously. "Now, get the fuck out my way!"

He shoved her to the side and stormed away with his footsteps thunderous against the gravel. Kizzie stood there in utter shock and felt utterly paralyzed by the confession she'd heard. A wave of weakness and vulnerability hit her like a thunder strike, and she dropped to her knees with her face awash with tears. It was hurtful to hear—to know what Omar had become.

Thou shall not kill! It was written.

She heard the door to the rooftop shut, indicating Omar's departure. She couldn't stop crying. The only thing she could think about was his soul. It was in jeopardy, and it was hell bound. He had been corrupted by something. Still, she couldn't believe it. She wanted to believe it was a lie, but deep down inside, Kizzie knew her friend was telling the truth. Omar was on a path of destruction, and she decided she needed help to save him. It was dire. She couldn't do it alone.

CHAPTER TWENTY-THREE

DANNY GREENE FINALLY felt that he had a breakthrough in his murder case. They had a suspect in custody. He had gotten a tip about a local thug named Snake. Snake and Brice had been at odds with each other for years now, and it was believed that Brice may have been a snitch, and because of this action, Snake did a bullet on Rikers Island for drug possession. Snake had been home a few months now, and word on the streets was that Snake wanted Brice dead. And Danny's source informed him that Snake was in the area that night during Brice's demise. And the bonus for Danny, Snake had a lengthy and violent rap sheet, and he was on probation.

Danny was ready to interview or interrogate the suspect. In interrogation room #2, he was handcuffed to the table, slumped in the hard seat, and looking impatient. Snake was an imposing figure who stood at six-two and weighed over two hundred and fifty pounds. He was a Black man with a thick beard and was a man that quickly stood out in a crowd.

Bunk and Danny stood outside the room. They both were ready to go into the room and interview Snake. Bunk was familiar with the thug's character. He said to Danny, "This muthafucka is serious, Danny. He ain't no fuckin' pushover, and he's no rookie to this place or an interrogation."

"And neither are we," Danny replied.

Danny was ready to cut into him, ask him questions, and determine if his source from the streets was correct.

The two men readied themselves for an intense interview with Snake. Bunk entered the bland-looking room, followed by Danny. It was like a prison cell with its shade of grey, from washed-out concrete to almost steel blue. Every line was straight, every corner sharp, and the chairs inside the room were as comfortable as a train station bench.

The two men sat opposite Snake behind the gray table. Snake continued to slump in his seat, gazing at the detectives aloofly.

Danny spoke first, politely. "Hello, Snake. I'm Detective Danny Greene, and this is my partner—"

"Man, fuck y'all!" Snake rudely interrupted him.

Danny didn't react or falter from the rude interruption. He took a deep and needed breath with his eyes still on Snake. He kept his cool and continued, "Like I was saying, this is my partner, Bunk Foster."

"We've met before," Bunk oddly smiled at the suspect.

"What the fuck y'all want from me?" Snake exclaimed. "I ain't do shit!"

"Unfortunately, your name came up in my murder investigation," said Danny coolly.

"Yo, I ain't kill nobody."

"We'll be the judge of that," Bunk chimed. "Look, we're not here to beat around the fuckin' bush with you, Snake. Word on the street is that you killed Brice."

Snake angrily reacted to the accusation. He popped up in his seat like readied toast from a toaster, jerking his handcuffed wrist, yearning to break free from his restraints, and seething from the statement he heard.

"Fuck you! I ain't had shit to do wit' that nigga's death! Y'all ain't 'bout to pin that shit on me. Real talk, muthafucka!" Snake retorted.

"Well, we have a witness that says otherwise," said Danny.

"Who . . .?"

"You think we're dumb enough to give you their name?" Bunk replied.

"Listen, Snake, there are a lot of strikes against you right now," Danny uttered, taking control of the interview. "First, we know you were in the area when Brice was killed. Second, we know that you and he have had perpetual beef for years. And we know he snitched on you a while back, the reason you did a bullet on Rikers Island. So, you had every motive to kill him . . . shoot him multiple times that night."

"Yeah, I had my issues wit' that nigga. It ain't no secret. Fuck him, and I'm glad he's dead. Real talk. He and his crew were fuckin' bottom-feeders, do anything for a buck. But I was at a bitch's place nearby; that's why I was seen in the area that night," he said.

"So, you have an alibi?" asked Bunk.

"Fuck yeah, I do. I was fuckin this bitch that night . . . ate the bitch out and everything. Real talk. Man, I even got pictures and video of the bitch that night . . . some nasty shit we got into. She's a fuckin' freak like that. Real talk!"

"You lying to us, Snake? Because you know we're going to find out," said Danny.

"Ain't no reason to lie because I ain't kill the nigga. Y'all barking up the wrong fuckin' tree wit' this shit here. So, whoever's tryin' to put that shit on me, fuck them and fuck y'all!"

"See, this the thing. It's easy to get a bitch to lie for you. What thug nigga in Brooklyn can't get a bitch to lie for him . . . to solidify his alibi?" said Bunk.

"Muthafucka, didn't I just fuckin' tell you that I got this fuckin' bitch on video fuckin' and suckin' me. Shit is time-stamped and everything. Real talk," Snake chided.

"Video, huh . . .?"

"Yeah, check that shit, and see how a *real* nigga fucks a bitch, unlike you two old dirtbag fucks," continued Snake. "And don't get jealous of my big dick either."

"We're going to look into your alibi and this video," Danny said.

"Yeah, do that. And besides, I had beef wit' Brice, not his entire crew. Shit, nigga, you think I got time to be hunting down niggas like that?" said Snake. "Fuck I look like . . . the fuckin' Terminator?"

It made sense.

"I only did a year on Rikers, and that ain't shit . . . no real fuckin' time to do," Snake continued. "And from what I'm hearing on the streets, whoever killed Brice and his peoples, it's probably over that rape shit."

"Rape . . . What rape?" asked Danny.

"Y'all muthafuckas are stupid and clueless. Real talk! Got me in this bitch, locked up and shit, and y'all don't shit 'bout out there. Yeah, word on the streets is that Brice and his niggas raped some church bitch a few weeks back . . . and they beat her rather good. Fucked her whole shit up. But the bitch ain't telling on these niggas," Snake said.

"Why not?" Danny asked.

"I don't fuckin' know. Maybe she's fuckin' scared. But on the other hand, maybe she liked that shit," Snake exclaimed.

"You know her name?" Danny asked.

"Muthafucka, no, I don't know her fuckin' name. I don't know the bitch. So y'all assholes got the badge and the gun and go by fuckin' detective, right? So y'all go figure that shit out! Real talk!" Snake griped.

Danny's gut told him that Snake was most likely telling the truth. He wasn't their guy. The rape and beating of a church girl were new information to him. And he believed that if Brice and his crew did brutally rape a young woman, that gave the killer motive to strike—revenge. He felt whoever was close or connected to this mystery girl was their killer.

"We done here?" Snake asked irritably.

"One more thing," Bunk uttered. "What do you know about a missing .357 Magnum?"

"What . . .? A .357? Nigga, I don't know shit about any gun, especially no .357."

Danny was caught off guard by his partner's question about the gun.

"Well, do me a favor. If you hear anything about that gun, let me know," said Bunk.

Snake scoffed. "Do you a favor . . . You funny, nigga."

Done, both men stood up from the table and removed themselves from the room. Bunk said to his partner outside the interrogation room, "Well, that was fun."

"Why are you looking for a .357 Magnum?" Danny asked him.

"It connects to an old case of mines, and I was just fishing. I didn't expect to get much from him about it," Bunk replied.

Bunk pivoted and marched away. But Danny stood there thinking, pondering—he felt there was more to it than what his partner said. It was odd that Bunk mentioned a .357, the same caliber of gun that most likely killed Brice, Mo, and Chuck. And none of their autopsies recovered a bullet. Things were getting stranger by the minute. But Danny knew that one member of

Brice's crew was still alive. Tip. He needed to speak to Tip and either warn him or investigate him. Either way, Danny felt he was getting closer to solving his case.

CHAPTER TWENTY-FOUR

IT WAS A cruel practice, but it was profitable—dogfighting. Science was excited and obsessed over it. He was adept at breeding and training a puppy to become a vicious beast in the ring. It had been a thing of his for years now. He started breeding dogs for fighting in his early teens when he used to help his older cousin train pit bull terriers in Bushwick, Brooklyn. And although it was malicious and illegal in every state, Science had a knack for it. And like his reputation in the streets for moving serious weight, he cemented a reputation in New York City as one of the best to do it—breeding and training dogs to win—to tear their opponents apart like they were rag dolls.

The bricked building in Sunset Park was the core of Science's dog breeding and training. It was a private kennel with various dogs, from young pups to fierce veterans. From corner to corner of the spacious building, locked away in cages, were American pit bull terriers, Staffordshire bull terriers, American Staffordshire terriers, and bulldogs. These animals had explicitly been bred over generations to enhance aggressiveness.

Science walked the grounds with a cattle prod in his hand. He meticulously inspected his dogs, his prize possessions, for any flaws or weaknesses. He was conversing with his acquaintance in the drug business about dogfighting and breeding while his armed goons were everywhere.

"Taking a dog from birth to fully train for fighting can take two years. And top breeders can sell puppies from a successful bloodline for more than a thousand each . . . sometimes ten thousand or more. This is a lucrative business, nigga, if you know what you're doin' and how to do it right," Science proclaimed.

"Yeah, I see," said the man.

Science stopped where there was a caged pit bull. It was large and muscular—scary. The dog's teeth had been filed down to make them as sharp as possible to inflict maximum damage. Around its neck was a heavy chain with a heavyweight attached to it. The purpose of this was to increase the dog's upper-body strength. And each dog was kept close to the other but just out of reach to increase their antagonism.

Science glared at the pit bull. It looked like it had seen one fight too many, and it had won them all.

"This my special bitch right here," said Science about the pit bull. "His name is Terror . . . I named him that for a good reason."

Science crouched near the cage and heartlessly, and without warning, he started to poke the dog with the cattle prod. The results were snarling and fierce teeth showing, barking, and Terror was ready to attack. It looked like he was prepared to break free from the cage and release his aggression on anything. Science continued the cruel act with the cattle prod for about a minute; then he stopped. He turned to the person he was talking to and said, "You can't let any of your bitches slack; always fuck 'em up and let them know who's boss."

On the other side of the room, one of Science's handlers was hanging a tire from the ceiling. It made their dogs tug on hanging objects to increase their jaw strength.

"My nigga, did you know that Ancient Romans pitted dogs against each other in gladiatorial contests?" said Science.

"Nah. I didn't know that," replied the man.

"Yeah. Dogs have played functional roles in society. Muthafuckas had been used for hunting companions; they defended fuckin' properties and fuckin' protected livestock against poachers and wild animals. And in England, fuckin' dogs were a force to attack bulls or bears, a practice called bull-baiting that was outlawed in 1835," said Science.

"You know your history about dogs and the sport," replied the man.

"Yeah. I do. A dog . . . a bitch; they're loyal, reliable, and fierce no matter what. And they know how to protect their master from any harm coming their way, and they are willing to die in the process," said Science. "Unlike some people I know."

Science unexpectedly pushed the man into the dogfighting ring and locked him inside. The man was shocked.

"Science, what's going on, man?"

One of Science's dog handlers loomed on the opposite end of the ring, gripping two leather leashes. Two vicious, strapping, and snarling-looking pit bulls were at the end of those leashes. The man in the ring grew extremely nervous. He looked Science's way with panic written on his face. He tried to escape from the pit, but two of Science's men drew guns on him, forcing him to stay inside.

"Science, what's up with this? What's going on, man?" he asked fearfully.

"You think I'm stupid? That's what's goin' on," replied Science. "You know how I feel about niggas stealing from me, right?"

"What . . . I ain't take shit!"

"And you lying to me now."

"Nah!" he shouted.

"I'm already taking losses on the streets from rival crews, and now I'm supposed to take losses from my own peoples? I'm not fuckin tolerating that, nigga," Science exclaimed. "And unfortunately, I'm 'bout to make an example out of your ass right now."

"C'mon, Science, don't do this shit. Not like this. If you gonna kill me, just shoot me," he begged.

"And where would the fun be in that?" Science replied unsympathetically. "Meet Snow and Blizzard; they're fierce, strong, and guess what, nigga? I ain't feed them in over a week. So right now, you're looking like a five-course meal to them."

The man was shivering in his shoes and frantically begging for his life. But his pleads for mercy fell on deaf ears. Science and his men wanted to see a gruesome performance, and they were about to get one.

Science nodded to his dog handler, indicating releasing the beasts and letting the show begin. There was no hesitation. The handler released the dogs, and they charged ferociously at their target with malice. Immediately, the man tried to run, but there was no way out. So, he pivoted sharply and went on the defense—any good *that* would do with two vicious, hungry, full-grown pit bulls rushing at him. The first dog grabbed his right knee with its sharp teeth and went berserk on his leg. It nearly took him down, but the man tried to stand firm and fight them off. The second dog grabbed his second leg and tore into his flesh with its teeth, generating panic and a crackling sound of pain and fear from the man. He punched the dogs heatedly and tried to tear the pit bulls off his body but to no avail. Their aggressiveness was nearly demonic. They were attacking him with incredible strength and hunger. He went down eventually, and they were tearing into him all over, with chunks of flesh and bone flying everywhere.

Science and his crew stood there unflinching and watched a man being ripped apart by the two pit bulls. One dog bit the man's mouth under his lips and chewed on his ears, tearing one ear off. Next, they bit into his face. And with his last breath, the victim desperately tried to pry their mouths off his face, but his defending effort to survive was fruitless. The dogs were killing him—devouring him inhumanly with their mouths thickly coated with the man's blood.

Soon, the frantic screaming stopped, and there was silence, despite the grunt of the dogs still feasting on the victim.

"Science!" Ray called out. "We got company."

Science turned his attention from the dreadful display and saw Ray entering the location. He was flanked by the fraternal twins Zack and O'Malley—skilled killers. The twins glanced at what was happening in the dog ring, seeing a substantial amount of blood and a partially dismembered body, but they looked unaffected and undaunted by the sight of it. They've seen worse, and they've done worse. The appalling scene at the bodega on Saratoga Avenue was their doing—their handiwork.

"Like what you see?" Science joked.

They both scoffed—"Amateur."

"Yeah, I bet. Y'all two muthafuckas are on some cartel shit, I see. That job at the bodega, loved it. Shit definitely sent a message," said Science with praise.

"We aim to please," Zack said.

"And to be paid," O'Malley voiced.

"Yeah. I got the rest of y'all money," said Science.

He nodded to Ray, and Ray removed himself from the conversation and disappeared into a neighboring room. Science continued to entertain the twins. He was impressed with their work style and wasn't shy of saying so. Ray didn't take long to return with a small black duffle bag filled with cash. He handed it to O'Malley. The twin unzipped it, glanced at the bundles of cash inside, and nodded, approving the payment.

"We good?" Science asked.

"Yeah, we're good," O'Malley replied.

"Listen, I was thinking, how would y'all two like to be on my official payroll?" Science asked. "A hundred thousand a month, each."

"We're independent contractors. You know that," said Zack.

"Yeah, I know that. The problem is, what's to stop anyone else from hiring y'all two to come at me . . . say, for instance, Anton and Kenya?" Science fretted.

"That's not our problem," said Zack.

"Yeah, I know it's not, but I want to be cautious in the future. Y'all feel me?"

"Tomorrow night, we're leaving town, going out west to do another job," said Zack.

"Then when will y'all be back in New York? After that, I might need y'all services again," Science said.

"You know how to reach us. Nothing's changed," said Zack.

"Yeah, nothing's changed," Science replied dryly. "A'ight, no doubt, it was good doin' business wit' y'all niggas."

Zack and O'Malley turned to leave. But the moment their backs were turned to Science, Science subtly nodded to one of his soldiers, and the reaction was violent. Science immediately threw a plastic bag over Zack's head, and one of his goons repeated the same action with O'Malley. The twins fought wildly for their survival, trying not to suffocate, and they were strong—not going down without a fight. But a cattle prod was shoved against their necks, jolting the two men's struggle—their animalistic battle. Finally, they dropped . . . and their suffering had only just begun. As the plastic bag was suffocating them over their heads, their brains were bashed in with a metal rod. Therefore, the plastic bags became heavy and polluted with blood and gore.

"What the fuck, Science!" Ray cried out. "What the fuck did you do?"

"Fuck 'em. It had to be done. I can't take that chance at them coming at us," Science uttered.

"You know they gonna have peoples looking for them . . . You know what you just started?"

"Listen, I ain't worried about that. And besides, they won't be found; I'll make sure of that," said Science. "And far as we know, they came and collected their money and left here all in one piece."

Ray looked skeptical. The Douglas brothers had connections with a fierce organization called the Black Hand. They were respected, feared, and valued. Ray felt that Science's paranoid actions had targeted them and doomed them.

"It's business, Ray. You know how that goes," Science proclaimed coolly.

CHAPTER TWENTY-FIVE

TIP HAD HIS hands placed safely on the hood of the unmarked police car as the plainclothes detective went rummaging through his pocket. It was a routine stop and frisk on Brooklyn Street, an action Tip thought was illegal. He grimaced as the detective roughly patted him down and turned his pockets inside out.

"Yo, what the fuck is this about, Officer? Y'all know y'all are violating my rights, right?" he griped. "Man, I can sue y'all fo' this shit. I ain't got shit on me. I ain't do shit!"

The detective ignored his grievance and continued violating his rights. Two other detectives stood on the side, watching their partner work. Tip was a powerful and intimidating-looking man. They were ready for him to take things left—make a simple procedure go completely wrong. They were itching for it, for him to fuck up because it would give them a reason to arrest him. Their hands were placed slightly against their holstered weapons, skillfully poised for the unexpected. But Tip was no fool, and he was clean.

"He's good," said the pasty-looking detective with blond hair to his two partners.

"I told y'all fools, I ain't got shit on me," said Tip.

"Still, someone wants to talk to you down at the precinct."

"Fo' what . . .?"

"Not our business; just get in the car," said the detective in a demanding tone.

Tip knew that he didn't have a choice. The look the detectives gave him said it clearly: we can do this the easy way or the hard way. And it looked like they were yearning to do it the hard way. Tip relented and climbed into the backseat of the unmarked Dodge Charger. He scowled and remained silent. If he was nervous, it didn't show.

Danny Greene got the call from the street detectives that they had Tip in the backseat of their car, and they were bringing him to the precinct. Danny was delighted. He needed to have a profound talk with Tip for two reasons: one, he wanted to try to save his life, and two, he'd looked into the rape of a young girl named Kizzie, and he was appalled at what he heard and saw. So, Danny visited Emily Paul from the Special Victims Unit. Emily was the detective investigating the brutal beating and rape of the young girl.

"She refuses to give up her attackers," Emily had said about Kizzie. "But this is not uncommon with rape and assault victims. They want to forget what has happened to them and move on from it. And a lengthy trial is a nightmare to go through, for them to relive it all over again."

Danny was listening.

"Often, the most compelling evidence comes from the testimony of the victims, who sit at the witness stand in a courtroom filled with strangers and describe the horrors they endured. And sometimes, it will be in excruciating detail. Kizzie didn't want to experience that. But I believe that it also was something else with her. Fear, maybe, but it felt like she was protecting someone because of that fear. And we can't force a victim in a sex case to testify."

Danny saw the pictures of Kizzie, and they were unspeakable. Emily explained to him what she'd had gone through—what she had suffered.

"She was a virgin when it happened," she had mentioned. "And she might not be able to have kids in the future."

"Was there any DNA . . . semen, hairs, any kind of fibers found on her?" Danny had asked.

"Her body reeked of it. Her attackers didn't use condoms, and we found some skin underneath her fingernails, and they were a match to a . . ."

"Brice," Danny answered for her.

"Correct."

"But without her testimony and cooperation, it was hard to proceed with the case. And then there was the sudden demise of our suspect, or suspects."

They continued to talk, and Danny took in the information given to him wholeheartedly. Emily Paul finished with, "As I said, it becomes a he-said-she-said situation. And when our victim wants to move forward and move on, there's nothing in the law that says a victim must testify."

Danny took a deep breath and readied himself for a one-on-one talk with Tip. He was in the interrogation room alone. He wasn't under arrest, and he wasn't handcuffed. Danny wanted to talk. He valued information.

He opened the door to the interrogation room, slid inside with purpose carrying a tan folder, and immediately shot his attention to Tip. The man was physically built—powerful looking, solid, and assertive. He sat upright in the metal chair, leaned forward with his elbows on the table, looking attentive to his situation. Danny sat opposite him across the table and placed the tan folder in the center. Tip wasn't curious about what the contents were inside.

"Why I'm here?" Tip asked.

"First, let me introduce myself. I'm Detective Danny Greene. I work homicide, and I want to thank you for coming in to talk with me," Danny politely spoke.

"Like I had a choice. And homicide, I ain't kill nobody," Tip replied.

"I just want to have a word with you, Tip . . . Is that what they call you?"

"Yeah."

"You're not under arrest or anything . . ." said Danny.

"So, I should just get up and walk the fuck outta that door right now, right?"

"It's your choice, but I advise you not to."

Tip scoffed. "Man, what the fuck you think I'm gonna tell you if I'm not under arrest? And I ain't no snitch!"

"Nobody is asking you to tell on anyone. In fact, I brought you in here to save your life."

Confused, Tip replied, "What the fuck you talkin' about?"

"C'mon, Tip, you have to know by now that your life is in danger," Danny said, then paused. He wanted to see Tip's reaction. But instead, the man continued to sit there coolly, undaunted by his words.

"I'm good, man. I ain't got no worries out there. These are my streets."

"Are you sure about that?" replied Danny. He then opened the folder to reveal and spill the 8x10 glossy photos across the table—for Tip to see with his own two eyes.

"What's this?" asked Tip.

The table had become inundated with gruesome crime scene photos—nearly a dozen. In the pictures were men he knew—friends Brice, Chuck, and Mo. Their bodies were riddled with gunshot wounds, blood, and their frames and faces were contorted in death. They had horror manifested across their faces. Each one was unsightly and horrible.

"What the fuck you showin' me these for, man?" Tip griped.

"I need you to see what's happening out there . . . the kind of fate your friends suffered. You're the only one left, Tip. Someone is after you. And by the look of these photos, that someone is very angry with you. So, can you explain why you and your friends have a target on your back?"

"Man, I don't fuckin' know!" he exclaimed.

"Are you sure about that?"

"Like I said, I don't' fuckin' know a damn thing!"

Danny exhaled sharply, and he kept calm. He had more to show him. He reached into the tanned folder again and removed a set of different pictures and placed them in front of Tip to see. Danny sat there and keenly observed Tip's reaction to the photos. Photos of Kizzie's beaten and battered face. Images taken after her horrifying rape, a rape Danny knew Tip took part in. He glanced at the pictures, and he didn't flinch.

"I don't know that bitch," he protested.

"Are you sure about that? Her name is Kizzie. Good girl . . . churchgoing, educated, and smart girl. And she was a virgin until you and your friends brutally beat and raped her and destroyed her chances of having any kids or a normal relationship with someone. And how long do you think it will take for whoever found them to find you soon too? So, tell me the truth. Who did y'all piss off? Who's connected to her? Does she have a brother, a cousin?" asked Danny seriously but calmly.

"Like I fuckin' told you before, I don't know that bitch, and I don't fuckin' know what the fuck you talkin' 'bout. I ain't lay one fuckin' hand on that girl," Tip argued.

Danny wasn't about to expose his frustration to Tip. He mastered self-reliance and patience. He exhaled. Tip was stubborn or naïve, maybe both.

"Stubbornness and stupidity are twins," Danny uttered.

"What . . .?" Tip replied.

"Exactly."

"I'm not under arrest, right?" asked Tip.

"No. You're not," he admitted.

"Good! Cuz I've had enough of this shit! Been in here fo' too fuckin' long, and I hate the fuckin' stench of a pig on me," said Tip sneeringly, standing up abruptly.

Danny remained seated, his eyes on Tip moving toward the door, relentless and stubborn to the threat on his life.

"You walk out that door, and I promise you, I'm gonna have your 8x10 glossy photo displayed on this table soon," Danny warned him.

"I'll take my chances," Tip replied gruffly.

Tip continued to scoff at the detective and exited the interrogation room. Danny huffed. He was disappointed, but Tip wasn't his only choice. He had other tricks up his sleeve to try to solve this case and track down his shooter. His next move on the chessboard was to visit Kizzie. He had her address, and now it was time to see her and put the pieces together. And one thing he wanted to solve was the mystery of the gun—the .357, and the chaos it was leaving behind . . . contorted bodies in the morgue with charred organs and missing bullets from autopsies.

CHAPTER TWENTY-SIX

"I SAY GOD IS good! God is good!" Pastor Richard Morgan shouted out joyfully to his congregation. "I'm gonna repeat it; God is good!"

"All the time!" the congregation hollered with a corresponding and harmonizing response.

"Repeat it, repeat it; God is good!"

"All the time!" they shouted.

Pastor Morgan marched around on the platform in his long black and blue clergy robe. He was glistening with joy. He was jubilant with praise, and he was preaching triumphantly.

"There's triumphant in this place tonight! Do y'all hear me . . . TRIUMPHANT!" he shouted.

The congregation agreed, and it was a packed house. The most packed the church had ever been. Nearly all the pews were filled with people early Sunday morning.

"And that triumphant can only come because of God's doing! God is the way. He is the provider, the healer, the ultimate, and the definitive!" continued the pastor.

He put a little extra pep in his step, jumped down from the platform, and came closer to his congregation. The choir, which was few, stood behind him with equivalent praise and joy. They were ready to break out into a praiseworthy song. They were prepared to sing like they were on the show *American Idol.*

"I'm excited this morning. You all wanna know why I'm excited this morning?" said the pastor.

"Tell us why you're excited, Pastor," someone shouted from a pew. "Tell us!"

"Oh, I'm going to tell you why I'm excited this morning. Because there's proof of God's love, God's healing, and one of God's miracles inside this church this morning," he exclaimed with vigor. "Oh yes, there is. God is good!"

He continued to prance around in front of the congregation, clapping his hands and stomping his feet. He continued to preach and spread joy. And then he stopped and stared at her . . . stared at Kizzie seated in the front pew with her grandmother.

"I'm excited because we have Kizzie here this beautiful Sunday morning. This is God's angel right here. God has brought her through the valley of the shadow of death and delivered her back to us this beautiful Sunday morning. He delivered her from such a tragic experience," Pastor Morgan hollered. "And Kizzie is living proof that God is good and that God can bring us through anything . . . any bad experience, any pain, and tribulation. With Him and His love, there are no worries, no forever pain, but there is Triumph and Victory!"

"Amen! Amen!"

"Preach, Pastor! Preach!" someone else shouted.

"Let us all stand to our feet and give her a huge welcoming applause and praise for her strength," said the pastor.

Kizzie sat there with a slight smile while Pastor Morgan placed her in the spotlight. But while everyone stood to their feet to give her worthy applauds to welcome her return, she sat there aloofly. She seemed strong, but inside, she felt fragile. The nightmares were happening to her almost every night. And she couldn't stop thinking about Omar and his dramatic change—the predicament he was in.

There was a roar of jubilance surrounding Kizzie. Her grandmother took her hand into hers and squeezed gently, giving her comfort and support. And as the applauding and praise continued, Kizzie felt overwhelmed by the response. It was a reaction she didn't expect or want.

"Kizzie, come on up here and give us a few words . . . some words of encouragement," said the pastor. "Give us your testimony."

Kizzie hesitated. *Oh no*, she thought. She wasn't up for it. She wanted to remain seated and listen to the sermon, hear the choir sing, and praise Him—God Almighty. But now, she'd become the center of attention.

"C'mon, Kizzie, come up here and say a few words," Pastor Morgan continued to press.

Kizzie glanced at her grandmother, who had a confident smile plastered across her face. She continued to hold her granddaughter's hand in hers. Then, finally, she nodded, the slight nod and smile saying to Kizzie, *Go ahead, chile, give your testimony. Speak.*

Kizzie slowly stood up and walked toward the platform. She was nervous. She turned around and gazed at the sea of faces looking at her. Each face was smiling at her, admiring her, and wanting to feel encouraged by her words. And for a moment, Kizzie stood there in silence—nervous. She wanted God to give her the strength to say something—*anything*. But there was nothing to say. They were waiting, anticipating some grand speech from her, but there were more moments of silence. Pastor Morgan kept his eyes on her, not wanting to feel embarrassed by bringing her up not to say anything special.

Maybe it was too soon to bring her up to speak.

Kizzie grabbed the microphone gingerly, looked at the faces staring at her, and the only thing she could say to them was, "God is good."

That was it. There was nothing else, no magnificent and majestic speech of survival and God's grace, and whatever else they expected from her. They weren't there. They had no idea what she'd experienced and the nightmares spinning around in her head. And then there was Omar; Kizzie couldn't stop worrying about her best friend.

So, all she could say to them was *God is good.*

She removed herself from the attention and went to sit back down with her grandmother. Pastor Morgan stood there fleetingly in awe and question. But the show must go on. He returned to the podium and worked his charm and grace, repeating Kizzie's words, "Yes. Yes, He is. God is good. Thank you for that, Kizzie, because God is good. He is magnificent!"

And just like that, the attention shifted from Kizzie back to the pastor and his words. Kizzie sighed. Once again, her grandmother took her hand and gently squeezed and smiled at her, giving Kizzie the comfort and support she needed.

After the sermon, Kizzie remained seated in the pew, looking pensive. Her grandmother was conversing with an old friend. And folks were piling out of the building on a sunny Sunday afternoon. The pastor was chatting with a few folks when his eyes turned Kizzie's way, noticing she was still seated and not looking like her old self. He excused himself from the conversation with the ladies and walked toward Kizzie with a look of concern. He sat beside her and asked, "Is everything okay with you, Kizzie?"

She puffed out; her worries manifested.

"I need to talk to you, Pastor. It's important," she replied.

"Of course. We can talk in my office. Can you give me ten minutes? Meet me there."

She nodded. The pastor stood and approached another group of ladies waiting to speak with him. Kizzie stood up behind him and went to her grandmother to tell her she would meet her at home; she needed to talk to the pastor. Her grandmother understood but showed some concern.

"Are you sure you'll be okay to walk home by yourself?"

"Yes, Grandma. I'll be okay. It's Sunday afternoon, right?" she even joked. "Besides, I need to start getting out more and get my life back on track."

Her grandmother smiled. They were words she wanted to hear. "Yes, Lord, that is great to hear. You are a strong woman, Kizzie."

Kizzie turned and walked away while her grandmother's eyes remained on her. She watched Kizzie disappear through the brown rear door leading to a short, narrow hallway to the pastor's office.

The office door opened slowly, with Kizzie poking her head inside and announcing, "Hello?" No answer. She entered the office. It was small and warm, with a sea-green carpet and a dark walnut bookcase lining the entire right-hand wall. Books were piled everywhere. The place was cluttered with the detritus of university degrees from various colleges signifying his esteemed education and intelligence. Manila folders sat on top of an old, dark desk, where a Dell laptop stood in the corner of his desk.

Kizzie sat in an old armed chair at the desk and waited. Hanging on the wall behind the pastor's old leather-armed chair was a framed saying, *"Faith isn't believing that God can. It's believing that God will."*

Her attention remained on the saying for a moment, and then it was interrupted by the pastor entering the office.

He immediately sat in his chair behind his desk and smiled at Kizzie. Then right away, he said to her, "I'm glad you're back, Kizzie. And I'm sorry if I pushed you up there during the service earlier. I didn't intend to force you to do something you weren't ready for. Godspeed, right?"

She managed to grin. "It's good to be back. But it's fine, Pastor. I know everyone's excited to see me again."

"We are," he said. "So, what is it that you needed to talk to me about that's important?" he asked.

A heartrending look took place on Kizzie's face right away. Pastor Morgan picked up on it and said, "You can talk to me about anything, Kizzie. It's why I'm here."

She sighed deeply, her eyes diverting from his gaze. How could she explain it to him—the situation?

"It's Omar . . . Something is going on with him, Pastor Morgan. He's changed, I mean, really changed for the worst," she said.

"You know he's been on my mind lately. He doesn't come to church anymore."

"You need to go see him."

"I plan to."

"I mean, you need to go see him *right now*, Pastor. It's serious. I think . . ." she paused, not wanting to say it or didn't know how to say it without it sounding crazy—the unthinkable because it was something you only see in the movies. But she huffed and continued. "I think he might be possessed."

The statement didn't make the pastor flinch. Instead, he sat there coolly, focusing on Kizzie and taking in what she had just said to him in disregard—possessed!

"That's a powerful statement, Kizzie, to say about Omar," he said.

"You haven't seen him lately, Pastor. He's becoming terrifying."

"And what proof do you have to believe he's possessed?"

She wanted to tell him about the murders, but there wasn't any evidence of him committing them. And he didn't honestly confess to her. Instead, she remembered him shouting, "*There's your fuckin' truth, Kizzie.*" And he shoved her out of the way. So, it was hard for her to explain everything. But she believed that the only person she could turn to with such damaging revelations was her pastor.

"For someone to be possessed, do you understand how strong of an accusation that is, Kizzie?"

"Yes."

"I'm no expert on the subject, and I can't execute an exorcism on someone even if he might be possessed," he said. "That is way out of my league, Kizzie."

"He needs help, Pastor. I'm afraid something is going to happen to him . . . something bad," Kizzie cried out.

"Listen, I'll go by to see him soon."

"It *needs* to be soon, Pastor Morgan, before it's too late."

"I promise, Kizzie. I'll visit him. I will place it on the top of my to-do list."

She nodded, feeling he was going to keep his promise. But the look on her face was still depressing. She was worried, and it showed.

She spent fifteen minutes in the pastor's office talking. The day was growing late, and Kizzie knew she needed to get home soon. She didn't want her grandmother to worry about her. She was still healing and mending from her wounds.

"Thank you for seeing me, Pastor," she spoke politely.

"Anytime, Kizzie. My door is always open for you," he returned wholeheartedly.

She stood and made her exit from his office. The church was now empty and quiet—a bit too quiet for her. She found herself alone, and suddenly it started to look like a long walk from the church to her home. She hadn't made that walk since the night it happened—that incident that gave her nightmares. The pastor was still in his office conducting business, and she didn't want to bother him with her worries. He'd given her enough of his time, she felt.

Kizzie stood in the foyer looking apprehensive until she heard Deacon Fry say, "C'mon, Kizzie, let an old man like myself accompany you home. And I won't be taking no for an answer this time."

He extended his arm to her, indicating for her to grab it and attach herself to him. She smiled. She was delighted. She took hold of him, and they left the church together.

CHAPTER TWENTY-SEVEN

DETECTIVE FOSTER CLIMBED out of his black Cadillac Deville with the lit cigarette in his hand. He exhaled sharply and then took one last pull from it. The nicotine was needed like always. Then he flicked it away and waited in the designated area in Brooklyn—near a park in Dyker Heights. It was a chilly and cloudy night, with the stars in the sky becoming nonexistent. The sky was blanketed with gray, hiding the full moon in its grandeur behind them. He was early, as always, and he was patient. He leaned against his Cadillac and observed the area.

Dyker Heights was an affluent residential neighborhood in the southwest corner of Brooklyn. The area had a suburban character with detached and semidetached one- and two-family homes, many of which had driveways and private yards, tree-lined streets, and very few apartment buildings. It was a direct contrast from Brownsville, Brooklyn—day and night. Here, residents could breathe and live their lives generously and without restraints. They weren't crowded with violence and bloodshed. But unfortunately, there was a war raging in the Ville. One that if it happened in a peachy neighborhood like Dyker Heights, where there was so much blood being spilled on the streets that it could drown a city, then there would have been martial law in the streets and considered a state of emergency. But Bunk knew that the lives in the Ville were expendable—disposable.

He'd been a detective for many years and a cop for even longer. And he had seen the good, the bad, and the ugly, and now he was witnessing the unthinkable. Shit in Mexico was currently happening in his city—*his* borough. The other day, they'd found a body swinging from a light pole—a modern-day lynching. How the fuck it got up there without anyone seeing the action baffled Bunk. The body had been severely tortured and mangled; a young Black male met a gruesome fate. His death made the headlines—front-page news, bringing more negative attention to the neighborhood and his precinct. It wasn't good. Killings and negative press and attention meant harsh backlash from the superiors. Yeah, it was dominantly Black and impoverished, and Black lives didn't matter to many politicians and developers. But when the homicide rate starts rocketing in specific regions and soon reaches the stratosphere, creating a bad light on the city itself, that's when they want to wake up and notice, and that's when they want to step in and do something about it when the crime rate starts infecting the city's currency and its reputation.

Bunk knew it was only a matter of time before the bubble would burst. Black men were dying—young Black men, but when the violence started to spill onto the innocent and into affluent neighborhoods, *that's* when shit hit the fan.

Five minutes passed when Bunk noticed the black-on-black Range Rover with tinted windows on black 23-inch rims approaching. He could hear rap music blaring. He knew it was them. He stood up from leaning against his Cadillac and waited for it to stop. When it got near him, the back-passenger window came rolling down and becoming visible like he was some Mafia Don was Anton. He stared at Bunk and said, "Get in. Let's go for a ride."

Bunk walked to the other side and slid into the backseat to join Anton. The interior was luxury at its finest, with brown leather seats, a moon roof, and the latest amenities. Anton's leg was still in a brace, but he now walked with a cane instead of crutches.

"I had surgery on my leg the other day," Anton told Bunk. "Muthafuckas keep cutting and ripping away at my shit like I'm some science project."

"I see you're getting better," said Bunk.

"Better . . . Nigga, this ain't better; this is weak," he griped.

"Listen, I ain't for the small talk and this damn ride along, Anton. You know that? What the fuck do you want from me?" Bunk asked with impatience.

"You know that nigga they found hanging from the light pole the other night? That was my little cousin," Anton said.

"Sorry to hear about that."

"Why they do him like that? I don't know if it was Science or Kenya's doing. My cousin was like a little brother to me. I raised that boy from when he was eight. He was only eighteen, and they did him like that," Anton spoke with profound grief.

He paused momentarily, trying to hold back his grief, tears, and emotions.

"That's the game, though, right? What they call collateral damage," Anton continued. "But fuck that. I'm tired of these fools, Bunk. So, how much?"

"What . . .?" Bunk replied, looking baffled by the question. "How much what?"

"Everyone has a price, and I know you have yours. I want everyone involved in my cousin's death, every fuckin' rival—anyone that looked at me wrong—dead. And I know you're the man capable of that, Detective Foster. You have the resources and other dirty and corrupt cops at your beck and call. So just name your price to get it done, and I'll pay it," said Anton with gravity.

"And I need this done now, not later. So whatever shit you doin' now, cut that shit, cuz this is important."

Bunk scoffed at the offer.

"You find something funny, Detective?" Anton griped.

"Yeah, I do. I ain't your fuckin' personal security service, or one of your fuckin' hit men on your damn payroll, Anton. Yeah, I'll take your money to provide a service, but I'm not one of your bitches, so don't ever disrespect me like that again," Bunk retorted.

Anton chuckled. "Nigga, you became one of my bitches when you took money from me. So don't get this shit twisted. We in this together . . . till death do us part."

"That's a threat to me, Anton?"

"You know I don't make threats, Detective; I make promises," he replied.

"Listen, you ignorant fuck. I've been around a long fuckin' time and done seen piss-shit niggas like you come and go . . . and you keep fuckin' around with me, you might just come and go real soon, *capeesh*?" Bunk promised him with gusto. "Now, I know you're emotional about your little cousin's death, but that will pass, and it will soon be back to business. Remember that. Business, what you got with me and on these streets. You fuck that up, and I'll fuck you up!"

Anton seethed. "It ain't gonna be much business if niggas keep coming at me like this."

"You're right; the murders are too much, Anton . . . creating negative attention and attracting too much attention, and business will go down."

"It's why we need to get a handle on this shit, Detective. Science and Kenya, the longer they stay breathing, the more money I lose . . . *we* lose, and this ain't gonna get nothin' but worse."

"Why the reason you need to let go of this personal vendetta with the man that shot you and not go looking for this gun," said Bunk.

"Nah. Fuck that. That bounty is still active on that muthafucka, and I still want that gun."

"You're stubborn, Anton. You know that?"

"The reason why I'm here today," he countered.

"As I told you before, I hope to be playing for the winning team," said Bunk.

"You're my Jordan, Detective," Anton smiled. "You make wins happen no matter what obstacles are put before you, right?"

Detective Foster gave him a glaring look and departed from the Range Rover. The vehicle drove off, and he stood there lost in thought—what next? The money coming from Anton was good. He was putting it to good use, his early retirement. But he was becoming sick of the badge and the gun every day. The bodies piling up . . . the stench of murder victims always upon him. The menace inside the urban communities spread uncontrollably like a virus and a wildfire and became overwhelming. He wondered, *Is it worth it?*

The Ville was on a one-way trip to hell—the community was on fire with violence and plagued with gangs and drugs. Bunk wanted to get paid, get rich, and get as far away from the Ville and Brooklyn as possible. Maybe go west after his retirement and live in an affluent and gated community. And buy a boat. He could spend his days fishing and his nights drinking beers and watching old western flicks. And the animals could keep killing each other. It was their nature, he felt. They would continue tearing each other apart over drugs and property they didn't own, making Black mothers cry. After that, he planned on it not being his problem anymore. Bunk felt he'd done his part to make the streets safe again, but it was inevitable: animals were meant to be animals. And it was their nature to be violent, and being a homicide detective in a vile place like Brownsville was an uphill and unwinnable battle.

Though it started as a discouraging task and an uphill investigation, Detective Greene felt that he was finally making some headway in the murder investigation of Brice and the others. He stood tall and valiantly in front of the towering Tilden Houses Project with his badge and gun showing dazzlingly, indicating to all around him who he was.

The community was bustling with activity, with the blazing sun gradually descending. Nearing the horizon, it burned the sky a gorgeous and powerful mix of amber and bloodred. A gentle breeze made the leaves rustle in a rhythm, blending with the urban noise. It was a time of day that seemed magical. It was a beautiful day with a looming change of seasons after a violent and bloody summer.

Greene approached the towering building that soared into the sky like a beast. The locals were out and about, shooting him quick looks that didn't welcome his presence in the area—a cop—thy enemy. Ironic when the community was held hostage by killings and violence coming from the gangs and drug dealers. Some innocent folks were being sucked into the tragedy of urban warfare. But Greene ignored their foul looks and kept walking with an air of confidence and dominance about him.

He entered the dilapidated-looking lobby with trash spewed about and gang graffiti decorating the walls. It was a sour atmosphere, with two fiends, a man, and a woman, exiting the stairwell with high and higher written on their faces. It was apparent they had just finished shooting up. They shot an awkward look at Greene with his dark suit and the badge and gun on his hip, and he shot a stern look of authority their way. His face made them nervous, and they quickly directed their attention away from his and hurried out of the lobby. A cop to them was bad news.

Detective Greene shook his head with displeasure, sad to see such young life wasted on drugs and foolishness. But he wasn't there for them or any drugs. He was there to visit Kizzie. He knew her address and didn't want to waste another day without getting her statement. He pushed for the elevator to descend where he stood and waited. He would be alone this visit. His partner Foster had other business to attend to, and it was apparent to Greene that Foster wasn't too keen on investigating Brice's murder.

"Waste of time and energy on that asshole," Foster kept reminding him.

But it wasn't a waste of time to Greene. It was his job. He was focused and determined when it felt like extreme chaos around him—fire and brimstone. It was about the job and profession they'd signed up for, not the victim and their background.

Danny Greene exhaled as the elevator ascended toward the desired floor. Alone, quiet, he had a lot to think about. Visiting Kizzie unannounced was a risk because she was a rape victim, and he didn't want to trigger anything with her with questions about the incident. Nevertheless, he proceeded, understanding that she was in a delicate situation.

Before he knocked on her door, he took a deep breath. This was a critical moment for him; he knew it deeply. He knocked and waited. And then he heard, "Who is it?" The voice sounded older, elderly—her grandmother.

"Hello, ma'am, I'm Detective Danny Greene, and I would like to have a few words with your granddaughter," he announced himself politely.

"Detective . . .?" the grandmother uttered with some bewilderment.

"Homicide," he made clear.

Now she was utterly baffled. She opened the door slightly with the security chain still attached to it. The two got a good look at each other, and it was clear that he was a cop—nicely dressed and a handsome detective. The grandmother even smiled at him; his presence felt kind and gentle.

"I'm sorry to bother you, but I wanted to know if I could have a few words with your granddaughter."

"Why does a homicide detective want to speak to my granddaughter?"

"It's . . . It's somewhat complicated."

"So, make it uncomplicated, Detective," she countered. "My granddaughter has been through a lot, and there's no rational explanation for the murder police to come visit her."

"I understand, ma'am. But I believe her unfortunate incident has crossed over into my world," he said.

"How . . .?"

He sighed slightly, trying to find the right words to explain it to her. "I'm investigating the murder of a Brice—"

"I know who he is," she interrupted him agitatedly. "I don't want to hear that boy's name, Detective."

"I understand. But as you know, he was murdered a few weeks back."

"And this involves Kizzie how? So, you think my granddaughter had something to do with that boy's death?"

"No . . . not directly."

Baffled, she replied, "Not directly?"

"There's been a string of killings lately, each one involving the men that allegedly raped your granddaughter—"

"Allegedly!" she exclaimed. "No, there's nothing *allegedly* about it; they raped my granddaughter, Detective—almost killed her. She's been through a lot these past few weeks. And she's just now starting to leave the apartment to get her life back. So now you want to come knock on my door and interrogate her after what she's been through?"

"No. Not interrogate, ma'am. I simply want to ask her a few questions," he replied sympathetically.

"Well, I don't think that's a good idea," the grandmother disputed.

"It's okay, Grandma," the detective heard someone say from behind the door. "I can talk to him."

"You sure?" she asked Kizzie.

"Yes."

The grandmother unhooked the security chain, opened the door wider, and stepped to the side, revealing Kizzie standing behind her. Detective Greene gazed at her with purity and nearly in awe. She was beautiful and strong, knowing what she'd been through, yet still standing and trying to put the pieces back together in her life.

"I'm Kizzie," she spoke humbly.

He smiled at her. "Hello, I'm Detective—"

"I know your name," she chimed. "But I don't believe I can be much of any help to you."

"You never know, Kizzie. I just need you to answer a few questions, and I'll be on my way. But first of all, I'm terribly sorry about what happened to you. It's tragic, and if you need anything from me, all you need to do is ask."

"I'm fine. What do you want to know?"

He was on the right track so far. Kizzie remained standing at the threshold of the doorway with her arms folded across her chest—a protective or defensive posture. She seemed strong and willing, but he knew not to push things with her.

He started by asking her, "Why did you refuse to cooperate with the detectives handling your case? Were you threatened?"

"I already told that lady detective with that unit. I don't want to talk about it," she replied harshly.

"Okay. Are you aware of any enemies that your attackers might have had?"

"No. Why?"

"It's just a formal question," he replied. "And do you have any close friends?"

"No, Detective," she lied.

He knew she was an only child; both parents were gone, and her grandmother had been raising her since she was young.

While he asked his questions, her grandmother stood closely behind her and observed. Kizzie was doing well handling herself. Detective Greene continued to ask a few questions, nothing complicated or challenging. Kizzie's response to them was straightforward and minimal. She didn't know anything, and she wasn't involved with anything. She had no information on who would want to implement revenge on her behalf. She didn't associate with any known criminals or thugs. As the report said, she was a churchgoing, God-fearing Christian attending college and working hard—but now trying to recuperate from her incident. She was the epitome of a square—a good girl, and not even a tragedy like rape polluted her image.

"Well, I thank you for your time, and I'm sorry for the inconvenience," he said ever so politely.

"You're welcome," Kizzie responded.

Nothing in her character or nature suggested to the detective any wrongdoing. Her body language was accurate, showing nothing suspicious. He smiled and turned to leave. Then with an afterthought, he turned back to ask her, "And about your neighbors? Are you close with any of them? Would anyone of them implement revenge because of what happened to you?"

Then he saw it, a slight hesitation on her part—maybe a thought who. She knew someone. To the subtle eye, it was noticeable; her mind fleetingly shifted to someone of interest—a suspect.

"No, Detective," she lied.

His intuition told him she was lying, but he couldn't pursue it further. But he knew she was lying about that question. Moreover, her body language changed subtly after he asked her that question.

"Okay, and once again, thank you for your time," he said, finally leaving.

He took the stairs to the lobby and exited the stairwell when his cell phone rang. It was a call he needed to take. Answering the phone on his way out of the lobby, he accidentally bumped into a young, hooded male entering the building.

"Pardon me," said Greene to the male.

The young male showed no response or anything; he was cold and detached, moving mechanically. Greene stopped gawkily and stared at the male for some strange reason. There was something about him that seemed off—strangely off. He watched him disappear into the stairwell, and Greene wondered what floor he was going to.

Did Kizzie know him?

"You still there, Greene," said the caller on the other end, interrupting Greene's concentration.

"Yeah, I'm here."

"Unfortunately, I lost sight of him," said the caller.

"How . . .?"

"He moves around a lot, goes into places where I would stand out."

Greene sighed heavily. "It's okay. You did your best. Where did you lose him?"

"Some underground club in Bushwick."

"Okay. Thanks. Appreciate the favor."

"No problem."

Their call ended. Greene had called in a favor to a private detective to follow Tip around town and snap pictures of his comings and goings. Unfortunately, the captain and the department were against applying the extra manpower and the hours to follow a local thug. So, Greene decided to take matters into his own hands, and he called in a favor to a friend for help. He predicted that Tip was a man living on borrowed time, and he was a man with a habit. So, it was only a matter of time before this killer came after him—to finish what he'd started. Unfortunately for Greene, his private investigator was a middle-aged white male, limiting him from entering certain places in the urban/Black community without raising suspicion.

CHAPTER TWENTY-EIGHT

You can't hide from who you are
The light peels back the dark
You can run, but you won't make it far . . .

IT WAS THE lyrics to "When the Truth Hunts You Down" by Sam Tinnesz. Omar sat in his dark bedroom with music playing from a small radio. With the .357 Magnum placed on the bed next to him, the souls of its victims trapped in the weapon like small prey in the jaws of a giant snake, he could feel his body heating up. It felt like he was on fire inside, like the blazing sun beating inside his chest. The air around him felt stale, and he was sweating profusely. The darkness, the lust, and the sexual affair with Malaka were becoming comforting and encouraging. Omar was nearly naked, in his boxers, his scarred body thin and looking sickly. Yet, he had never felt so powerful and wanted. His body was ravaged with such a desire for it—for her—that he rarely ate, and he became highly antisocial. He didn't want to feel any completion or end with the entity. He wanted it to last forever.

The entity, the blackness, was perfect—a visual desire that gave revered awe. Omar's mind became plagued to appease it. He wanted to feed it with what it truly desired, become alive and complete via the deaths of others, and Omar's rage and vendetta were the perfect feeding source. His hatred for them—his bullies, society, the weak; his core for vengeance was strong. It was exponentially connecting with Omar that it hadn't done with others. Its unity with the individual was exceptional but came with a grave cost, unbeknownst to Omar.

It felt like his skin was on fire. He removed his boxers, quickly walked to the bathroom and turned on the cold water in the bathtub. He didn't let it fill up entirely until he jumped in to cool off, to soothe the burning sensation overcoming him. He submerged himself at eye level into the cold water, a cold and dark abyss. He became silent and still, and his breathing became shallow. Silence and darkness were present. It was the kind of dark that encouraged him to fall asleep when he closed his eyes. There was the simple sweetness of existing, being, and breathing with his eyes closed—something limitless. He had blocked out the light, the noise—and he had long lost that feeling of being inadequate and vulnerable.

With his eyes still closed, he submerged himself underwater.

When he opened his eyes, Omar found himself in dystopia, a hellish world in which everything was imperfect, and absolute chaos and slaughter reigned. Everything had gone wrong. It was a nightmarish world where the souls of the weak and damn were being devoured and tortured. Everything was ablaze, smoldering debris and dark, billowing smoke reaching the sky. And rubble and destruction were sprawled for miles, along with thousands of rotten and decaying corpses—men and women completely ripped apart. The sky was black; the stench of death and rotten flesh was so overwhelming that it was vile and revolting. Souls and meat were being subjected to castigatory suffering. And there was even twisted perversion and sexual debauchery happening with the bodies—demonic creatures were having violent sex with men and women. At the same time, their ravenous, sharp fangs tore into their covering and flesh with malice. One foul-looking creature with a hairy humpback, bonelike fingers, and a long snout chewed on a man's genitals.

Omar found himself roaming in this nightmarish world. He was naked and cold, but surprisingly, he wasn't afraid. Loud, catastrophic screaming that seemed perpetual and rustling noises, crackling, and crunching came from all directions. Materializing were hellish-looking creatures—creatures that were hungry and lustful and vicious. The more there were, the more screams he heard, and in those empty screams was the pain of the indifference. An overabundance of men and women were there, individuals who sold their souls for wealth, ease, and power and instead, found hell.

He continued to walk farther into the dark and frightening abyss and suddenly stopped. He took one look at it—at her—and recognized this terrifying creature that locked eyes with him from a short distance. Underneath it, with its legs straddled around a tortured being, was a naked man being ripped apart and eaten alive by it. It had been gnawing at the head as a child nibbled at cotton candy. It was Malaka in her proper form—vicious, evil, and scary. It stared at Omar with its glaring red eyes and mouth caked with the man's blood and fleshy tissue. She had pointed ears, bony, scaly claws and scaly skin, a long tail, and half-cleft feet. It also had a giant wingspan, and it looked at Omar. It suddenly altered its position, crouching. And it studied Omar as if it might drop its present feast and seek a juicer, fresher morsel at any moment.

This creature reeked of raw sewage and rotten fish and slowly advanced toward Omar. With each dawdling advance that belied the speed it was capable of, it growled at him with ferociousness. Omar stood there paralyzed by its fiery gaze. But then he snapped out of it and started to slowly back away from it. It lurched closer to him, and it seemed aggravated that its food was backing away. It thrashed its tail in a fury. Omar's heart beat thunderously inside his chest. He could sense her predatory approach and its excessive desire to attack and devour him. It wanted to completely rip him apart and consume his soft flesh with teeth that looked like they could tear through anything—bones, wood, lead. It didn't matter. Somehow, he knew that it wanted to become alive, and he would become the vessel for it. It needed a conduit to his realm, and he was it. His hatred, his revenge, insecurities, his yearning for strength, and the murders he committed were vigorously feeding this demonic being. It was ready to come into his world and feast as it did in this hellish abyss that Omar found himself trapped inside.

It pounced his way with terrifying speed, knocking him to the ground with a crackling thud, knocking the wind out of him. Then before it could feast on him, a bright flash happened, and his eyes instantly opened.

He was back—home, inside the tub, in a daze.

Though the water was meant to be cold, it heated up quickly like boiling water on a hot stove, the liquid simmering inside the tub with him in it. Intense steam started to rise from the tub like it was on fire, and it inundated the bathroom. Omar sat composedly, roasting slowly inside it and staring ahead pointlessly, his mind captured by something unseen. Soon, looming into his view, emerging from the steaming water on the opposite side of the bathtub, facing him, was Malaka. Again, she was in her human form, and her gaze was intense toward him. Menacing. Wet. Her dark skin glistened like sunshine, and her naked body was perfect. Enticingly, she stood up from the tub and stepped out of it. Omar's eyes were hooked on her. Though he remembered the images of her in the alternate realm/reality, the vile act she was implementing and attacking him, he was still fascinated and in awe over her. He still yearned for it.

He too stood up from the steaming tub naked and joined her near the door where she stood. Then with his attention fixed on her, he said, "You're beautiful."

She didn't respond; her eyes gazed into him like she was searching far beyond his mortal condition. She didn't just look at a man but looked into him as if she knew his desires. And then, without warning, she pulled him into a passionate and interlocking kiss—the kiss of death, a burning flame of their perverse love. Omar's entire body craved more. He was entirely under her seductive enchantment. He was outright aroused. When she pulled her mouth away from his, his lips quivered while her hands cornered both his sides. Her soulless eyes continued to stare at him.

"Please, I want you. I *need* you," he said with edginess.

Omar wanted to lie with it, and he wanted to be with her. He wanted to be inside of it. He wanted to feel pleasure and bliss—to orgasm inside of her like a flowing river. But it teased him. Tonight, it wouldn't give him the sexual desires that he craved.

"Bring me life," she spoke. "Complete me."

Omar nodded, understanding. "I will."

He could feel the tears stinging when it denied him what he desired. She was intoxicating. Her physical appearance was imposing. Omar knew he wasn't dreaming this time. She was real—or was she?

Under her enchantment, Omar stepped out of the bathroom and entered the bedroom to dress and grab the .357. He clutched the gun firmly, ready to put it to use once more, prepared to take someone's life, to feed the weapon of destruction, and appease Malaka's longing and hunger. The violence, the bloodshed . . . The more he killed with it for her, it gave her further supremacy and authority to cross from her hellish realm into his—to feed.

It was time to finish what he'd started.

Tip climbed out of the passenger seat of his friend's Dodge Challenger, putting a Hennessy bottle to his lips and taking a massive gulp.

"Damn, nigga, you gonna kill ya liver wit' that shit," said Fuzz, the driver of the Dodge. "But save me some, nigga."

"Nigga, you good," replied Tip. "We 'bout to go up in here and see some pussy and get shit poppin'." He handed Fuzz the fifth of Hennessy, and the two men walked toward the Purple Pussy strip club, an underground and known spot on Fulton Street.

It was a beautiful fall night. Summer had ended a week ago, and now it was an autumn breeze with changing leaves. The air was fresh but without a chill, and back to school for many kids. And though there had been a change of season, it was still the same in the Ville: a violent drug war and murders happening regularly like night and day.

Parked a block from the club, the two men talked and shared the fifth.

"I heard you got picked up by the police the other day," said Fuzz. "What the fuck was that about?"

"Niggas fishin', that's all. Tryin' to question me about some rape and talkin' 'bout saving my life."

Fuzz laughed. "Yeah, I heard sumthin' 'bout that a few months ago. Brice and y'all wildin' out like that. Miss my nigga, though."

"No doubt," Tip agreed. "I do too."

"Yo, fo' real, though, did y'all niggas really do that shit . . . rape and beat a church bitch like that?" Fuzz wanted to know. "And if so, was that pussy heavenly?" he joked.

Tip laughed. "Nigga . . . Yeah, we did that shit. I fucked that bitch last, though, and that pussy was still tight. Nigga, she made me come so lovely. You should have been there, my nigga; got you some of that good-good pure pussy too."

Fuzz laughed. "Y'all were some thirsty niggas."

"Pussy is pussy, no matter how you get it. But shit, we probably did that bitch a favor and showed her what some real dick feels like," Tip added.

The two men continued to talk and laugh. They were approaching the club entrance. Security searched both of them, and they paid the ten-dollar admission and entered their desirable paradise. Rap music blared throughout the club, the underground location where scantily clad women walked about flirting with men. The stage was occupied by a curvy stripper swinging around the pole with agility. Tip smiled. He was in his element—around some pussy.

"Yeah, yeah, I'm fucking something tonight," he said. "I'm gonna need two bitches tonight cuz I'm horny as fuck."

Fuzz laughed.

"You buying drinks, nigga?" asked Tip.

"You a broke-ass nigga up in here tryin' to get some free pussy and free drinks," said Fuzz.

Tip chuckled. "Fuck, yeah . . . Free pussy is the best pussy, or I might just rape a bitch again."

It was tasteless humor that both men found amusing. Fuzz replied, "I don't do sloppy seconds, especially if I'm buying."

"Nigga, I don't mind fuckin' last, as long as I'm fuckin'. Shit, I like to take my time in that pussy too, anyway."

Fuzz and Tip hit the bar and immediately ordered two shots of Patrón, two beers, and Fuzz opened up a tab. It would be their night to enjoy the scenery of appealing flesh and engage in some debauchery shit. The women were pretty, sexy, and lively—nearly a dozen doing what they needed to do for tips and cash. Tip downed his shot of Patrón and then gulped his beer like it was the last one left. He immediately ordered another one, and then his eyes danced around the room, gazing at every piece of ass in movement. He licked his lips, rubbed his crotch, and felt an erection brewing in his pants. He was ready to take one or two ladies home with him tonight—more like right now. Tip was known to be aggressive with women, and there was no such thing as "no" to him— "no" meant "yes." He and Brice shared the same animal and womanizing characteristics; it's why they got along so well. They were savages when it came to taking something that didn't belong to them—including pussy.

Tip was on his second shot of Patrón and his second beer when she suddenly caught his attention from the opposite side of the room. She was beautiful, exotic looking, with glistening black and silky-smooth skin. Her eyes were hypnotic, and her lovely features surrounded straight but beautiful shiny black tresses. Her hair flowed liberally, and it enclosed her face perfectly. In addition, she had long, defined legs that seemed endless. She was utterly stunning and had Tip in absolute awe. Immediately, he knew he had to have her.

He removed himself right away from the bar and chased after her, but as he got close, she seemed to disappear bizarrely. He was baffled until he spotted her again on the opposite side of the room, moving through the place gracefully like she was in her own world—unnoticed but with an aura of mystery about her. Tip hurried her way, following her with eagerness to introduce himself to her and then take things from there. But the closer he got, it seemed the more skillfully she would withdraw from him. However, he was utterly engrossed by her dark beauty. He followed her down a narrow hallway leading him away from the activity inside the club toward their own conviction. He drifted down a flight of stairs into the location's basement, which was dim and confined.

Finally, he caught up with her, saying, "Hey, what's ya name, ma?"

She turned and smiled at him. Quiet. She was tempting and foreign—mysterious. Their eyes and attention connected. Tip was more impressed by her up close. She was utterly naked in front of him, tempting him. He wondered whether she had been naked the entire time. If so, bold.

"I like that, ma. I like what I see. You nice, fo' real," he said.

She approached him with her seductive stare burning into him, enticing him. Tip damn near had his jeans unzipped, ready to pull out his dick for her when he felt a compelling force push him against the wall. He figured it was her.

"Damn, you strong, ma," he said, impressed. "I like that shit."

She moved intimately closer to him. She continued to seduce and touch him fervently in places that naturally aroused him. Her attractive touch reached down to his crotch and between his legs. He liked the feeling so far. He liked where things were going—what she was thinking. They had privacy *and* time.

"You never told me your name, ma," Tip said.

"My name . . ." she spoke.

"Yeah, what's your name? Damn, I wanna fuck you," said Tip, feeling absolute pleasure from the satisfying massage she bestowed against his hard dick.

He closed his eyes, exhaling, waiting for her to do some nasty things to him—waiting for her to propel him into sexual bliss.

"Go ahead, ma . . . suck my dick."

He felt fortunate to find a bitch like her.

It was the sarcastic laughter and the cocking back of the gun that made Tip open his eyes to reveal the truth . . . to see his fate. She had lured him into a trap—some being that wasn't there anymore. Instead, he was staring down the barrel of a .357 Magnum. Gripping the gun was Omar with a ferocious look about him—anger and rage. Shocked and knowing his fate, the only thing Tip could utter was, "That fuckin' bitch set me up—"

Boom! Boom! Boom! Boom!

Omar pumped four fierce slugs into his face and head, destroying everything about his features. The first bullet shattered his entire right eye. The second nearly tore off the right side of this face. The final two bullets slammed into his forehead and cheek with such force and rapid succession that Tip's body stood a few seconds before collapsing at Omar's feet.

Omar glared down at the body with indifference. He felt it was some of his best work. The lake of blood against the concrete floor was crimson thick. Tip was a bleeder. It felt good . . . the power, the destruction—death. Tonight, Malaka would be his desire. Tonight, she grew stronger.

PART THREE

"Our whole being is nothing but a fight against the dark forces within ourselves. To live is to war with trolls in heart and soul . . ."

CHAPTER TWENTY-NINE

THE CORONER PULLED back the bloody sheet to reveal the body underneath. What the detectives saw wasn't for the faint of heart. It was bothersome. The body with four gunshot wounds to his face—at close range and in a pool of blood that was almost dried—gave the room a sickly sweet butcher shop stench. What the slugs to a .357 magnum could do to a man's face was something out of a horror movie—it was nightmarish. Tip's handsome features were rotting away. The remnants of his face were frozen in a rigid snarl.

The only thing Danny Greene could do was shake his head and sigh.

"Jesus," someone uttered at the gruesome sight. "Someone really hated this guy. His face . . . It's almost not there."

Another man viewing the body had a churning mixture of digestive fluids and a previous dinner fill his mouth. He became weak and nauseated and had to rush from the scene. The evil that men do to each other—it was sickening.

Danny crouched closer to the body and looked more deeply at the mess someone left behind. The ghastly sight of a man's face thoroughly chewed away by gunfire didn't make him falter with queasiness or cringe. He stood there with his attention to the detail of someone's rage. How ugly it was. He locked eyes with the body. This was hatred, revenge, he thought. It was personal.

"You tried to warn this fool," said Bunk. "Some niggas are just too ignorant and stupid to understand when a gift is given to them. Dumb nigga probably thought he was Superman. He probably deserved it. This fool won't be raping anyone anymore," Bunk scoffed.

Danny had heard enough. He stood up impulsively and shot a look at his partner that manifested enough was enough.

"What is your problem, Bunk? That's someone's life taken, and you, a homicide detective, mock him," Danny exclaimed.

"Look at what these animals keep doing to each other! Look at his fuckin' face. I'm supposed to show sympathy to a nigga that rapes girls and does nothing but creates destruction and malice in his own neighborhood?" Bunk countered. "As I said before, Greene, this shit we're doing, it's an uphill and losing battle. These niggas keep killing each other like it's a drink of water, and we're left behind to clean up the mess and try to put the pieces back together."

"Then quit!" Danny suggested.

"Oh, I'm almost there, Detective. I'm almost fuckin' there," Bunk replied, offended.

Bunk marched away upset, leaving Greene standing there with his thoughts—and maybe his doubts. Not too long ago, he had Tip in the interrogation room and warned him that his life was endangered. Three of his friends were already dead, and Greene figured that might incentivize Tip to leave town or cooperate with the authorities. But the man had chosen his fate. And as Greene had promised, the 8x10 crime scene photos of his horrific murder would soon be displayed across the table during an interrogation to discourage someone else.

Greene huffed again. Four men died, and he felt no closer to catching their killer. He had a hunch, but suspicion wasn't concrete proof or evidence in carrying out an arrest or a conviction.

"Who found the body?" he asked the cop who was first on the scene.

"The owner."

Danny took in the area, the crime scene, with a trained eye. It was in the basement, underneath everything, underneath the party happening above. So, it was easy for him to deduce how Tip ended up in the basement. Someone lured him there.

"Any surveillance footage?" asked Danny.

The cop scoffed. "At a place like this?"

"Yeah. It figures," Danny replied. "And where's the owner?"

"In his office upstairs. He says he came down to get a few things and found him like this. Freaked him out," said the cop.

"And the patrons . . .?"

"We got a few we're questioning now. But understand, Detective, the area we're in, and the illicit activity happening inside the club, not too many chose to stick around."

Greene nodded his head. He understood. Many males who frequented places like this had questionable and shady backgrounds; some might be on parole and have warrants. And the last thing they wanted was to witness a murder and have the police question them.

The body was covered, concealed in a body bag, then positioned on the gurney to be taken to the morgue. Danny Greene had a lot to do, a lot to cover. He strode upstairs into the main area to have a few words with the club's owner, a man named Snaps.

"I have never seen shit like that before," Snaps said, still shaken by the scene.

"Do you remember seeing anyone suspicious lurking about?"

"Nah, I mean, I run a business with bitches, right? Shit can get crazy sometimes, but not like this."

"Would there be any reason for one of your customers to leave the event and enter the basement?"

"Shit is off-limits, Detective. I don't know how that fool got down there. He wasn't supposed to be there."

"I think he was lured down there by one of your girls."

"Nah, my girls don't fuck with the basement."

"Are you certain?"

"Listen, I run a tight shit here, and my bitches know that downstairs is off-limits to everybody," Snaps replied with certainty.

Danny took a mental note of that. He figured it had to be a woman that caught Tip's attention but felt that maybe she was a customer there, not a working girl.

"I want to show you a picture of someone; let me know if you recognize this person," said Greene.

"Yeah . . . a'ight."

Danny pulled out his cell phone and pulled up a picture of Kizzie. "Do you know this girl? Have you seen around?"

Snaps stared at the picture and shook his head. "Nah, I never saw the bitch a day in my life. Who she anyway?"

Danny ignored the question. It wasn't his business.

"Thanks for your cooperation, and if you remember anything else, please call me," said Danny, handing Snaps his card.

"Yeah, sure. Whatever," Snaps replied matter-of-factly.

Danny turned and left the man's office. He had a lot of ground to cover. The officers detained a few girls for questioning, and only a handful of males and employees were there. He needed to take a statement from every one of them, which was time-consuming, but it was the job. He was good at investigating and solving cases—and reading people, their behavior, and movements.

But what became puzzling to the detective now, with each man involved in Kizzie's rape dead, what was next for this killer? Would they continue killing? Danny was worried about the subsequent moves of this killer, who moved in the shadows and with efficiency. Whoever it was left no evidence or any trace of their existence behind. With its purpose fulfilled, would the killer now disappear suddenly, never to be heard from again? That was what worried Danny, his investigation becoming a cold case. It was the last thing he wanted.

Danny Greene left the building and climbed into his vehicle, his mind swimming with the case—with what he just saw. The image of Tip's face was destroyed like that; the gun was powerful and dangerous. He knew that the autopsy would reveal the same thing, something he couldn't explain—something bizarre.

He huffed and sat behind the wheel for a moment. He was listening to his instincts, and they told him that the girl, Kizzie, was involved somehow, maybe not indirectly. Danny felt someone close to her, someone who cared about her and who she cared about, was executing these violent murders on her behalf—implementing their own brand of justice. His gut made him think about her neighbors—male, he figured. She was the only child, had no cousins, and her only living relative was her grandmother; of course, the woman was too old to be behind this.

Greene then thought about that day in the lobby when he passed that young male who displayed odd behavior. It stayed glued to his memory, knowing something wasn't right about that individual. If he wanted to find this revenge killer, Greene knew it started at that building—Kizzie's location.

CHAPTER THIRTY

THOUGH THEY WERE all dead, it wasn't over, and Omar had gotten vengeance. But his soul was still restless. He still carried that thirst for murder. The lust for bloodshed was so rooted inside him that it spread like cancer. He was hungry for more. Malaka was an addiction, a needed source of inspiration and stimulus. He satisfied her, and she pleased him unquestionably. He was with her last night. The orgasm he experienced was overpowering once again, memorable. Like always, he wanted more of her—to escape into her ungodly realm of ecstasy. Twisted as it was, Omar enjoyed it.

She had emerged from the darkened corner, out of nowhere, entering his realm from hers. She no longer needed him to be asleep, with his consciousness vague. She was stronger now, able to cross over into his bedroom, into his world like an open door. She walked toward Omar naked as he sat at the foot of his bed, with him anticipating the expected—mind-boggling pleasure and power. Her dark skin was shimmering, and her appearance nearly godly, though she came from a hellish place. She straddled him masterfully, squeezing his dick between her pussy walls, sliding her aching folds over his dick. She rode him with undisguised pleasure. Omar's eyes rolled into the back of his head when he was inside her. It was needed—to be alone with her, intimate with her, and experience that wild wave of pleasure.

He'd grunted, huffed, and puffed, never wanting the feeling, the experience with this supernatural being, to end. The slow rocking motion she'd implemented on top of him allowed his hard erection to glide flawlessly. The scratches and marks she'd left on his back and against his chest became deeper and more concentrated. And when he came, he'd howled and quivered like he was having a seizure, feeling his soul sink deeper into some profound abyss.

"I need you," he had admitted.

She'd whispered into his ear, "Keep killing for me."

He nodded.

To continue his warped relationship with her, he would do anything . . . mass murder if needed.

Omar stood alone on the rooftop of his building. It had become one of his favorite places to be. It was a dark night, with the clouds stretching over the sky, giving it a hazy, ominous feel, along with a breeze that had some dampness to it. It wasn't there a short while ago. But it was cool and fresh.

The .357 Magnum was tucked in Omar's waistband. It had become like a heartbeat to him. The roar of the gunshot coming from it was his lifeline. Each bullet fired, becoming a pulsating vein of destruction, and each soul he sent to the afterlife came with its consequences.

He took a pull from his Newport and just stared aimlessly at the borough of Brooklyn, all of it lit up at night like a Christmas tree. So below him, many people move about with their average and natural lives. So much temptation about targets for him to pick from—enemies he wanted to destroy, the chaos he yearned to ensue. He took one final pull from the cigarette and flicked it away.

He entered the stairway and descended toward his floor. He passed a young male clad in black seated on the concrete stairs smoking a cigarette. Omar paid him no attention . . . until he heard the man say, "I see you, nigga."

Omar turned toward him, their eyes locking. He remained silent, wondering who this person was.

The young man stood up with his burning cancer stick and continued. "Your name is Omar, right? Yeah, that's you. I see you, nigga."

"Who are you?" asked Omar.

"They call me Dubai. I'm like the watcher around here cuz I see everything. And I see you, know what you're about, nigga. Your moms died a few weeks ago. You're that church boy. Yeah, it was always quiet, unassuming, and didn't mess with anybody until they fucked with you and raped your friend. And you made them fools pay."

Omar stood there in thickened silence, with his attention heavily on Dubai. He didn't corroborate what Dubai was saying. Instead, he had an aloof attitude. Dubai was a man of average height and not much of an imposing figure. He was thin with corn rows. He looked unassuming and inconspicuous. But when he looked at you, his eyes told a different story—someone with experience and knowledge.

"Look at you; you changed, nigga. Yeah, you're a killer now." Dubai chuckled. "You're a fierce one too. Them fools didn't even see you coming. And they never will. But you got a contract out on you; you know that, right? Anton, Science. They're looking for you, and they want you dead."

Omar continued to remain silent. He looked undaunted by Dubai's words.

"And look at you. I tell you niggas is after you, and you don't flinch, don't give a fuck . . . impervious to my words. I see it in your eyes, that fire for violence. It burns thick through your soul, right?"

Omar knew he was intelligent. But his words, the way he spoke, and what he knew, he wondered where he'd come from and what he wanted.

"Still quiet, huh? Yeah, you have never been the talkative type," said Dubai. "But silence is good. I knew a lot of talkative muthafuckas that didn't know how to shut up, so guess what? A bullet eventually shut them up. And that .357 tucked in your waistband . . . unique, right?"

"What do you want from me?" Omar asked finally.

"Yeah, straight to the point. I like that. But what I want, we want . . . Why do something for free when you can get paid for it? You had your fun, got your revenge. Now, I'm giving you the chance to outsource your talents," he replied.

Omar was listening.

Dubai continued. "You like a shark; got a sniff and taste of that blood in the waters, and I know you want more. I see it in your eyes . . . the hunger to hunt, to kill. It's in you now. It is. And how long you think you're gonna last by yourself? Science might not be the sharpest knife around, but he ain't stupid. And Anton, you crippled that nigga when you robbed him, so imagine what he'll do to you when he finds out about you."

Omar remained undaunted by Dubai's words. He stood in front of him with glaring eyes and clenched fists. Dubai threatened his life. He could kill the man right there, appease his hunger—its hunger, but he didn't. There was something strange about Dubai that Omar couldn't put his finger on.

"I figure you might need a little incentive to take me seriously about the offer," said Dubai. "So, here's your incentive."

He tossed a small brown envelope to Omar, and when opened, it revealed cash inside.

"That's twenty-five hundred for you," Dubai said. "Easy money already."

Omar stared indifferently at the cash in the envelope. It wasn't about the money but the sensation, the supremacy.

"The world is yours, nigga . . . at least this one is. Don't fuck things up for yourself," Dubai continued.

What did he mean, this one is? Omar thought. He wondered; did he know something he didn't? Was he aware of Malaka? Who was Dubai, and what was his true purpose?

"Make the smart choice. Get rich off this shit. I'll see you around," Dubai said, then descended the stairs to leave Omar pondering about the offer—his fate.

CHAPTER THIRTY-ONE

KIZZIE'S FACE WAS glued to her laptop screen as she read various materials on the signs and stages of demonic possession. It was a hard pill to swallow about Omar, but her gut instincts told her he was being controlled by something. She had no idea what it was, but she knew it was evil and wanted to destroy her friend. It had already changed his entire character. He wasn't fun to be around anymore. He had become aloof, unapproachable, and unfriendly. And he didn't have faith or belief anymore. She was scared to be around him because he had become unpredictable.

Mental illness had crossed her mind, but Kizzie knew it wasn't a mental illness that Omar was suffering from. Instead, this thing was powerful, and she felt it was changing her friend into something demonic—a murderer. She kept quiet about the latter because it was still disturbing for Kizzie to know that Omar had become a killer. But what she read about possession was equally disturbing.

She read aloud, "When the demon takes control of its host, certain behaviors will crop up that will distinguish the possession from something else like mental illness."

Kizzie was hooked on the subject of possession with odd behavior, night terrors, and a negative reaction to prayer. She remembered how negative Omar would turn when anyone mentioned God or wanted to pray about something as if he had an allergic reaction to it. And then there was his odd behavior; he started smoking. Omar *never* smoked. He hated cigarettes. Kizzie remembered how his eyes would water and turn red whenever he was around someone smoking. He found cigarettes disgusting. And his personality had grown bizarre; there were mood swings and hanging out at night. And the one disturbing thing that lingered on Kizzie's mind was Omar carrying a gun. The Omar she once knew did not know anything about guns. He'd never shot a gun. Guns used to make him nervous. She remembered how the sound of gunshots would send shivers through Omar. He was a nerd, a mama's boy; a churchgoing, good Christian kid who wanted to praise God and live his life peacefully. He wanted to leave Brooklyn. He had dreams of going west, maybe opening his own business somewhere. Now what plagued her friend was this thuggish, violent, and demonic being that was hell-bent on carrying out revenge and destroying everything around him.

Kizzie continued to sit in her bedroom at her desk with her face in her laptop. She focused on every word she read. There were three stages of demonic possession. The first stage was manifestation and infestation. The demon is seeking approval at this stage, authorization to stay. And it almost needs permission to begin to reveal its true self. After that, it will slowly increase in tempo as the demon gains strength and the chosen individual loses theirs.

The second stage was oppression. This is where the entity makes its true identity known and moves into full attack mode. It can be physical, mental, and psychological, even bordering on the psychic, and is designed to break the affected person's will to live. In the second stage of possession, sleep deprivation occurred, along with increased paranormal activity, bites, scratches, and even sexual assaults.

The more Kizzie continued to read, the more she found it accurate and possible that Omar had possession-related symptoms.

She felt hesitant to read about the third stage of possession, but she needed to know. So, she read out loud to herself, "In this final and most dangerous stage, the demon now has sufficient power and hold over the individual to 'close the deal,' so to speak."

The article continued to say that the person affected will have little to no self-worth, will, or faith left. And that this evil entity would often be in control, and the influence may well be hearing voices telling them to harm others or themselves. This entity, this demon's goal, is to drive the affected to suicide and take as many people as possible with them on the way, thus condemning their souls to an eternity of hell.

Kizzie couldn't read anymore. She closed her laptop with grave concern. Something had to be done, and she hoped that Pastor Morgan could help Omar. It wasn't just his well-being that was in jeopardy, but his entire soul.

She removed herself from the desk and went to the window. It was late, nearly midnight, with a silver moon high in the sky in a velvet blanket of black. Kizzie knew that Omar had a habit of leaving at night—most likely to do the unspeakable. She'd heard about the murder of Tip, one of the men that had raped her. His gruesome death, with half his face destroyed by gunfire, had spread through the community like wildfire. There were rumors of why he was killed—because of this rape. It was running rampant throughout the hood. They all were dead: Brice, Mo, Chuck, and now Tip. There was a murderous vigilante in the Ville, creating grave concern.

Kizzie sat on her windowsill with her attention outside. She couldn't sleep. The nightmares that she was having were becoming disturbing—too real. It felt like someone, or something, was coming after her. What it wanted from her; she didn't know.

She was afraid to know. She didn't want to go back to sleep. She thought it was risky, but she had to do some investigation of her own. She donned a long robe and left her bedroom and apartment purposefully. She knocked at Omar's door, thinking he wasn't home, but she had to make sure. After a minute of knocking and no answer, Kizzie took the elevator to the lobby and knocked on the superintendent's door. She didn't care that it was late. This was urgent.

"Mr. Reynor, it's me, Kizzie. Can you open the door, please?" she hollered. "I know it's late, but this is important."

Kizzie continued to bang on his door until she heard the locks unfastened, and the door swung open rashly with an angry building superintendent looming into Kizzie's view.

"Kizzie, do you know what time it is?" he exclaimed. "What in the hell is so important that it brings you to bang on my door at midnight?"

"I need a favor," she uttered.

"A favor . . .?" he repeated with a deep frown. "You come to my door at this time of the night for a favor?"

"It has to do with Omar."

"Omar. That boy has gotten all kinds of weird ever since his mother died."

"I know. But I need to check on him, Mr. Reynor . . . to do some kind of welfare check," she said.

"A welfare check . . .? Police do that, Kizzie, and you and I aren't the police," he replied.

"I think he's suicidal," she mentioned with concern. "He's my friend, Mr. Reynor, and I'm afraid for him. I want to see if he's okay. I'll be in and out."

Mr. Reynor sighed. He looked at Kizzie and her trickling tears and relented. "Okay. Just this one time, Kizzie. Only because you're a good girl, and I know you mean well."

"Thank you, Mr. Reynor."

"You owe me one, Kizzie."

"I know. And I promise I'll get my grandmother to make you one of her pumpkin pies and velvet cake."

The mention of pie and cake delighted his ears. He smiled. "Don't play with my feelings, Kizzie. You know how I feel about your grandmother's velvet cake."

"I know, and I'll get her to make one for you."

In his late fifties, Mr. Reynor was an aging Black man with a potbelly and a grizzly beard. He had an affable personality, a fondness for Kizzie's grandmother, and was adept at fixing anything, which was why he'd been the building's superintendent for over thirty years.

He went back into his apartment, grabbed his jingling keys and a shirt, and followed Kizzie to Omar's apartment.

Standing outside Omar's door, a weird feeling sent chills through Mr. Reynor. He couldn't put his finger on it, but something wasn't quite right. He looked at Kizzie and asked, "Are you sure about this?"

She nodded. "I just want to make sure he's okay. I'm in and out."

"Okay."

Mr. Reynor put the master key inside the lock, turned it, and opened the door. He hesitated at the door's threshold as Kizzie made her way inside. She turned to him with bafflement and asked, "You're not coming inside?"

"No. You said you'll be in and out, right?"

She nodded.

He was fine where he was.

Kizzie stepped farther into the apartment. What was once a place she was familiar with—a second home to her, had now become foreign and unfamiliar. It had been months since she stepped foot inside Omar's apartment. The living room was dark, still, and too quiet. Suddenly, the front door slammed shut like a rogue gust of wind had caught it. The problem was . . . There was no wind. It scared Kizzie and Mr. Reynor. They were now separated by the shut door and baffled by the strange encounter.

"Kizzie, are you okay?" Mr. Reynor hollered from the hallway.

"I'm fine," she replied.

Kizzie stood in the center of darkness, alone. It felt like the apartment was under a constant shadow, as if any sunlight or light had shrunk away. The windows in the living room were black, the furniture the same but appeared older and dirty, and the walls looked like they were rotting away. She went into the kitchen, and everything was sparse. Opening the fridge, Kizzie nearly vomited. The food was so old that it was covered in mold and looked foul, and the smell was unbearable.

"Oh God, that's nasty," Kizzie spewed as she felt nauseated.

It wasn't just the rotten food coming from the fridge that smelled. Instead, a foul stench was invading her nostrils—like a body or rotten flesh. She went from the kitchen to the hallway. She didn't bother calling Omar's name; she figured he wasn't home. Or maybe she was mistaken. Perhaps he was sleeping in the bedroom and didn't hear her knocking earlier. If so, she wanted to check on him but at the same time investigate things. Kizzie was eager to find the root of her friend's problem, to find out if her hunch about her friend being possessed was correct. But how would she find out by snooping around in his apartment and the bedroom?

When she pushed open the bedroom door, it was so dark in his room that it was hard for her to see. She reached for the light switch on the wall and flicked it up, but no lights came on. The room remained dark. She flicked it up and down several times, but nothing . . . still dark. She wondered if he paid his light bill. Did he pay anything at all? But from what she could see in the dark, the room was sparsely furnished; only a mattress was placed against the wall and an old dresser with a mirror. The windows had been blacked out. And there was an equivalent stench like in the kitchen and the living room. And it looked like the walls were discolored due to a lack of routine cleaning. There were no amenities in his bedroom or throughout the apartment.

As Kizzie stood in the center of the room—snooping around, she thought she heard a woman's voice come from somewhere. She couldn't pinpoint where. But it was raspy and ominous. Creepy. Suddenly, the air inside the room became stale—nearly toxic. She couldn't breathe. There was an intense tightening inside her chest, and she became very dizzy and felt sick. The overwhelming feeling made Kizzie drop to her knees, trying to grasp something nearby to steady her, but there was nothing to hold onto. Her hands hit the floor, and she found herself on all fours, choking, gasping, and maybe dying somehow.

Get up! Get up! she told herself. She screamed to herself.

It felt like something was trying to drain her life from her. Something didn't want her there, inside Omar's room.

She coughed and tried to stand, but it felt like gravity was cripplingly her. Her vision became blurry. It felt like she was drowning and suffocating at the same time. But she was determined not to pass out—not to close her eyes and succumb to such a crippling feeling that came out of nowhere. Whatever it was trying to hinder her, Kizzie fought it. Finally, she was able to recite the Lord's Prayer.

"Our Father in heaven . . . hallowed be your name. Your . . . your Kingdom come . . ."

She heard intense growling that boomed through the room. It seemed like the prayer had angered it, and the tightness inside of Kizzie's chest became more intense and unbearable.

"Your will be done, on earth . . ." she tried to continue.

She then heard it say, "He's mine!"

Kizzie continued to pray. "Give us this day . . . our daily bread and . . . forgive us our debts . . . as we . . . also have forgiven our debtors."

It felt like the room started to shake around her, and this frightful darkness began to swallow up the room. This evil being was looming closer, itching to destroy her. But Kizzie continued to finalize her prayer with, "And lead us not into temptation but . . . but deliver us from evil . . ."

Subsequently, she felt a burst of strength, and she could breathe again. She didn't waste a second more on her knees. She sprang to her feet and bolted from the bedroom faster than lightning could strike, and she flew toward the front door, swung it open quickly, and flew into Mr. Reynor's arms with tears in her eyes. It shocked Mr. Reynor. He hugged her back and asked, "Kizzie, what happened in there? Are you okay?"

Kizzie couldn't talk. She cried. She couldn't explain it to him, but her assumption was correct. Her friend was possessed by something demonic.

Pastor Morgan sat at his desk in his office and read the Bible verse, Luke 8:30 . . . *Then, Jesus asked him, "What is your name?" Legion, he replied, because many demons had gone into him.*

He then read the verse from Peter 5:8, which read, *Be alert and of sober mind. Your enemy, the devil, prowls around like a roaring lion looking for someone to devour.*

That word "devour" stuck on him profoundly and worryingly—"to swallow or eat up hungrily, ravenously to consume, recklessly or wantonly—the mind devoured by fears." He thought about Omar and his sudden absence from church. Something had exhausted his faith, his belief in the Lord and

Jesus Christ. He knew Kizzie was right. Something was going on with Omar, and it was troubling. Since his mother had passed, Omar wasn't the same person, and Pastor Morgan started to feel guilty. He should have been there for Omar. He should have given him counseling and spent more time helping Omar heal from losing his mother. The boy was like a son to him, and he needed help.

The pastor sat and read many verses and articles about demons, possession, and other ungodly things.

How could he tell if someone was demon-possessed?

Pastor Morgan knew he needed to recognize the difference between a possessed person and someone struggling with a mental illness. So he decided to visit Omar at his place. Pastor Morgan knew he couldn't wait a day longer. This was imperative.

He leaned back in his old chair and sighed heavily. It was a lot to take in. It was a lot to worry about, but he was a Christian man, knowing to put it into God's hands and not fret. Nevertheless, the pastor felt it was time to act—for he believed that faith without works was dead. He looked at the time and saw that it was 8:00 p.m.—late, but still early with the days becoming shorter because it was fall. He had spent two hours in his office reading the Bible, praying, and asking the Lord for guidance on handling such a disturbing situation.

Deciding to call his wife before he made his move, he reached for the cell phone on his desk and dialed her number. It rang twice before she picked up with a delighted, "Hey, honey, what's up?"

"Hey. I know it's already late. But I'm going to be a bit late coming home tonight. I need to take care of something," he said.

"Is it really important?"

He sighed. "Yes. It's Omar; I'm going by his place after I leave here and check on him."

"It's been a while since he's been to church."

"I know. Something is going on with him, something that came to my attention, and it can't wait," said Pastor Morgan.

"Okay. Just be careful. Call me the moment you leave there," she said.

"I will. Love you."

"Love you too."

Their call ended, and the pastor stood up and collected his things. He exited his office and walked through the church to ensure everything was secured and okay. He picked up a few Bibles and hymn books left in the pews, stacked them neatly where they belonged, then left the building, locking the door behind him. He stood in front of his church momentarily, reflecting on a thought—a doubt, maybe. The air was crisp, with the clouds a little grey and coinciding with the dropping leaves from the trees, indicating summer was gone and fall was now taking over. He zipped up his jacket and looked back at his church—The Tabernacle, where his flock came to worship and find support, and then he strolled toward the soaring projects nearby.

He moved through the urban community and the projects with self-assurance and optimism, though things looked bleak because of a drug war. He had been preaching in the neighborhood for years, becoming a pillar in his community. He'd helped start numerous foundations and outreach organizations. He always wanted what was best for his community. That's why it was so disheartening to see it destroyed by drugs, gangs, violence, and murders. But it was more heartbreaking to see the same youth he knew when they were young, some who even attended his church when they were knee high, to see them now caught up in the streets—in such negativity. However, it was a lot more shattering to the pastor when he gave the eulogy at these same kids' funerals. Their lives were cut short because of gun violence and gangs.

Pastor Morgan arrived at Omar's residence. A few locals were lingering out front, including some young teens with nothing better to do with their time than drink and gamble. He shot a welcoming grin their way and said, "Good evening, gentlemen," and only one smiled back and greeted, knowing the pastor.

"Hey, Pastor Morgan," said the teenager.

The pastor entered the lobby with an unexpected nervous feeling. It was out of his league, demonic possession, but Omar needed his help.

He pushed for the elevator clutching the Bible in his hand and released another sigh. He uttered a Bible verse as he waited for the elevator to descend. "Be strong and of good courage, do not fear nor be afraid of them; for the Lord your God, He is the One who goes with you. He will not leave you nor forsake you."

The elevator finally arrived, and he stepped inside with the stench of urine attacking his nostrils and getting closer to a daunting task. He had to quote another verse to himself. "The Lord is my light and my salvation; whom shall I fear?"

The door to the elevator closed, and it ascended to what he believed was necessary redemption. Omar had been absent from the church for a while now, but the pastor still considered him family and a member. He had watched the boy grow up. He had witnessed his struggles—his trials and tribulations. He could no longer sit back idly and watched someone he loved and cared for fall plunge into despair and transgression.

"Faith," the pastor uttered to himself. "If you can believe, all things are possible to him that believes."

He knocked on Omar's door several times and waited patiently for him to answer.

"Omar, it's me, Pastor Morgan; please open the door. We need to talk."

He continued to knock. It was getting late, but he was determined to see and talk to Omar before returning to his wife.

"Omar, I know you're home. Let's talk," he continued. "I'm . . . We are all worried about you. And if you don't open this door tonight, I'll be by here every night until you do. Then I will sit outside your door and pray and deliver God's word—"

The apartment door opened rudely, and Omar appeared in front of the pastor's eyes, looking sunken and gaunt; behind him, darkness. He glared at the pastor and roughly asked, "What do you want, Pastor?"

Pastor Morgan was taken aback by Omar's appearance for a fleeting moment. He looked nefarious with a perpetual frown and cloaked in some inexplicable malice. His eyes were dark, almost characterless. It was a stark change for Omar. He was a completely different person, not the good kid, God-fearing mama's boy he was known for.

"Can I come in?" asked the pastor. "We need to talk."

"About what . . .?"

"First off, we are all worried about you, Omar."

"Y'all don't have to worry about me," he replied.

"But we are. And I want to come inside and talk to you." Pastor Morgan was resilient. "Besides, I know you must be lonely inside that apartment. And I didn't come all this way to hear no and be turned around."

Omar continued to frown, knowing the pastor wasn't taking no for an answer. "I'm just tryin' to warn you, Pastor."

"Warn me . . . Warn me about what? What is going on with you, Omar? What's going on inside the apartment? But if I leave here, I'll be back tomorrow with my wife and a few other church members who are worried about you. So, either we can talk inside, or—"

"Come in for a minute," Omar relented.

He stepped to the side, allowing Pastor Morgan access to the apartment. He closed the door right away, looking unsettled. Pastor Morgan stood in the living room and looked around. It was dark and static, and a disturbing smell invaded his nostrils.

"What happened to the lights? And what is that smell?" he questioned.

"You have five minutes, Pastor," Omar said with touchiness.

"Can we sit and talk?"

Omar led him into the kitchen. Pastor Morgan took a seat at the raggedy table. Omar sat opposite him with a heavy frown, obviously reluctant. The kitchen was dull and bleak—lifeless of his mother's special touch, departed of her preparing a home-cooked meal with gospel music playing, sunshine, and happiness. The pastor grew nostalgic, remembering how good a cook Ms. Richards was, putting together something special while having so little.

"She was a special woman, you know. And we all miss her," said Pastor Morgan, referring to his mother.

"She's gone, and that's it, Pastor. She left me, and I don't care anymore," Omar replied frankly.

"She's in a better place right now. Her soul and spirit are with the Lord—"

"I don't want to hear that nonsense right now, Pastor," Omar interjected offensively. "Not in this place anymore."

"I see. What has changed you, Omar? To see you living like this . . . in the dark, saddened, alone with this sudden hatred in your heart for the Lord. This isn't you. You were a good kid; your mother wouldn't want this for you. Seeing you like this would break her heart. Yes, she's gone in the physical, but her absence here means that her presence is with—"

"Listen, don't speak that in my home," Omar warned him through clenched teeth. "I don't want to hear it."

"You used to sing in the children's choir, Omar. You used to attend Bible study and Sunday school. You had a bright future. You still do. Whatever's in you, possessing you, it needs to stop now," Pastor Morgan exclaimed. "Rebuke it and remove it from you!"

"You need to leave, Pastor," said Omar sternly.

"No! I'm not going anywhere. I came here for a reason, to save you . . . to save your soul from the damned. I know this isn't you, Omar. I know something is controlling you. I don't know what it is, but I'm here to help you . . . help you fight and remove whatever's corrupting you and endangering your soul," exclaimed the pastor.

"I don't need your damn help!" Omar shouted, his voice nearly demonic. It shocked the pastor.

The pastor was stunned and taken aback by Omar's hostile and antagonistic demeanor, but he stood firm and undaunted. He wasn't going to be easily scared away or become simply agitated. A friend needed his help, and it gave him unwavering faith to do so.

"Submit yourselves to God. Resist the devil, and he will flee from you," Pastor Morgan spewed a random Bible verse.

"Leave, Pastor . . . Please, I'm begging you before it's too late," Omar warned him wholeheartedly.

Once again, Pastor Morgan remained stubborn. He didn't budge from his chair. Instead, he stared at Omar assertively and loudly exclaimed another verse. "Behold, I have given you authority to tread on serpents and scorpions and all the power of the enemy, and nothing shall hurt you."

"She wants to hurt you, and nothing is going to stop her," Omar exclaimed.

Pastor Morgan ignored what Omar was saying to him. Determined, he continued to pray. He continued to shout the Lord's name. He was adamant about destroying whatever was changing the boy and manipulating his mind.

"He who dwells in the shelter of the Highest will rest in the shadow of the Almighty. Therefore, I will say of the Lord, He is my refugee and my fortress, my God, in whom I trust—"

"Stop it!" Omar screamed. "She's coming!"

Darkness came into the room like thick velvet curtains of the theatre. It changed the ambiance of the kitchen. There was something in the dark that became unsettling. Creepy. Pastor Morgan felt an icy chill run down the back of his spine like ice water was dripping down on him. He gazed at Omar. The boy sat there still, looking absorbed by something. His eyes were soulless. He was quiet—too quiet. Pastor Morgan tried to continue the Bible verse.

"Surely, He will save you from the fowler's snare and the deadly pestilence . . ."

Omar sat there entirely still in the kitchen chair, looking spaced out. He wasn't alone. Unexpectedly, a pair of hands loomed from the darkness behind him, coming from around and over Omar's shoulders. They reached down to his chest sensually. It was something unreal, something the pastor saw with his own two eyes.

"I warned you, Pastor. Now it's too late," said Omar chillingly.

Pastor Morgan tried to remain undaunted by the terrifying sight—something supernatural and demonic. There was a dark presence by Omar, gradually making itself visible. His eyes were glued to the shadowy figure standing behind him, something ominous. Nevertheless, the pastor continued his prayer relentlessly.

"He will cover you with his features, and under his wings, you will find refuge; his faithfulness will be your shield and rampart . . ."

His prayer angered it. The pastor wanted to take Omar away from it. A mammoth roar boomed from the shadows, and a profound and compelling force thrust the pastor from out of the chair, and it nearly sent him flying across the room. Instead, he landed on his side. He was more shocked than hurt. The ominous entity appeared from behind Omar, materializing from the darkness. It was a naked woman, dark and beautiful. But he knew there wasn't anything attractive about this being. It was manipulative and evil. And Pastor Morgan refused to be afraid of it.

"I rebuke you in the name of Jesus!" shouted the pastor.

"You are a foolish being," said the ominous entity, Malaka.

"I'm not afraid of you!" Pastor Morgan shouted.

"You will be," she roared.

Omar sat there still and indifferently to what was happening around him. Things were out of his control. It was out of his power. The succubus had grown stronger and had an appetite for murder and chaos. Omar had become its vessel into their world—their realm. It desired to come to life in this realm and feed, to be born.

It approached Pastor Morgan as he hugged the floor; his eyes were aimed at the evil being, and he was still spewing out prayers and Bible verses. He continued to anger the succubus. This dark figure advanced toward him with malicious intentions. Its eyes were hooked onto the pastor with rage and disgust. Her nakedness and perversion were disturbing. It was in direct contrast to everything the man of God stood for and believed. She towered over the pastor in her rawness with a flowing mane of hair like a lion. Then she crouched near him with her nudity to taunt him.

"He's mine," Malaka exclaimed. "Yes, I fucked him, Pastor. Imagine it, his virginity taken by me . . . by something you truly despise. Imagine it, him inside of me every night, fornicating with me, ejaculating inside of me, and impregnating me. Do you envy him, Pastor?"

"You are an abomination!" he shouted.

"Do you believe that? When was the last time you had some pussy?" she mocked.

She subsequently straddled the pastor after her vile statement. "You wanna fuck me too, Pastor? Do you wanna feel inside of me? I can make you feel good too. I can give you what He can't . . . What she can't."

He remained relentless and stubborn. "You are a curse. Our Father, who art in heaven—"

Before he could complete the prayer, Malaka stood up abruptly, knowing Pastor Morgan was one soul she couldn't have or corrupt. She scowled at him. Her demonic being was fleetingly revealed to the pastor, its true identity, and it was appalling.

"Fine!" shouted Malaka. "If you won't accept pleasure, then experience pain!"

There was a place in the living room that sprouted thicker with darkness. The darkness seemed to spread and gave off a profound chill. And coming from that blackness were terrifying demonic noises that echoed toward the pastor.

"Enjoy your fate," Malaka uttered with dripping sarcasm.

She and the pastor locked eyes heatedly, and a ball of terror formed in his stomach. And then, some unseen force propelled him toward the thick darkness as Malaka stood there and watched. The dreadful darkness swallowed him. He screamed. It was a piercing and chilling sound coming from the pastor—and from the terrifying darkness came loud crunching, snarling, and flesh being ripped apart.

Malaka smirked. The torturous sound of a man being ripped apart was appealing to her. He would no longer be an interference. With Pastor Morgan gone, the terrifying darkness began to subside, and the living room shifted back to its normal state—and rapid silence. Omar was still seated in the kitchen chair, looking unapologetic about what happened to Pastor Morgan, a man he had known nearly his entire life.

Nevertheless, it needed doing. The pastor was warned, and he was becoming trouble for him—for them. She stared at Omar and grinned.

His future was sealed. He belonged to her. She promised him power, sex, and wealth as long as he remained faithful to her. She was a jealous bitch.

CHAPTER THIRTY-TWO

"I CAN'T BELIEVE YOU got me sitting out here on some wild goose chase," Detective Foster griped to Detective Greene. "You're fishing, Greene."

"Maybe I am, but I have a hunch about this suspect," Greene replied.

"Brice and his crew had many enemies. And you believe that your primary suspect in these killings is this meek, churchgoing kid, someone I understand recently lost his mother. This little corny nigga doesn't have a criminal record, not even a damn misdemeanor. And now, suddenly, this unassuming muthafucka is an adept killer? Nigga probably never picked up a gun a day in his life, let alone shot one," Foster mocked.

"A murderer can come in all shapes and sizes . . . and this person has a motive," Greene countered.

"They raped his girlfriend, so that's motive?" Foster wasn't buying it.

"She wasn't his girlfriend, just a friend," he corrected.

"And that makes it more plausible? Nigga wasn't getting any pussy. The nigga was a mama's boy; probably still can't pee straight," Foster quipped.

"If you have so much doubt, why bother coming along?" Greene asked him, upset.

"We're partners, right?"

"Most times it doesn't feel like it," Greene replied matter-of-factly.

"Look, I know we don't see eye to eye most times—"

"Try all the time," Greene interjected.

"You have your way of doing things, and I have mines. I've been doing this for a long time, and I closed many cases, and some went cold. So, what I'm trying to say is that you have a good eye, Danny . . . a sharp eye, and you care about your cases . . . putting the dead before anything else in your life."

Danny wondered where he was going with this.

Bunk continued with, "Don't let this job, solving these cases, be the only important thing in your life . . . the only thing you care about. I did once . . . lost a beautiful wife and time with my twins by doing so. I haven't seen them in two years. Bitch got fed up with me choosing the job over family, packed her shit, and took my kids out west."

It was the first time Bunk ever opened up to him, especially about his family. Danny Greene sat there and listened.

"You're a good man, I see that . . . and a great cop, but get yourself a girlfriend, Greene . . . Go home to something sweet like pussy and find some balance in your life," Greene continued. "Because these muthafuckas out here, these streets, they will take something from you mentally. Change you."

Danny sat there impassive, listening to Bunk's blunt advice. They didn't have many moments like this when they shared personal information about themselves. They had been partners for nearly two years and were like day and night. They both were good at their jobs but had different views toward the work, the people, and the community.

"I appreciate the advice," Greene replied nonchalantly.

They continued to talk while they sat inside the Chevy parked outside the projects. It was a sunny autumn day with a bit of breeze. Activity around the Ville was bustling in the morning with children on their way to school. The early hustlers/drug dealers were out and about slinging their drugs to numerous drug fiends that haunted the area. It was an open market—a drug haven happening right before the detectives' eyes, but they weren't interested in narcotics. They were homicide, and the murders happening in Brooklyn, especially in Brownsville, were spiraling out of control.

"What's your interest in the gun?" Danny asked.

"The .357 . . .?"

"Yeah."

"I think it connects with a few of my old cases," Bunk again lied to his partner.

While conversing, Danny caught a woman from the corner of his eye walking across the street. When she emerged into his full view, she was moving fast with a sense of urgency. She had somewhere important to be, it seemed. It looked like she woke up and hurried out of the house quickly, not bothering to get dressed, with rollers still in her hair, clad in a long housecoat and slippers. She rushed by their parked Chevy and walked briskly into the projects. The first thought from both men was crackhead, but there was something different about her, something off and off-putting. Danny's eyes lingered on her, and he caught this strange feeling that she was heading somewhere that would be of their interest. Without telling his partner, he exited the car to follow her. Bunk was bewildered by the sudden movement. He too left the vehicle and followed behind Danny.

"What's up, Greene?"

"I'm following my instincts," he replied.

"What, by following this crazy-looking woman?"

Greene followed her to Kizzie's building, and when she entered the lobby, he knew he was on to something. The woman impatiently pushed for the elevator to descend. She seemed worried and rattled with concern. It looked like she hadn't slept all night. She was in her late forties, and from what Greene could see, she wasn't there to buy drugs. Instead, it seemed like she was there to confront someone. But who?

Impatient, the woman decided to take the stairs. She hurried into the stairwell, not caring about anything but her destination. Both men followed her. Bunk thought they were going on a wild goose chase, but he kept his comments to himself this time. Their day was becoming more interesting by the minute.

When the detectives reached the floor she'd disappeared on, this woman was banging on an apartment door with the bottom of her fist and yelling, "Open this door, Omar! Where is my husband? Open the door. Please!"

She was adamant. She wasn't going anywhere. She was confident that her husband was somewhere inside the apartment.

"Omar, open this door. Where is my husband? He told me that he was coming here last night and didn't come home!" she shouted.

Mrs. Morgan continued to bang on the apartment door. She shouted so loud that she could have woken up the dead. It was their suspect's place. Detective Greene's hunch was correct, and next door was Kizzie's apartment.

Greene cautiously approached the woman; his partner stood watchfully behind him, wondering what was happening.

"Ma'am, is everything okay?" asked Greene.

Mrs. Morgan turned around with her face awash with tears and anguish. She was worried about her husband.

"My husband didn't come home last night," she cried out.

"And you're certain he's inside this apartment?" Greene asked.

"Yes! He called me last night right before he told me that he was going to see Omar," she expressed.

She spun around and started to bang on the door again—much louder and more demanding this time. She was determined to get an answer, and it was apparent that she wasn't going away until someone opened the door. The commotion attracted Kizzie's attention. She opened her door and was shocked and taken aback to find Mrs. Morgan, the pastor's wife, knocking angrily at Omar's door.

"Mrs. Morgan," Kizzie uttered. "What . . . What is going on?"

Teary-eyed, she turned to Kizzie and said, "My husband is missing."

"What? He's missing?" she replied, confused.

"He called me last night and told me he was going to see Omar before coming home. But he didn't come home." Mrs. Morgan continued to bang on the door and rant. "It's not like him. He always comes home and calls me to tell me where he is. Something's wrong; something happened to him last night. I know it. Please, Lord, give me strength . . ."

Detective Greene intervened with, "Ma'am, let us handle this for you. We'll get to the bottom of things."

She didn't want to leave in front of the door. Mrs. Morgan was growing hysterical with apprehension with every passing minute. Detective Foster calmly wrapped his arms around Mrs. Morgan and politely steered her away from the door with some reassuring words. She seemed reluctant to comply, but both men assured her they were going inside the apartment to look around. Greene took over. He knocked a cop's knock and said, "This is Detective Greene with Homicide; open up this door right now, or we'll break it down."

Curious, Kizzie stood at the threshold of her doorway. She didn't want to get any closer to that apartment after what she'd experienced the other day. She was convinced that something evil inside that apartment had utterly consumed her best friend. With Pastor Morgan assumed missing, guilt started to swell inside of her. She felt responsible. But she remained silent.

Detective Greene continued to knock, and he shouted out harsher warnings. He was adamant about entering the apartment. Now he had a plausible reason. Maybe a man's life was at stake. His second knock didn't produce any results. He shot a glance at Foster. It was now or never. Greene was ready to shoulder or kick in the door, force his way inside. He didn't know what to expect, but he was prepared for anything. And then the mystifying happened. The apartment door opened, and a slender, sickly-looking male stood there. Omar, they presumed.

"What the fuck y'all want?" Omar cursed at them.

Omar was shirtless, and his torso was swathed with scars and bruises, some looking fresh. He seemed unarmed and unassuming.

"You live here?" asked Greene.

"Yeah," Omar replied, being short with them.

"Are you alone inside?" Greene continued.

"Yeah."

"Do you mind if we take a look inside?"

"Where is my husband, Omar?" Mrs. Morgan shouted at him. "I know he came to visit you last night. What did you do to him?"

Omar shot Mrs. Morgan a cold and callous stare as if he had no history with her and replied, "I don't know what you're talking about. No one came to visit me last night."

"You're lying!" she shouted.

"Listen, we're not trying to make things difficult here. We just want your permission to come inside and look around," said Greene coolly.

"Sure. Whatever. I don't have anything to hide," Omar replied.

He stepped aside and allowed the detectives to enter his apartment. Mrs. Morgan was ready to rush inside. She was frantic and desperate, but Foster stopped her at the threshold and said, "It's best for you to wait out here, ma'am. We can handle this."

She wanted to resist. She tried to help look for her husband. Kizzie shot Mrs. Morgan a concerned look—a strange look. Mrs. Morgan picked up on it and asked, "Kizzie, did you see my husband last night? Do you know something?"

"No. I didn't see anything, Mrs. Morgan," she answered.

"Are you sure?"

"Maybe you should come inside and let the detectives do their job," Kizzie offered.

Mrs. Morgan was beside herself.

"Kizzie, I need to find him."

"I know, Mrs. Morgan; they'll find him," she replied. "Just come inside with me, and let's talk."

She got through to Mrs. Morgan, and the woman entered her apartment. But she stood nervously by the door, pacing back and forth while the detectives were inside Omar's apartment looking for her husband, hoping he was still alive.

Detectives Greene and Foster weren't shocked by the apartment's shitty décor. It was the projects, and people were poor. But what bewildered them was the darkness. The windows were completely blacked out, with no sunlight trickling into the living room or anywhere inside. There was a lingering blackness that felt uneasy to the detectives—and a foul smell coming from somewhere. It was so dark inside the apartment that both men had to pull out their small flashlights.

"You live alone?" Foster asked him.

Omar nodded.

"I want a yes or no answer from you," Foster said sternly.

"Yes."

"And last night, you had no visitors?" Foster continued his impromptu interrogation.

"Yes."

"Why do you have it so dark in here?" Greene asked him.

Omar smirked. "You afraid of the dark?"

"Are you trying to hide something?" Foster interjected.

Omar remained quiet and calm, but his presence was eerie. He also remained shirtless with his scars and bruises on display. There was something off about him—something creepy. Whatever innocence he had seemed long gone.

The detectives started in the living room, entered the kitchen, moved down the hallway, and thoroughly searched the bedrooms and closet. They came up empty. There was no one else inside the apartment. Nobody. And though the place seemed uneasy and mysterious, there was no indication of any foul play. But Detective Greene knew something was wrong even though there wasn't any tangible evidence to show for it. Omar was hiding something.

He approached the odd man and asked, "Do you own a gun?"

"No," Omar quickly responded.

"What's your relationship with your neighbor Kizzie?"

"She's a friend."

"Are you in love with her?" Foster asked.

Omar smirked and then responded, "She's a friend."

"Is she a good enough friend that you would kill for her if someone wronged her . . . especially after raping her?" Greene speculated.

Omar kept his reply simple. "She's a friend. And I'm sorry that happened to her."

While they were talking to him, Detective Greene saw something move fleetingly in the shadow of the living room from his peripheral vision. His attention was fixated on that area, but there was nothing there. He knew he wasn't going crazy, but the vibe from the apartment was incredibly eerie.

They continued questioning him, but Omar remained adamant about being alone last night and not having any visitors. And unfortunately for them, surveillance footage in the area was either nonexistent or broken. So there was no footage of the pastor arriving or corroborating Mrs. Morgan's story. And they had no evidence or reason to arrest Omar.

"Church boy, huh?" Greene uttered.

Foster knew his partner was on to something. He didn't want to believe it, but Omar's demeanor was off-putting and daunting.

The detectives left the apartment unhappy. The moment they stepped out, Mrs. Morgan burst from Kizzie's apartment with a look of desperation, maybe some hope.

"Was he in there?" she anxiously asked them.

The look on their faces told her of her worst fear. He wasn't inside.

"There was no sign of your husband inside the place," Foster said.

"No. No! He's *got* to be inside there somewhere! Please, keep looking for my husband," she shouted.

She attempted to run inside the apartment, but Greene immediately held her back. She was becoming a mess. She was confident that Pastor Morgan was inside the apartment or Omar did something terrible to him—maybe secretly disposed of his body. Omar stood in the doorway when Mrs. Morgan heatedly looked his way and screamed, "What did you do to my husband? He treated you like a son, Omar! Where is he?"

She fell to her knees in profound grief. Kizzie was there to comfort and console her. In their hearts, they knew something terrible had happened to the pastor. Omar stood there calmly, and it looked like he didn't care. Kizzie knew her best friend was gone entirely. And she felt guilty for suggesting that the pastor check in on Omar. Tears started to trickle from her eyes.

"Please, find my husband," Mrs. Morgan cried out.

CHAPTER THIRTY-THREE

SCIENCE TUGGED AT his dog's leash, an American Bully, the pocket type, as it tried to chase after a nearby squirrel. It was a powerful dog with a short, smooth, glossy coat. The beast was one of his favorites. Science loved his dogs, but he loved this one the most. He named him Master, and this was one of two dogs that he didn't involve in dogfighting. Some would say that he treated his two dogs better than he did some people.

It was a lovely fall afternoon, and Science took Master for a walk in the East New York Park called Paerdegat Park. It was a tree-filled park that boasted sports courts, benches, a playground, and facilities. And it was a school day and a workday, so the park was mostly empty, giving Science some privacy to walk his dog and conduct business. Science had a few of his goons nearby watching his back. They were armed but subtle about it. And though the act looked innocent and routine, he was there for a purpose—a meeting.

He walked Master toward the baseball field and sat on a nearby bench with Master sitting too.

Almost immediately, a black Maybach drove up and parked at the entrance to the park. The doors opened, and several men climbed out. Science's attention was fixed on the activity. He sat coolly with Master as three men approached the park, each looking serious and in a dark suit. One of the men approaching looked the part of a serious Mafioso wearing a three-piece suit over a Gordon Gekko-style white-collared shirt. When they came near, Science stood up with a calm gaze aimed their way. He was familiar with them, and he knew the reason for their visit to see him.

It was expected.

The man in the three-piece suit was named Ferranti, a powerful-looking Black male with a dark goatee and a bald head. He stood at six-one and was physically fit. A diamond Rolex gleamed around his wrist, along with a diamond pinky ring. His eyes were frosty, indicating he was a man you didn't want to mess around with. And he was an extremely wealthy male—some predicted that he had a net worth shy of a billion.

Standing next to him was his partner in crime, Mason, another well-dressed Black man with a violent pedigree. Mason had long dreadlocks, dark skin, and darker eyes that seemed perpetually intimidating and predatory, and there was a presence about him that was frightening yet intriguing. He rarely spoke, had large hands, and was an adept killer. Together, these men ran and controlled a ruthless, deadly, and highly wealthy organization called the "Black Hand." They were a lawless, clandestine society engaged in many criminal activities. One of their treacherous trademarks was cutting out the tongues and even the hearts of snitches. As a result, the Black Hand was feared and highly respected. Their members and brutality rivaled the Mexican cartel and the Italian Mafia . . . *combined.*

Ferranti and Mason were a mystery to many. Their backgrounds were unknown. And though their organization was powerful and wealthy, it was highly mysterious.

"So, what's this about?" Science asked.

For Ferranti and Mason to meet him, Science knew it was of paramount importance. They remained largely invisible. These men had their hands in the drug trade and were responsible for sixty percent of the drugs distributed into the tristate area. They were an organization of contract killers and assassins—employing some of the best around. So when two of their killers suddenly went missing, they brought the big dogs out of the dark to find answers.

Ferranti had an icy glare toward Science, one that could send chills down the devil's spine.

"I find it strange that two of our men go missing after they implement a job for you," said Ferranti.

"I don't know what to say about that. I'm shocked too that they went missing," Science replied with false concern.

"So, you have no idea where they could be?"

"I paid them what I owed, Ferranti, and they left. Where they went after that, that's none of my business," he lied.

"They've been missing for two weeks now."

"I don't know what to tell you," said Science.

Ferranti had an intense look about him, firm and not blinking as if he was reading Science's soul and consciousness. It was so intimidating that it could make a charging bull falter and turn around. He was a man hard to lie to, but Science kept the lie going, and he was trying to make it believable.

Mason remained silent, his attention fixed on Science. He was a dog ready to bite. He was a man that wouldn't hesitate to kill someone in public. And standing behind them was a suited goon on alert, his attention on a constant swivel.

"I ain't stupid to fuck with you and yours, Ferranti. You know that. Zack and O'Malley did a job for me, did me a favor, and I appreciate it. But you think I'm stupid to go against the Black Hand? I know what y'all niggas are about; shit, who doesn't?

Man, I heard the cartels don't even fuck wit' y'all," continued Science wholeheartedly.

"If there was any evidence of transgression on your end, you would already be dead," Ferranti uttered.

"Yeah, I know," Science replied.

Ferranti wasn't keen on staying out in public too long. Though he had heavy security with him, he was a cautious man. He had to personally meet with Science and look him in the eyes to read thoroughly and sense Science's vibes when he questioned the whereabouts of his two missing assassins.

"We good?" Science asked.

Ferranti didn't answer him. Whatever he was thinking, whether or not he believed Science, it didn't show on his face. He remained expressionless. The men held each other's gaze, and Science wasn't faltering. He kept his rock-hard look and firm composure. He showed no weakness or vulnerability. It was absolute death for him if the truth was revealed.

Ferranti pivoted and walked away dispassionately, not giving Science his answer. Mason delayed leaving for a split second, maintaining his cold, icy stare on Science. It was a tense moment, not knowing what action such an influential underworld figure would implement. *Has Ferranti subtly given him the go-ahead to murder him right there?* he wondered. And then Mason smirked, and briefly, the man's eyes altered into a soulless black, which was utterly unnatural and freaked out Science.

What the fuck! he thought.

Mason then spun around and walked away from the area, leaving Science with an ambiguous answer and creeped the fuck out. He stood there clutching the leash to Master and watched both men climb into the backseat of the Maybach, and it drove away. Science knew he was on thin ice. He also knew they would come to question him about the twins. But he asked himself what had just happened and what was the strange thing with Mason's eyes. How did they change suddenly like that? He had never seen anything like that before—a man's eyes, his pupils go from brown to a dark onyx color. It was unreal. But he shrugged it off; he had more compelling problems to worry about.

He turned the opposite way and walked toward his goons waiting nearby.

Anton and Kenya were wreaking havoc on his business. And the war with both men was starting to take a toll on him.

I got my niggas 'cross the street livin' large
Thinkin' back to the fact that they dead
Thought my raps wasn't facts 'til they sat with the bars

Bookie took a pull from the blunt and enjoyed the strong zest of loud weed as the rolled blunt burned between his fingers. He leaned back in the passenger seat with his cohort, Jo-Jo, behind the wheel of the dark blue Benz. They listened to "Money in the Grave" by Drake. It was another fall day in Brooklyn, sunny and a bit breezy. It was early afternoon, and the streets were bustling with folks, traffic, and businesses. Bookie took another deep pull from the blunt and passed it to Jo-Jo. He then looked to his right, gazing out the window, eyeing the string of folks moving about on the busy sidewalk. Then he saw her amongst the people, an old flame named Nyah. Bookie smiled and shouted to Jo-Jo, "Yo, stop the car!"

Jo-Jo was confused, thinking something was wrong. "Huh?" he replied.

"Nigga, I said stop the fuckin' car!"

Jo-Jo stopped the car abruptly, and Bookie quickly leaped from the passenger seat like there was a troubling situation and chased after Nyah.

"Yo, Nyah!" he hollered. "Nyah!"

He caught her attention. She turned around and saw one of Brooklyn's deadliest killers coming her way. However, she didn't feel threatened by Bookie. Instead, she smiled at him and stopped for him. "Hey, Bookie, what's up?"

"What's good, ma? I ain't seen you around in a minute," he said. "Where you been at?"

They hugged each other and started to converse. Bookie's eyes lit up with a desire to see her again. It was the most he smiled in weeks. He was always serious about his business on the streets, spreading misery and death with a longing. But seeing her again, he became someone else.

"You know, trying to go back to school and taking care of my mother. She's sick now. She's on dialysis," she replied.

"Damn, sorry to hear that. But anyway, what you doin' right now? You busy?"

"Just going into the store to get a few things for my mother," she replied.

"Yo, I'll walk with you."

She shrugged and smiled. "Okay."

Bookie walked with her toward one of the many bodegas crowding the block. She had his undivided attention. He laughed with her as they entered the store. But unbeknownst to Bookie, he caught the attention of some rivals nearby standing across the street.

Seeing Bookie with Nyah, three men felt they had the opportunity of a lifetime to gun down one of Brooklyn's notorious hitters. Each man was amped, ready to make their name on the streets and in the game. Then seeing Bookie vulnerable with a young, pretty girl, they were prepared to strike. They stood idly across the street from the bodega Bookie had entered. Each man was armed with a semiautomatic pistol, including an extended clip. They scowled in the direction of their rival, itching to strike.

"When he comes out of that joint, we fuck him up," uttered one of the gunmen.

"No doubt."

They waited for ten minutes until Bookie and Nyah finally exited the bodega. Bookie was still distracted by her beauty and presence, helping her with her items. At the same time, Jo-Jo remained seated in the Benz nearby, listening to loud rap music.

With their guns in hand, the three scowling gunmen quickly made their way across the busy street, approaching to kill him where he stood.

Bookie chatted and laughed with Nyah, being in a good mood with her. But then he looked ahead and immediately saw the triple threat coming his way. His reaction was swift; he dropped whatever he was carrying and desperately reached for his weapon tucked in his waistband as the first shot was fired.

Boom! Boom!

Bak! Bak! Bak! Bak! Bak!

A shootout immediately ensued, and chaos and panic were everywhere, with people running, hiding, and screaming. Bookie crouched in a defensive position and heatedly returned fire. He cursed and became the readied killer that he was known for. Bullets went flying everywhere. And hearing the shots, Jo-Jo emerged from the driver's seat with a .45 in his hand, and he joined Bookie in the shootout. It became the O.K. Corral in Brooklyn.

Bookie wasn't going down without a fight. He was a formidable and vibrant rival. Though it was three against two, Bookie made sure to even things with his intensity. And what was supposed to be a quick kill didn't happen. Instead, the three goons found him hard to kill as bullets whizzed by their heads. Bookie charged their way with such ferocity that it looked like he was nearly invincible.

"Fuck this!" one of the gunmen shouted, retreating.

The other two speedily followed his lead, retreating from the scene in haste as Bookie continued to fire in their direction, but to no avail. They had gotten away. Bookie stood there in the middle of the street, seething. *The audacity of these muthafuckas!* he thought. There was a lot of shooting, but no bodies dropped.

Soon, he heard a sharp and piercing scream behind him. It was a woman. Bookie spun around toward the woman's scream, smoking gun in hand, and what he saw was terrifying—shocking. It was a mother on her knees, clutching her small daughter in her arms. The little girl had been shot in the chest by a stray bullet. The woman was hysterical.

"Bookie, c'mon, nigga. We gotta go!" Jo-Jo shouted.

Bookie snapped out of it and hurried toward the car. He leaped into the passenger seat, and Jo-Jo sped off.

After the smoke cleared, folks hurried to the little girl's aid as her mother tightly held her in her arms, crying her eyes out. They wanted to help, but it was clear to everyone that she was dead. She was only nine years old.

Nisha Smith was nine when she died from a stray bullet to the chest. The community was not only saddened by her tragic death, but they were also outraged—enough was enough! The violence and murders were out of control. The political leaders, pillars of the community, residents, a few celebrities, and hundreds of people gathered in the streets of Brownsville to protest gun violence. It was a large crowd that spread for several blocks. They carried lit candles in memory of Nisha Smith. They held up signs that demanded peace in their community and urgent gun control. And they lifted many pictures high in the air of the little girl killed that day.

They marched down Rockaway Avenue shouting and chanting. One activist leading the charge shouted into the microphone, "What do we want?"

"Gun control," the large crowd shouted.

"When do we want it?" the activist yelled.

"Now!" the crowd roared.

It was a continuous chant, and they made a glorious statement. People were tired, angry, and scared. It felt like their community and streets were becoming hell on earth. The public and brazen shootouts and murders some of these drug crews and gangs were committing were gruesome and damn near rivaled the brutality seen only in Mexico.

The crowd had intensely swollen at the location where Nisha Smith was killed. An abundance of flowers, memorial candles, teddy bears and toys, and pictures of her were everywhere. Many were speaking, singing, and praying. And the media was present at the scene with their cameras and anchormen and women positioned ubiquitously. Kizzie was also present at the protest and rally. When she heard the news about the little girl, she was devastated. The fact that it happened in her neighborhood was more catastrophic. The Ville had enough problems already, but the killing of an innocent little girl, accident or not, was uncalled for.

She stood amongst the crowd, holding a candle for the vigil and praying. Her eyes watered up—so sad. She lifted her head, looked around, and it didn't take her long to notice him there too—Omar. He stood there alone, camouflaged in the crowd with an impassive look about him. He saw her too. He seemed so dark. They stared at each other briefly until Omar smirked and disappeared out of the blue. He gave her the creeps. She cringed and started to cry, not just for the little girl's soul, but because she never thought the day would come when she would be so afraid of her best friend.

CHAPTER THIRTY-FOUR

THE SUDDEN DISAPPEARANCE of Pastor Morgan spread through the community like wildfire. A week had passed since his disappearance. And along with his wife, church members were distraught and deeply worried. A few witnesses had seen the pastor enter the building that night, several young boys outside gambling, but they never saw him leave the building. Detective Greene was baffled by it all. He and his partner had combed Omar's apartment. Unless there was some secret room or Omar had cleverly gotten rid of the body, there was no reasonable explanation for the incident. Pastor Morgan was a pillar in the community, and there was no reason he would leave everything he loved. He was a respected and liked man, so the mystery spiraled through the urban community . . . Where did he go?

Greene and Foster sat at their desks in the precinct. With a gang and drug war happening, murders rose in the area, and everyone was busy working on a homicide case, drugs, or an incident. The Ville community had become a hotbed for violence and hatred. It seemed like a veil of rage had come down on the city, and everyone was angry and in despair.

Greene leaned back in his chair. His mind was spinning with wanting answers, speculations, and trouble. What was happening in the community? Things weren't adding up.

"A man doesn't just vanish, right?" Detective Greene said to his partner.

"People disappear every day, Greene," Foster replied. "Maybe the pastor just wanted to go away. He got a sidepiece somewhere, a nice piece of pussy, and he said fuck it. He doesn't wanna preach anymore."

Greene shot him a look saying, *Nigga, seriously?*

"Anything's possible. Look, he's a man too, and pussy is a powerful drug," Foster continued to joke.

Greene didn't laugh.

"That kid had something to do with this," said Greene.

"Look, he is a creepy muthafucka. I agree. And he's weird, but you can't arrest a muthafucka for being creepy and weird. We searched that apartment and came up with nothing."

"It still doesn't mean a crime wasn't committed there."

"What? This muthafucka is now, all of a sudden, some criminal mastermind? This trained and incognito killer wants revenge, so he takes out four hard-core goons, known killers, and knows how to skillfully dispose of a body from his apartment? And he's clever enough to avoid any detection and the authorities?" said Foster. "I'm sorry, Greene, but I'm not buying it."

"So, you want me to let it go?"

"Either you get some hard-core evidence on this kid, or you need to find a different angle," Foster replied. "And besides, we got bigger issues with this nine-year-old girl being killed by a stray bullet the other day. The department wants to make a show, make noise, kick in doors, and make arrests. They want the muthafuckas responsible in handcuffs like yesterday."

The tragedy saddened Danny. It broke his heart. A nine-year-old girl was killed in his district; it was uncalled for. And though it was an accident, it was still senseless violence that didn't need to happen. Young Nisha was a victim caught up in a drug war between burgeoning criminal organizations. It was the reason Danny didn't want to have kids. The fear of the world corrupting them, or worse, death taking them away from him far too soon.

"We need to make a statement out there . . . Make some serious noise by fuckin' up some heads, fuck it. Maybe become as violent as them to show and prove to these fuckin' idiots and animals that *we're* in control—*not* them," said Foster. "Fuckin' Black-ass animals, and I swear, any one of them ever decides to come for me, I won't hesitate to take that muthafucka down."

"We start acting like them, then we become them, Foster," Greene countered.

"Who do you think is winning out there, huh? Them or us?"

Greene sighed.

Foster continued, "You would be a fool if you think that what we do, what we're doing, is making some change out there. Most times, I feel like a glorified babysitter on these streets. We make a case go from red to black, and guess what? There are *ten other* open murder investigations right behind that one. We lock up one or two animals, but there's a dozen more to follow right behind that one. There's no structure out there, no fuckin' order. It's just the fuckin' jungle, Greene . . . That's it, a fuckin' jungle with animals preying on each other."

As Foster was going into one of his usual rants, Greene tuned him out. He was used to it. His partner was griping about the streets, about the animals, and then reminiscing about the heyday of policing when cops could be cops and do whatever it took to solve an open murder investigation. Including implementing their own brand of justice—violent justice to make the streets safe. Their superiors would look the other way.

"Detective Greene," a uniformed female cop called out to him.

Greene looked her way.

"There's someone here to see you . . . a young girl," said the lady cop.

"A young girl . . .?"

"Yeah, she says it's important and only wants to see you."

Greene was bewildered. He wasn't expecting anybody.

"You got a hot date that I don't know about?" Foster joked.

Greene didn't laugh. He stood up from his desk and walked toward the room exit and out into the hallway, moving by a group of uniformed cops chatting and laughing. He descended the stairs toward the main entrance to the precinct and spotted his visitor when he entered the lobby. It was Kizzie. She was sitting on the wood bench alone. She looked adrift, her attention wandering on some profound thought that was probably trapped inside her head, maybe haunting her.

Her long skirt and buttoned blouse were unassuming, indicating that she didn't want any attention—especially male attention. She sat there still and silent, and she looked utterly uncomfortable. When a male officer moved by her too closely, she would slightly jump and cringe. It was apparent that she didn't want to be there.

Greene walked toward her with a smile. He didn't want to spook her. But she was there for a reason, and he needed to find out what it was.

"Kizzie," he said politely. He extended his hand to greet her with a handshake, but she didn't accept it. Instead, she continued to sit there with her arms folded across her lap, slightly hunched over and defensive. "I heard you wanted to see me."

She stared at him. She didn't stand. Greene gave her the space she needed, not crowding or towering over her because he knew she was still fragile. But he also knew that it took courage for her to come see him at the precinct. But her sudden silence made him nervous. Whatever she was there to tell him, he felt she might be having second thoughts.

"Listen, I'm here to help, Kizzie. Remember that," he said politely.

She sighed heavily and uttered, "It's about Omar."

He was listening. But she paused again. Danny could see it, her thoughts drifting back and forth to some dangerous place in her mind, information troubling her.

"Is there somewhere we can talk privately?" she asked him.

"Of course," Danny replied.

He gestured to a nearby empty room. She stood up and followed him into the room. Danny closed the door behind her and asked her to sit if she wanted.

"I would rather stand," she replied.

It was fine by him. She clutched a blue jacket in her arms like she wanted it to be some barrier between them. But instead, she was nervous and scared. It showed.

"Don't be nervous, Kizzie. You came here for a reason; what is it?" He didn't want to rush her.

She locked eyes with him and spewed from her mouth, "It's about Omar. I know, I mean . . . I think he did something awful."

Finally!

"Awful? What do you mean awful?" he asked. "Does it have something to do with the missing pastor?"

"It's my fault," she confessed, her voice shaky. "I . . . I met with Pastor Morgan to tell him that something was going on with Omar. He wasn't himself. He was dangerous; I believed he was even possessed by something. So I told Pastor Morgan that he should talk with Omar. And he did. And now he's missing."

"You think he killed the pastor?"

"I . . . I don't know. But I know he's killed those men," she said.

"Those men? Who are you referring to?"

"The men that raped me," she mentioned.

"And you know this how? Do you have proof of this?"

"He . . . He said it to me that night when I confronted him on the roof. He had a gun on him, and there was this crazy look about him . . . like he was possessed. But he told me that he killed all those men for me . . . because they raped me," she stated. "And the way he talked about it, it was as if he enjoyed it . . . killing those men."

Danny Greene was ecstatic to hear such news but kept his composure. "Do you know what kind of gun he had on him?" he asked.

She shook her head. "No. I don't know anything about guns."

Of course, she didn't. But he was confident about where things were headed.

"Do you think he has that gun on him now?" asked Greene.

"Yes. I believe so. It was like . . . He's become obsessed with it. He needs help, Detective, serious help. I want my friend back. That's all; I want my friend back," she cried out.

He could see her pain. "We'll get him the help he needs, Kizzie. I promise you."

The look in the detective's eyes was sincere and believable. What Kizzie was telling him solidified his hunch about Omar. He figured the kid used to be a good guy, but that wasn't the case anymore. Whatever took hold of him, it had now ruined his life. He was now a hard-core killer.

Detective Greene escorted Kizzie out of the precinct. She was emotional. She wanted things to end well, but she knew the truth. There was a high possibility that her friend was gone entirely and lost, and he was going to jail for murder.

At that moment, Kizzie felt truly alone.

"Do you need me to take you home?" Greene asked her.

"No. I'll walk."

"Are you sure?"

She nodded. "I just need to walk and pray about things," she replied.

He understood. He stood there and watched her walk away, but he was eager to get an arrest warrant for Omar. He was confident that Omar still had the gun on him, the .357 Magnum. But the tricky part of the case was unnatural. With no ballistic report to match the weapon to the murders, how could he prove that the gun killed all four men? It was bizarre, but Detective Greene was willing to move forward. He had a motive, and he had a witness, somewhat. The pieces were falling into place, and now it was time to map out the entire puzzle.

Greene was about to turn and walk back into the precinct, but something or someone caught his immediate attention from across the street. A Black man in a black trench coat stood there, gazing at him strangely. It was odd. The detective didn't see him as a threat, but the stranger's focus was definitely on him. He was tall with a bald head and a thick beard. The man stood still like a statue, and it was clear that his attention was fixed on Greene.

Who is he? Greene thought. There was only one way to find out. Greene decided to approach him to ask him about his business. He waited for the traffic to clear. Then he stepped onto the street, and a city bus passed, briefly obscuring his view of the man. But when the city bus passed, the man in the black trench coat was gone. It was as if he had vanished into thin air. It was odd and uncanny. Detective Greene didn't know what to think of it. But the deeper he dug into this case, the stranger things became.

CHAPTER THIRTY-FIVE

FOUR APPEALING AND expensive black SUVs were parked outside a Brooklyn warehouse in Flatlands during the night. Two men dressed in long black trench coats stood outside on watch and guard duty. Several significant players and crime figures were inside having an undisclosed meeting. Nearly a dozen men sat at a long table in the open room's center with many pillars. And each man seated at the table carried some firm seriousness with them and a dangerous pedigree that was respected amongst everyone. And among these men were Anton, Science, and Kenya. Peace reigned among the three of them as they were in the presence of members of the Black Hand. They were the ones that requested all three men be present in the same room at once. And two representatives from the Black Hand organization were Amarok and Aspen, two high-class members who spoke for Ferranti and other superiors.

Amarok and Aspen were two masculine figures with thick facial hair and long dreadlocks. They had a strong presence, clad in expensive dark suits indicating their wealth and power. While everyone was seated at the table, they stood tall and almost sinister-looking. Their black eyes concentrated on each drug kingpin before them and their associates. A crisis had happened. Their business was in jeopardy, money wasn't being made, law enforcement was amped up in the streets, and several political leaders called for justice and arrests.

"Who is responsible for killing the little girl?" asked Amarok.

"Not my peoples," Kenya uttered, staring intensely at Anton.

"And you think it was mine?" Anton shot back.

"It was your boy Bookie with the smoking gun," Science chimed.

"Dumb muthafucka," said Kenya.

"Fuck y'all niggas," Anton cursed angrily.

"Quiet!" Aspen shouted.

The room fell silent.

"This needs to be corrected. Ferranti is not happy at all with this shit," Aspen continued.

"What, you want us to bring the little bitch back to life?" uttered Science with apathy.

"Show some respect, muthafucka," Kenya exclaimed.

"Or what, nigga . . .?" Science retorted. "You weird, freak muthafucka. Do that voodoo shit now, nigga. Who you think ya scaring wit' that bullshit play magic?"

Kenya glared at Science with intensity. He wanted to murder him right there, but he was able to keep his composure. Ferranti and the Black Hand were an organization he didn't want to piss off.

"Yo, Science, go fuck your dogs and fuck you, nigga," Anton chided.

"Come to my part of town and meet my bitches, niggas. I would love to watch them tear your faggot ass apart . . . wannabe pimp-ass nigga. Nigga don't know if he wanna sell drugs or pussy," Science angrily countered. "Nigga, my dogs got more class than your ugly-ass bitches!"

"Yeah, you fuckin' them dogs too, huh?" Anton countered.

The three men went back and forth with insults and threats with their associates and goons close by, just waiting for the orders to pop off. Finally, it was apparent the three couldn't get along. Still, Ferranti demanded temporary peace between all three of them, and Amarok and Aspen were assigned to make it happen—by any means necessary.

"I *said* enough of this shit from all three of y'all!" Amarok's voice boomed through the room. He continued to stand in their presence. He wasn't about to hear their bickering all night. He was there for a purpose, and it would get done no matter what, the Black Hand's order.

"We fix this bullshit with y'all tonight. Or I guarantee, come tomorrow morning, none of y'all will continue to fuckin' exist," Amarok warned them. "Understand?"

Their utter silence meant they did. Each man's attention was on Amarok and Aspen.

What now?

"First off, we need an answer for the girl's death," said Aspen.

"You mean a scapegoat," Anton mentioned.

"The backlash from this incident and the taste for justice coming from the authorities need to be appeased somehow," Aspen said.

"And that means giving up my guy, Bookie?" Anton said.

"Good fuckin' riddance. He was a bitch nigga anyway, living on borrowed time," Science mocked.

Anton cut his eyes at Science—and if looks could kill, it would have been a massacre. Instead, Science returned a matching unpleasant and crazy gaze toward Anton. If a bell had sounded, the two men would have reacted to it and started fighting. But the Black Hand was there to keep things in order, to discuss an alternative to their problems and issues.

"You think Bookie gonna agree to shit so easily?" said Anton.

"He doesn't have a choice. He goes down for the killing of that girl, or your entire organization is cut off completely," Aspen warned him.

"Just like that?" Anton replied gruffly.

Aspen nodded. "He's got forty-eight hours. So I suggest you talk to him."

Anton knew he didn't have a choice. When the Black Hand demanded something, it wasn't a choice but a demand. Science smirked at the option Anton was given. It was hard for him to hold his composure. He wanted to burst out laughing and mock Anton, but it wasn't wise to do so.

"Second thing," Aspen continued. "All activity in the Ville and elsewhere will be divided between each crew equally."

"Say what?" Science shouted, becoming the knucklehead of the three. "That's fuckin' bullshit!"

"You have a problem with that, Science?" Amarok asked with a steely glare aimed his way.

Science frowned. He did, but he wasn't going to admit it. Reluctantly, he replied, "Nah, I don't have a problem with it. I'm good."

Aspen continued to talk. He didn't want to be interrupted again and clarified it to everyone. Each man in the warehouse listened as the man barked out more instructions for them to implement peace among each other—and how. Finally, each man consented to the terms the Black Hand gave. They were to be precisely followed by each crew, or else there would be dire consequences for anyone who didn't want to play by the rules. With the meeting completed, Science angrily pushed back his chair and started to leave the warehouse with his goons following. But Amarok stopped him, saying, "Science, we need to have a word with you. Everyone else is free to leave."

Science was baffled why they stopped him but let everyone else go. And as Kenya made his departure from the building, he stopped suddenly and looked intently at Amarok and Aspen. Of course, they didn't intimidate him, but he was a man of knowledge and understanding, knowing that the cards were in their hands for now and it was their show. So he smirked and uttered in Creole, "*Lapè, Jiska pwochen fwa* . . ."

Peace until next time, he said.

The two men stared at each other as if they knew something that the others didn't. But Kenya exited the warehouse with his crew, and so did Anton. Science continued to stand there, remaining baffled.

"What's up with this?" Science asked.

"Ferranti has requested that you come with us," Aspen said.

"For what?" he asked.

"Business," Aspen replied.

Science knew he didn't have a choice. He watched the others leave, including his men, while he felt he was held captive. There was no going against the Black Hand. His crew against theirs was like a lion going against a T.rex—both were powerful creatures, but the T.rex was bigger, stronger, and had many more teeth.

CHAPTER THIRTY-SIX

IT WAS THE search warrant that Detective Greene had been waiting for—a small accomplishment. The warrant was signed and secured by a reluctant judge. Still, Danny Greene persuaded the judge to sign off on the search warrant for probable cause. They knew there wasn't much evidence to go on—flimsy at best with information from the neighbor, Kizzie. But it was usable. The authorities and the people of Brooklyn were growing desperate for a change. They wanted the violence, the drug wars, and the murders to end if that was possible. The killing of Nisha Smith, the sudden disappearance of a prominent pastor, and the ghastly and gangland murders in Brownsville were making front-page news. The spotlight shone brightly on the Ville. The authorities needed to make some noise and appease their superiors and the good and hardworking people of the community.

Enough was enough!

A squad of officers was ready to implement a search warrant for Omar's apartment. Greene was hoping to find a .357 somewhere inside. He had gotten confirmation from Kizzie, his witness, if one can consider her a witness. Greene knew he was taking a considerable risk executing the search. But if they found the gun inside the apartment, there was a chance that Omar could be connected to the murders—or not. The uncanny and the unnatural were something he thought about with his case, and the autopsy results on all four men were the same—bizarre and inexplicable. Yet, he was determined to close this homicide case and bring about justice.

Several officers hurried inside the project building early that morning and urgently moved up the stairway. Greene and Foster were leading the charge. The narrowed hallway became crowded with a few officers. Detective Greene knocked on the door and called out to Omar, announcing they had a search warrant for the apartment. Again, Greene knocked on the apartment door firmly and loudly, and he continued shouting, "This is the police. We have a warrant to search the premises. Open the door now!"

They didn't get any response.

Silence.

Once more, Greene knocked loudly, making his presence known. But there was no answer within. The warrant was valid only for today, and he wasn't about to give up. He was entering the apartment with or without the tenant being home. Then the building's superintendent arrived on the floor with his jingling keys. He readily opened the front door to the apartment. Lately, the place had been giving him the creeps. And adding his two cents, he said to the police, "I haven't seen the boy around lately. He used to be a good kid, but something changed with that boy after his mama died . . . something weird."

His statement was ignored. Danny, Bunk, and the following officers entered the apartment with an objective. They spread through the place like scattering bugs, hurrying into different rooms and implementing their search for the gun. The area was dark and sparsely furnished with a foul odor to it. The detectives and the officers figured it wouldn't be a difficult search. There wasn't much to go through with the décor tenuous. Everything in the place was old, outdated, and filthy.

Detective Greene went into the bedroom to execute the search for the weapon. He quickly opened the drawers and went rummaging through each one, though there wasn't much to comb through, just some old clothes, books, and odd junk. Finally, he shifted toward the closet and searched through it methodically. Greene even checked for any secret compartments inside the bedroom, but there weren't any. The officers searched for that particular gun throughout the apartment; unfortunately, they didn't find anything—nothing illegal was inside it. It was just old, odd, and creepy. The place looked abandoned. Once again, it felt like another dead end for Greene's open murder cases.

Leaving the building disappointed, he sighed heavily. *What next?* he thought. Omar was gone, and no weapon was found inside.

"You happy, bitch?" Foster mocked him while walking by.

Greene stared at him. He was disappointed, and he felt like a joke. This case had become tiresome—an uphill battle with a slippery climb and a threatening fall. He was trying to hang on. He *wanted* to hang on, but it started to feel impossible. He had to wonder, was his suspect finally done with killing?

While exiting the scene, Danny noticed *him* again, the tall Black guy in the trench coat. Standing in the distance, he watched the police activity like a hawk. Greene deduced that this strange individual was following him. He wondered why. Seeing this odd stranger again, he didn't want it to happen a third time. Quickly, Danny Greene marched his way to confront the man in public. Whatever he wanted from him, Greene was about to find out.

"Hey, you!" Greene called out to him as he hastily approached. "Are you following me?"

The stranger didn't budge but stood his ground, focusing on Greene's approach. Greene kept his reach near his holstered weapon in case the situation grew ugly. The man coolly looked at Greene.

"Who are you, and what do you want?" asked Greene.

"I came to warn you, Detective. A threat looms . . . A war is coming to your world," the stranger uttered out of the blue.

Danny Greene was taken aback by the response. "What . . .?"

"You have been marked," the stranger continued.

He was baffled by the man's statement. *Is that a threat?* Greene replied, "Marked? Are you threatening me? What is this about? Who are you?"

"There are certain forces out there brewing, waiting for humanity's destruction," he said.

Now Greene was utterly baffled and confused. The first thing he thought was, *This man is crazy, maybe homeless.* But his appearance was well put together and neat. He was physically fit with powerful-looking arms and hands and had trimmed features. He looked like a man that could handle himself in a rough situation and maybe even take down multiple men at once.

"Enough with the damn riddles. Who are you? Who sent you?"

The stranger kept his intense gaze on Danny. It was awkward and intimidating, but Danny didn't scare easily.

"I just came to warn you. Unfortunately, you've been marked like the others," the stranger repeated.

The man turned to leave, but Danny wasn't about to let him walk away so quickly after what he considered a death threat. So instead, he reached out to grab the man, wanting to detain him for more questioning. "No, you're *not* going anywhere after you just threatened me," he uttered.

The moment Danny grabbed his arm, the stranger spun around quickly. He grasped Danny by his jacket, lifted him off his feet like he was a doll, and tossed him a few feet away with no trouble.

"Don't touch me!" the stranger shouted.

This man's unnatural strength astonished Danny. If he were a cursing man, he would have shouted, *What the fuck*! But, instead, the fleeting assault alerted the officers that were standing nearby. Seeing one of their own assaulted, they didn't hesitate to run to Danny's aid to take down this powerful-looking stranger. But the man took off with shocking speed, zipping undaunted through the traffic. And suddenly, he vanished.

"Are you all right, Danny?" asked a helping cop.

Danny was quiet, still stunned by the fast attack.

"Who was that?" another cop asked.

Back on his feet and a bit shaken up, Danny had no idea who he was. He kept his cool, but something spooked him. In this homicide case, his suspect, Omar, took him somewhere strange and scary—maybe too frightening.

The only thing Danny could do was stand there dumbfounded and get himself together. And though he was shocked and spooked, he was still determined to finish what he'd started. He felt he was getting closer to something.

Omar walked into the underground location in Brooklyn with a grim look about him. Clad in a dark hoodie, jeans, and black military boots, he immediately caught the attention of the few hood niggas inside, including Bookie. Bookie sat at a table in the back of the place, playing cards with a few of his homies. But then, he noticed this stranger entering the building—coming into what everyone else inside considered a private establishment—off-limits to anyone that wasn't crew.

Omar stood near the entrance in silence.

"Yo, you lost nigga?" someone asked him. "You know where you at?"

Omar didn't respond to the question. Instead, he stood there with his eyes fixed on Bookie in the back. Six men were inside; each was armed and dangerous, and they wouldn't hesitate to kill Omar where he stood.

Bookie stood up from the table and glared at Omar, shouting at him, "Yo, you heard the man, muthafucka . . . You lost, nigga? 'Cuz you fo' sure in the wrong fuckin' building."

"Bookie, right?" Omar finally spoke.

"Nigga, who asking . . .?"

Omar smirked. He could feel his blood boiling from the thrill of the hunt and the killing. He could feel Malaka's presence inside him, urging him to please her desires as she would incessantly please him. He could feel the power swelling tremendously inside him as he stood there among six threatening men ready to kill him. But he stood there undaunted. This was his moment to shine for her, and nothing was getting in the way of it.

Beforehand, he'd met with Dubai and Kenya. What he possessed, they wanted it in their favor. They wanted Omar to kill for them. Five thousand for every man he kills, starting with Bookie, Kenya had promised him.

"I can make you a rich man," said Kenya. "But I know it isn't just about the money with you."

Kenya knew about the gun—the .357 Magnum.

"That gun," Kenya continued, "used to belong to a man I know. So the power and influence it possesses are impressive. But there's a history behind it."

Omar didn't care about the gun's history or its past owners; it was his now. But Kenya did. It was a powerful weapon that Omar's feeble mind couldn't comprehend how powerful and destructive the demonic gun could be. Kenya knew that continued use of it from a mere mortal like Omar would eventually make him insane—and kill him. He knew what was latched to the gun—

the sexual succubus that unceasingly inclined the weapon's owner to kill for it. The more souls it collected via revenge, hatred, greed, power, and so on, the more powerful it became. The weapon had claimed nearly ten thousand souls in over seven hundred years when it was first crafted and designed as a .357 Magnum. But before it was a handgun, it was an ancient and cursed sword that had consumed the souls of men for centuries. It had been wielded by mighty kings, rulers, and emperors. Many wars were fought to control that power, and many lives were lost. The demonic weapon would gather the hatred and evil of mankind and convey it to the weapon's owner, altering him into the devil embodied.

Thou shalt become my demon blade of darkness that annihilates everything!

The weapon could bring out the worst in the user and possibly allow it to bring out the worst in others. The sword, which was now a gun, could absorb demonic power to grow stronger. The stronger it grew, the more powerful it became, even enough to kill divinities. And it was mighty against angels, fallen angels, and any supernatural and authoritative being, including Legba. The owner of the weapon can sometimes become an unstoppable force. The gun was able to enhance a man's strength and power. But a strong curse was placed on the weapon, which brought misfortune to its owner.

It was now shaped like a handgun to equate with the time of its existence; it awakened powerful demon energy—an intense momentum. As a result, when the projectile struck its target, it generated an intense burst of energy, which ultimately burned and exploded, initiating heavy damage. The damage inflicted could quickly disintegrate the enemy—and enflame their insides, scorching them.

Kenya had plans for the weapon. But he would have to wait. It was a weapon that he couldn't easily take from its owner. For now, he wanted Omar to become his pawn. So he sent him after Bookie. Though the Black Hand demanded Anton persuade Bookie to turn himself in to the authorities, Kenya wanted to disrupt that plan. He wanted Bookie dead.

Omar and Bookie locked eyes menacingly. It was easy to see that Omar was concealing a weapon in the waistband of his jeans. Everyone inside the place stood, knowing that this uninvited stranger inside their private establishment wasn't there as a friend. He was sent. It didn't take Bookie and the others to know rocket science to deduce why Omar was there. Alone. The tension inside the place grew thick, soon to turn into a deadly altercation.

Kill 'em all! she whispered to Omar.

He smirked at his foes, and then there was a brief flicker with the lights, creating bewilderment among the dwellers inside. When the lights finally stopped flickering, Omar had the .357 in his grip with his arm outstretched. He aimed at his first victim and fired—*Boom!* Shot the man between the eyes. Chaos ensued as each man hurriedly returned gunfire. But Omar was relentless, and as bullets dangerously whizzed by him, he was unscathed. He heatedly fired back and shot accurately at his targets, swiftly taking down another three men with headshots like he was the fastest gun in the west.

Bak! Bak!

Boom! Boom . . . Boom! Boom!

The gun performed magnificently, exploding like a powerful cannon in his grip. He was like death—the Grim Reaper himself, snatching away life with such handiness and taking all five men down effortlessly, leaving Bookie, the last man standing. Bookie raised his .45 at Omar and fired—but nothing.

Click! Click! Click!

The gun was empty. Now Bookie found himself staring down the barrel of the enemy's gun, becoming the prey instead of the predator this time. He scowled at Omar and griped, "So, they send a bitch like you to take me down! Fuck you and whoever sent you—"

Boom!

Bookie's right eye exploded, instantly dropping his body to the floor. Omar was a man of few words, no witty comebacks. Bookie's blood was thick and crimson, pooling on the floor like the others before him. The sight and smell of death were appeasing. Omar stood there straight-faced. Implementing death was power and strength at its finest. There was no going back to the man he used to be. On the contrary, the predatory transition was gratifying.

Omar continued to stand over the body of one of the most notorious killers in Brooklyn . . . and he smirked.

EPILOGUE

OMAR STOOD IN front of the mirror and closely stared at himself. He observed the nasty-looking scars that decorated his chest, abdomen, arms, and neck. Malaka had left its hellish markings on him, and he stood there in a deep trance. The .357 Magnum was placed on the dresser in front of him. The thirst for power, killing, and lust continued to swell inside him. There was no control over it. The feeling Malaka bestowed was like an addiction to crack cocaine, and there was no turning back. He was hers now, entirely. She'd promised Omar much more to come—from his sexual desires to absolute strength and power, but there were sacrifices he needed to make. He needed to make the hard choice—no distractions.

Malaka was a jealous bitch. She didn't want anyone or anything to divert his attention.

As Omar stood there gazing at his inflicted and troubled self, he was obsessed with wanting more and feeling more. Then, creepily materializing from behind him were a pair of hands—her hands that started touching him and seducing him. She appeared from out of nowhere, naked in her human form, whispering temptation and persuasion in his ear—influencing him greatly.

Kill for me!

Omar nodded. It was time, and there was no beating around the bush. His soul was utterly lost, and his humanity departed.

Malaka didn't want him to have any connections in his realm, for he needed to be free from any other influence and authority except hers. So, Omar reached for the .357, ready to execute the unthinkable.

Danny sat in the front pew of the church alone. He stared at the large cross with Jesus' crucifixion hanging on the wall behind the choir's seating. He sighed heavily. The Queen's church was empty and silent. It was just Danny, his prayers and his concerns, and God. He thought about the stranger's inhuman attack on him the other day. The strength he carried was unbelievable. He sorely needed direction. What was happening and what he was experiencing felt way out of his league and payroll. It had been weeks since Omar disappeared. The last incident the detective believed was connected to him was the multiple shootings in a private bar that left six men dead. There were no witnesses, but Detective Greene was becoming familiar with the brutality of the killings.

"I need guidance," he said to the cross. "What is going on? What is this world coming to?"

He sighed heavily again.

He was pensive.

As he sat there, his cell phone rang. His partner Foster. Greene answered with some uneasiness, knowing Bunk was calling to tell him about another homicide. It was late, after 11:00 p.m., and crime never slept.

"Yeah?" he answered inertly.

"You need to see this," said Bunk.

"What's the location?"

"Someplace you're familiar with," Bunk replied.

Greene took down the address, and Bunk was right. He was familiar with the location. He stood up from the pew, took one final look at the cross with Christ on it, and said a prayer. Then he pivoted and exited the church with the uneasiness he felt earlier growing.

Danny Greene parked his car on Livonia Avenue, arriving at the Tilden Housing Project in the Ville, where an abundance of police activity was happening at a specific building. The blaring police lights were blinding in the night. A crowd of looky-loos had gathered outside the entrance to the building. Their faces expressed concern and sadness, an indication of death. Greene moved past the group and through the impromptu police blockade, and entered the building. There were several cops in the lobby talking and sipping coffee. They showed apathy toward the crime scene nearby. It was just another day on the job and another murder in the Ville for them, where folks and cops jointly were becoming desensitized to the violence and murders.

Greene looked at the sergeant.

"Rooftop," the sergeant said off his look.

Greene pushed for the elevator to descend. Then he stepped into it with a heavy heart and a deep intuition. He lifted toward the last floor, exited the elevator to another group of nearby officers, and approached the roof via the stairwell. When he opened the door, and his hard-bottom shoes stepped onto the gravel, he immediately saw the body sprawled against the gravel. Foster was standing over her. Greene moved closer with the weight of gravity against his heart. His attention was fixed on the body—on Kizzie, lying there naked with a ghastly gunshot wound to her head. Her hands were tidily placed against her chest in a ritual position.

"I'm sorry, Greene," Foster uttered with deep empathy. "She didn't deserve this."

Greene crouched by her body and stared into her eyes. He knew Kizzie was a strong woman, and she'd been through a lot. Her death, though, was unexpected. It was apparent what the cause of death was. The hole in the middle of her forehead was gruesome, and leaving her naked in the cold was disrespectful. She was a good Christian girl, and some twisted pervert decided to violate her . . . again.

Greene stood up, and though it was a touching scene, he kept things professional. He looked at Foster and asked, "Any witnesses?"

"No."

Greene wanted to go in full throttle with the investigation, but then a feeling of guilt overcame him. He wondered if he'd put Kizzie in harm's way by questioning her, and what if the search warrant to Omar's apartment raised some speculation. What if Omar figured out it was her that reported him? Omar became the primary suspect for Greene. But he was in the wind.

"We're gonna catch this monster," said Foster.

Greene didn't reply to his comment. His mind was elsewhere.

"Cover her up," he uttered.

He walked away, moved toward the ledge, and gazed out. The city was lit and bustling; the holidays were approaching. Greene stood in silence near the ledge, his mind spinning like it was going stir-crazy. Once again, he noticed the same man below standing across the street, staring oddly at Greene. The stranger smirked at Greene, and then right before his eyes . . . He vanished into thin air.

"What the . . .?!" Greene stopped himself from cursing.

Greene then heard an unusual voice inside his mind, stating, "*You need to kill them before they kill you . . .*"

TO BE CONTINUED . . .

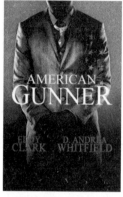

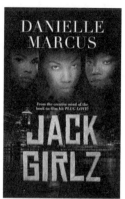

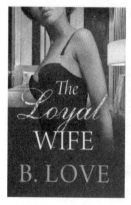